D1254143

HENRY JAMES'
Shorter Masterpieces
VOLUME 2

HENRY JAMES'

Shorter Masterpieces

VOLUME 2

Edited with an introduction
and notes by

Peter Rawlings

Fitzwilliam College
University of Cambridge

THE HARVESTER PRESS · SUSSEX

BARNES & NOBLE BOOKS · NEW JERSEY

First published in Great Britain in 1984 by
THE HARVESTER PRESS LIMITED
Publisher: John Spiers
16 Ship Street, Brighton, Sussex

and in the USA by
BARNES & NOBLE BOOKS
81 Adams Drive, Totowa, New Jersey 07512

British Library Cataloguing in Publication Data

James, Henry, 1843-1916
Henry James' shorter masterpieces.
Vol. 2
I. Title II. Rawlings, Peter
813'.4[F] PS2110

ISBN 0-7108-0698-1
ISBN 0-7108-0693-0 Pbk

BARNES & NOBLE BOOKS
ISBN 0-389-20503-6
ISBN 0-389-20505-2 Pbk

Printed and bound in Great Britain by
Whitstable Litho Ltd., Whitstable, Kent

CONTENTS

ACKNOWLEDGEMENTS

I SHOULD like to thank Mrs Jean M. Gooder for her valuable advice and Dr Eric Warner for his warm and vigorous encouragement throughout this project. I am particularly grateful to Mr Stephen Clark for his careful suggestions and reservations and to Mr Philip McGenity, Mr David Brown, and Mr Bob Cochrane for reading drafts of the introduction. My greatest debt is to Mrs Patricia Rawlings who knows the cost of this work.

Acknowledgements are due to the University of Chicago Press and Messrs Charles Scribner's Sons for quotations from *The Notebooks of Henry James* and from the Prefaces to the New York Edition, and to the Curator of Manuscripts, the Houghton Library, Harvard for permission to quote from a William James letter. An acknowledgement is also due to Oxford University Press for the Wordsworth quotations.

BIOGRAPHICAL NOTE

HENRY JAMES was born in New York on 15 April 1843 and died in London on 28 February 1916 less than a year after becoming a naturalised British subject. The family moved to Europe in 1855 where James was educated, desultorily, in Geneva, London, Paris, and Boulogne. 1858 saw the James family in Newport, Rhode Island, 1859 in Geneva and Bonn, and 1860 back in Newport. Henry followed his brother William (to become an eminent psychologist and philosopher) to Harvard, passing an unlikely term at Harvard Law School in 1862-3; their parents eventually migrated to Boston and then to Cambridge in 1864. This was also the year of James' first story and reviews. He embarked on a 'grand tour' of England, France, and Italy in 1869 but returned occasionally to America. He settled in London in 1876 there to remain, apart from regular visits to France and Italy in particular and two late trips to America, until moving to the relative seclusion of Rye, Sussex, in 1898.

James, who never married, had a ferocious capacity for work. He wrote twenty-two novels (two uncompleted), 112 tales, twelve plays, a vast quantity of travel essays and criticism of all kinds, and a bewildering number of letters. A characteristic concern in the 1870s and through into the 1880s — notably in *Roderick Hudson* (1875), *The American* (1877), *The Europeans*, and 'Daisy Miller' (both 1878) — was with the so-called 'international theme': the confrontation of American and European values. Although there was an oblique return to this theme in later novels — particularly in *The Ambassadors* (1903)

— *The Portrait of a Lady* (1881) can be seen as the culmination of a phase with which James had grown tired.

The Bostonians (1886), *The Princess Casamassima* (1886), and *The Tragic Muse* (1890) are among James' most heavily furnished works and, as he acknowledged in the case of *The Princess Casamassima*, owe a little to the documentary ambience of 'Naturalism'. During the 1890s the *mise-en-scène* of James' fiction became very much that of London and to an extent its *demi-monde*. This latter aspect is presaged in 'A London Life' (1888), one of James' finest stories, and perhaps reaches its zenith in the difficult but brilliant *What Maisie Knew* (1897) and *The Awkward Age* (1899). In the first half of the 1890s James was intensively occupied with the writing of plays and with the theatre, a large proportion of the tales of this period considering questions of the artist and society. At the level of popular success the plays were a complete failure.

The complexities of the later work are notorious; and many a reader has echoed William James' exasperated 'Say it *out* for God's sake . . . and have done with it'. But earlier in that letter (4 May 1907) *The American Scene* (1907) is described as 'in its peculiar way . . . *supremely* great'. And that comment seems appropriate to James' work as a whole.

INTRODUCTION

I

IN HIS introduction to The English Library Edition of Kipling's *Soldiers Three* in 1891 James' lament was that the 'short story is, on our side of the Channel and of the Atlantic, a mine which will take a great deal of working' (p.xix). Yet by 1898 his complaint was that the '"short story" has become of late an object' of 'almost extravagant dissertation'. The mine of the short story was certainly well worked in the 1890s and James added to the discussion of it in an essay making a distinction which implies some of the essential characteristics of most of his own tales in the two volumes of this edition (see volume I for a discussion of further aspects of James and the tale):

> Are there not two quite distinct effects to be produced by this rigour of brevity — the two that best make up for the many left unachieved as requiring a larger canvas? The one with which we are most familiar is that of the detached incident, single and sharp, as clear as a pistol-shot; the other, of rarer performance, is that of the impression, comparatively generalised — simplified, foreshortened, reduced to a particular perspective — of a complexity or continuity. The former is an adventure comparatively safe, in which you have, for the most part, but to put one foot after the other. It is just the risks of the latter, on the contrary, that make the best of the sport.
>
> ('The Story-Teller at Large: Mr Henry Harland', *Fortnightly Review*, April 1898.)

The remarks about the 'larger canvas' are a reminder that James had now begun to write novels again after the intensity of half a decade of play writing and a concentration on some of his best tales. In between the publication of *The Tragic Muse* (1890) and *The Other House* (1896), and more particularly the much shorter *The Spoils of Poynton* (1897), the tyranny of the three-volume novel had been broken with the refusal of the circulating libraries to accept any more. James continued to write shorter stories up until 1910 but revelled in the sharply innovative compression of novels such as *The Spoils of Poynton* and *What Maisie Knew* (1897). There was always though the impulse to develop, to expand, an impulse often straining at the leash in his tales, and soon to have its consequences in *The Awkward Age* (1899) and the great novels of the earlier 1900s.

The tales here continue to treat some of the themes which occupied James in the first half of the 1890s. But a motif in this volume is that of retreat, by choice or otherwise, and its costs and rewards. Literary production seems inevitably to involve compromise; and retreat from the market-place and into the purity of the imagination is seen not only as having its costs but of having costs which are too high for George Dane in 'The Great Good Place'. He is compelled to do battle again because of the very nature of the restored creative urge. And at the still point of this turning world of markets and compromise is the figure of Hugh Vereker and that extraordinary *tour de force* 'The Figure in the Carpet'.

II

'THE NEXT TIME' is set in the 1870s, the years of James' own attempts to subsidise his art partly by writing letters from Paris for the *New York Tribune*. The subject of this tale was suggested to James

> by all the little backward memories of one's own frustrated ambition — in particular by its having just come back to me how, already 20 years ago, when I was in Paris writing letters to the *N. Y. Tribune*, Whitelaw Reid wrote to me to ask me virtually *that* — . . . to make them, as he called it, more 'personal'.
>
> (*Notebooks*, p. 180. See *A Guide to Further Reading* for a full reference.)

The irony of 'The Next Time' is that the harder Ralph Limbert tries to write in a popular way the better his work becomes. His one great attempt, a beautifully structured anti-climax in the tale, to join Mrs Highmore's interminable production line of successful novels is valued by the narrator as 'an unscrupulous, an unsparing, a shameless, merciless masterpiece'.

The irony is deepened by the fact that Mrs Highmore's ambition, certainly from the later point of view of the tale, is to write just one masterpiece that will fail. Her situation is a neat inversion of Limbert's. She believes that the narrator's praise went some way to spoiling Limbert's chances in the market (and his criticism is even less 'popular' than Limbert's novels) and can do the same for hers; provide her with an opportunity, that is, for an 'exquisite failure' as opposed to that for a success 'as prosaic as a good dinner'.

The tale, however, asserts the essential independence of the quality of a work from its critics (as distinct from its actual dependence on the power of a man like Bousefield): 'Her appeal, her motive, her fantastic thirst for quality and her ingenious theory of my influence struck me all as excellent comedy . . .'. Although if the work is independent in this way from its critics, there is also an uncomfortable sense in which it is independent of its writers. Neither Mrs Highmore nor Ralph Limbert can exercise any control over the essential quality of their work because 'what was talent but the art of being completely whatever it was that one happened to be?'.

Ralph Limbert, still in search of a good dinner, moves to the country with his family but he eventually shunts them and their high living off to London and so can enjoy 'the supreme luxury of his frankly presenting himself as a poor man'. It is then that the voice of the market suddenly grows faint: 'he had merely waked up one morning in the country of the blue and had stayed there with a good conscience and a great idea. He stayed till death knocked at the gate . . .'. His pen drops over a 'splendid fragment' but thoughts of its consumption have gone. Although he continues to write, he writes in a seclusion which involves no thought of the situation of his work in the market-place. The question of whether or not such isolation is desirable or even possible for a writer is taken up again in 'The Great Good Place'.

There is a great deal of discussion of the word 'success'. The narrator's view and Limbert's is that 'the only success worth one's powder was success in the line of one's idiosyncracy' and that 'the man of his craft had achieved it when of a beautiful subject his expression was complete'. When Limbert's need to support his family grows desperate, this sounds like so much fine talk and his assault on the market is an attempt to change the definition of 'success' and to defy the law of 'his talent' by being obvious and popular.

For Mrs Highmore the quality of a work, be it good or bad, is a function of its place in the market; and this particularly includes what is said about it and the way in which it is said. In a curious way there is something of this logic in James' tendency to rationalise his failure as a playwright by establishing an equation between unpopularity and excellence.

No such rationalisation is necessary, however, for 'The Figure in the Carpet', an enduring fascination of which is that to read it is necessarily to engage in precisely that activity which so intensely occupies its characters and which to an extent it satirises. A story which in a large measure is concerned with the process of reading itself enacts that process.

The narrator of this tale is one of the most baffled detectives in fiction, and what helps to give it all a certain plausibility amidst the confusion is his tireless persistence. By the end, having given up at one stage, he is ready to begin again and with renewed obsession. But the nature of his pursuit changes. He quickly abandons reading Vereker's novels and spends the rest of the story attempting to track down those who might, he hopes, have made a better job of it.

Our access to events, with the exception of various laconic telegrams, is confined to this perplexed narrator whose attitude towards the 'idol' of Vereker's 'general intention' vacillates between atheism, agnosticism and obsession. The narrator, like the reader, is in the business of trying to make connections; his task is that of reading and perception generally: to construe, to construct, with all that that entails in selection and decisions about relevance and redundance. On this evidence it amounts to a mesmerising pursuit of the horizon.

Unlike Sherlock Holmes, a fictional relative in the 1890s, the narrator is hardly ever in the right place at the right time. A bizarre sequence of unexpected journeys and deaths seems to prevent his gaining the vital information. One of many virtuoso aspects of the tale is the way in which it constantly raises doubts about its own plausibility and in this way helps create a general air of infinite instability. Melodrama, with its intrinsic implausibility, is one device used. There are moments of melodrama — Corvick is killed by falling 'horribly on his head' — and more potently melodramatic cameos such as the younger brother's illness which causes the narrator's trip to Germany and France just as Corvick is returning.

It seems for most of the tale as if the narrator is excluded from the secret by marriage, particularly Mrs Corvick's (and Vereker's excitement about marriage and his secret prepares this little trail). Yet Drayton Deane, who marries the widowed Mrs Corvick, knows nothing — apparently. There is even a possibility, where all things are possible, that neither does Corvick and that he has simply implied his discovery to accelerate, even to make possible, his marriage. But then there is the complication over the engagement. The gyrations are eternal.

The central enigma is that of whether or not there is any secret to be discovered. And this is dramatised by a breathless shifting of the very terms of the enquiry. It is Corvick who first muses about a sense of 'something or other' in Vereker's work. And Vereker himself talks about his 'little point', 'the particular thing I've written my books most *for*', 'an idea', the 'finest fullest intention of the lot', a 'little trick', and a 'general intention'. The narrator decides that 'it was something, I guessed, in the primal plan, something like a complex figure in a Persian carpet', and consequently engages on a search as if for buried treasure. Vereker appears to approve of the image and adds one of his own: '"It's the very string," he said, "that my pearls are strung on!"'

Vereker is asked for clues. But what he does, ironically but appropriately unperceived by the narrator, is to provide a possible solution by implying, much as he likes a game, that the whole nature of the enquiry is misconceived. '"Is it something in the style or something in the thought? An element of form or an element of feeling?"', asks the narrator. His method is to analyse, to separate, to get to something that can be paraphrased, some kind of message which can be abstracted from the text. Vereker responds with '"Well, you've got a heart in your body. Is that an element of form or an element of feeling? What I contend that nobody has ever mentioned in my work is the organ of life".'.

As in 'The Middle Years' (volume I) it requires imagination, an acquaintance with the process of creation through art to penetrate through the superficial chaos to the essential unity. We come back to that task of the narrator to make connections. At this level what he fails to perceive in the author's work is that it is organically connected; the narrator, the reader, has to see the connection of part to part and part to whole, a connection of which Vereker, like James, is proud because it depends on a hidden art of selection and a growth from within to which few works can lay claim.

The irony of Vereker's position is similar to that of Dencombe's ('The Middle Years'). Their art is concealed by art; and Vereker quickly regrets beginning the process which might lead to its penetration. The art, the 'figure in the carpet', is in the composed nature of the composition and unless detected there is no evidence of the composer having been at work. Perhaps this is the pang which first made Vereker mention his secret to the narrator. As James put it in 'The Lesson of Balzac' (1905): it is

> the figured tapestry, all over-scored with objects in fine perspective, which symbolizes to me (if we may have a symbol) the last word of the achieved fable. Such a tapestry, with its wealth of expression of its subject, with its myriad ordered stitches, its harmonies of tone and felicities of taste, is a work, above all, of closeness. . . .
>
> (reprinted in *The House of Fiction*, edited by Leon Edel, London, 1957, p.84.)

Possibly Corvick perceived such a figure. It would certainly be appropriate that such perceptions could not be conveyed to anyone else. Perceptions are not transferable. If he did arrive at this solution, there is evidence that it was after a process of germination (he announces victory away from the texts, whilst thinking of other things) analogous to that of the author's with the originating idea for his work. Corvick's communion at the source then becomes, as in 'Nona Vincent' (volume I) and 'The Middle Years', a communion with an author and his intention.

And there are suggestions, here and there, that Corvick's is not really the mate-in-two approach of the narrator. He talks of 'notes of hidden music' and 'whiffs and hints' of 'he didn't know what'. The connotations of harmony are apposite if the 'figure' is the hidden unity of the work. There are also implications of aesthetic theories of the writer as a second creator whose works imitate the concealed unity and harmony of the universe. Creative writing of this kind depends on creative reading. It is possible, then, that Corvick's eventual communion with Vereker was similar to those in 'Nona Vincent' and 'The Middle Years'; yet if one is but a unique moment and the other is ended by death, there can be no certainty here that it has even taken place.

In some respects 'The Way it Came' is in quite a distinct vein from 'The Figure in the Carpet' and yet it has a similar enigmatic quality if rather more of an emphasis on the distorting conditions of the narrator's perspective. The supernatural strain of this tale links it with that whole group of stories, including 'The Turn of the Screw' (1898), which deals with the imagination in something like Wordsworth's 'vivid state of sensation'. Its theme of lost opportunities and of a life that might have been is characteristic of much of James' later work.

The tale begins with an account of how it has been extracted from some not particularly systematic diaries and divided up by the editor. This convention is subtly treated in that it is used as an opportunity to put the burden of inference on the reader and to generate expectations — 'these things would be striking, wouldn't they? to any reader' — about the tale as a whole.

In his Preface to the New York Edition of this tale (and in that edition the 'colourless' title is changed to 'The Friends of the Friends') James distinguishes himself from a writer like Poe by drawing attention to his own concern not so much with the events themselves but with a character's problematic reflections on them. Much of 'The Way it Came' is taken up with the consciousness of its narrator; or rather her retrospective consciousness of that consciousness. The editor tells us that 'she writes sometimes of herself, sometimes of others, sometimes of the combination', and we are early alerted to the fact that her combination of events, or 'evidence', with her own perceptions leads but to dubious conclusions.

We see something of this in miniature when '"the one, you know, who saw her father's ghost"' (the absence of names adds strikingly to the air of uncertainty) visits the narrator. Her long-estranged husband has recently died and the narrator makes an 'acute reflection' on the fact that despite her note to the contrary, obvious signs of mourning betray its effect. Later reflections show the extent to which her conclusion was a case of self-deception wrought by the eagerness of jealousy. Her reflections, interpretations, constructions all take place in a crucible of jealousy about the nature of any potential, ultimately ghostly, relationship between this lady and the narrator's fiancé. The tale is quite explicit about the fact that a great deal hinges on questions of interpretation and construction; for instance: 'he clung to his interpretation because he liked it better' and '"You hark back to the different construction we put on her appearance that evening"'.

There are two specific uncertainties. The first — whether the lady was alive or dead, or even *that* lady, when she visited the narrator's fiancé — is difficult for either the narrator or her fiancé to resolve because of uncertainties about time. The second problem is that of whether there is some kind of ghostly relationship at the end or whether this is a projection of the narrator's imagination heightened by jealousy. The tantalisation for the reader is in the narrator's belief that 'he had taken the line of indulgence, of meeting me half-way and kindly humouring me'.

One way of looking at the tale is to suggest that the two people, with affinities based on similar supernatural experiences, and kept apart in reality, ultimately become united only in the narrator's imagination. The structure of the tale is that of opposition (and the two characters are, in a way, quite crudely opposed; neither can be in the same place at once, and so on) and its transcendent reconciliation. Union, reconciliation, depends upon the synthesising power of the imagination. But the cost of that imaginative union here is its obstruction of another.

'John Delavoy' is concerned with the futility of pursuing the 'personal' at the expense of an author's work — having an obsession with an author, that is, which stops short of reading his books — and the way in which such a pursuit can kill both the author's talent and the author himself.

The story originated in James' own experience early in 1896 of having 'Dumas the Younger' turned down by the editor of the *Century Magazine* Robert Underwood Johnson. (It then appeared in the *New York Herald*, the *Boston Herald*, and the *New Review*, and was reprinted by James in *Notes on Novelists*, 1914.) In that essay, James held to his belief that a critic must grant a writer his 'case', his subject, and concern himself mainly with its treatment: 'to enjoy his manner of dealing with such material we must grant him in every connection his full premise'. Or as he had put it in 'The Art of Fiction' in 1884 (reprinted in Shapira's collection; see *A Guide to Further Reading*): 'questions of art are questions (in the widest sense) of execution; questions of morality are quite another affair'.

In 'John Delavoy' the editor is keen to publish anything about the writer but nothing about his work, which he regards as immoral. As James wrote in his notebook: editors such as Johnson 'want to *seem* to deal with' a writer 'because he is famous — and he is famous because he wrote certain things which they won't for the world have intelligibly mentioned' (*Notebooks*, p.246). This subject is treated with a consummate artistry largely achieved by the orchestration of some penetrating ironies.

The tale opens in a theatre and there, discarding a lady-friend in the process, the narrator animadverts on 'the manners and morals of London' and expresses his conviction that he 'didn't know what we were coming to'. His keen attention to the proprieties, which nicely sharpens the ironies of the scene where Beston tells him that his article is indelicate, does not prevent him however from supplementing his powers of observation with a pair of binoculars. And in this way he manages a full examination — 'yes, I was momentarily gross' — of Miss Delavoy. The perils of observation and the pliability of apparent evidence and information become clear when Miss Delavoy turns out to be a sister of the novelist rather than his daughter and a Lord Yarracombe is really Beston, the editor of the *Cynosure*. The texture of this opening scene then is observation; and this texture is thickened by the *mise-en-scène* of a theatre. On a variation of the play-within-a-play tradition the narrator watches Miss Delavoy watching a play. And in James acute observation, especially given the sexual undertones, is never far from voyeurism.

The irony of Beston's reaction to the narrator's article on John Delavoy is that although he regards it as indelicate — because it deals with 'those relations, with the question of sex' in Delavoy's novels — the real obscenity in his kind of periodical is to deal in any way with the work rather than the person. This irony is compounded by the fact that Beston is more than eager to publish an article on Delavoy consisting, according to the narrator, of 'anecdotes, glimpses, gossip, chat; a picture of his "home life", domestic habits, diet, dress, arrangements — and his little ways and little secrets, and even, to better it still, all your own, your relations with him, your feelings about him, his feelings about *you*'. This the public can 'stand'.

The narrator puzzles over the attraction of Miss Delavoy for Beston — she has 'a charm so fine and so veiled that if she had been a piece of prose or of verse I was sure he would never have discovered it' — and occasionally has glimpses of what this attraction might be: 'It's literal that as he stood there in his florid beauty and complete command I felt his infinite force, and, with a gush of admiration, wondered how, for our young lady, there could be at such a moment another man'. The narrator is set against the brute force of a man who sits at the head of 'the modern poetry of numbers'. It is the task of one of these men, if he is to marry Miss Delavoy, to displace the memory of her brother, to exorcise his spirit by having his work become known. It is really a question of what is published and how.

And at whose expense is the final irony? For Delavoy's portrait, together with a note by an 'anonymous hand', does appear in the *Cynosure*, and after the kind of publicity surrounding the narrator's wrangle with Beston which perhaps Miss Delavoy wanted. Her rôle in the affair is left open: 'the only thing I didn't do was to urge Miss Delavoy to write to her solicitors or to the newspapers'. Miss Delavoy marries the narrator and Delavoy's name has become known in a vulgar way (but earlier suggestions are that his work is now known too), although not in such a way as to associate the process with the narrator and his wife.

The indication here is that one consequence of artistic integrity might be eternal obscurity. To an extent, Beston represents the seductive lure of fertile popularity as opposed to its alternative of barren neglect. It is said at one point that Miss Delavoy 'might have been taken for the guardian of a temple or a tomb'. This is an account of the inevitable intrigue and compromise involved in turning it into a temple.

'Paste' is a slight tale and one example of the kind of art produced by James during his moments at the market-stall. His idea, acknowledged in his Preface to the New York Edition, was to reverse the situation of Maupassant's 'La Parure' (1884). In that tale a woman and her husband work for years to replace a necklace which has been borrowed and lost and which turns out to be paste.

There is evidence in Maupassant's 'Les Bijoux' (1883) that even the idea for his reversal of this situation was not new to James. A Madame Lantin has a taste for the theatre and for imitation jewellery. Her husband obliges and after her sudden death runs short of money. He sells a necklace only to discover that it is genuine. The implications for Madame Lantin's respectability are much the same as they are for the vicar's wife in 'Paste'.

Arthur Prime is a broadly unpleasant character whose mourning for his mother's death seems to be as genuine as the diamonds in 'La Parure'. He refuses to admit to Charlotte that there is any possibility of the pearls being real. If they are then his mother would have been *that* kind of actress. The pearls turn out to be genuine, of course, and some little twists towards the end make us realise what a gap there is between Prime's public uneasiness about his mother's character and his behaviour in relative privacy.

There is little connection between 'Paste' and 'The Great Good Place' other than that they were collected together by James in *The Soft Side* (1900). George Dane is in that long line of writers and artists in James' tales of the 1890s through whose creation he debates many of the problems of his own art.

Henry James moved to Lamb House in Rye, Sussex, in 1898. His brother, William, felt that the terms of the lease were rather poor and in a letter which attempts to correct Henry's impression of his view implies some of the significance that acquiring the house had had for Henry. William's 'great and good and holy' might well have suggested the title for this tale:

> But you, even now seem to be melodiously imploring us to let you have something in the world, beside the memory of your childhood's happiness, that you may still call your own. Whereas we . . . were simply rapturously overflowing at the thought of your finally owning Lamb House, and *all* we wanted was to help you get it cheaper . . . for your own sake we fairly revel in sympathetic feelings of ownership and assured possession . . . It is a great and good and holy and else a most prudent and financially sagacious thing, dear Harry, and I am proud of you for having already done it. (11 August 1899)

One of the delights in George Dane's 'dream' is the presence of a library where he can recognise 'from shelf to shelf every dear old book that he had had to put off or never returned to'. There is strong evidence that James himself was reading Wordsworth anew at the time of writing this tale. *The Excursion* (1814) in particular is close in theme to 'The Great Good Place', dealing as the poem does with the nature of the imagination in seclusion. Dane appropriates 'by theft' a line from this poem to try to give a sense of what it is that he has recovered: '"the vision and the faculty divine"'. And in the poem the lines are:

> Oh! many are the poets that are sown
> By Nature; men endowed with highest gifts,
> The vision and the faculty divine

Sections of *The Excursion* seem highly relevant to James' situation, lamenting as he did his lack of popularity yet anxious about the compromising effects on art of achieving or striving to achieve it:

> All but a scattered few, live out their time,
> Husbanding that which they possess within,
> And go to the grave, unthought of.
>   Strongest minds
> Are often those of whom the noisy world
> Hears least....

Wordsworth says in his 'Preface' that *The Recluse*, never completed but of which *The Excursion* was to be a part, was to have for its 'principal subject the sensations and opinions of a poet living in retirement' (*Wordsworth: Poetical Works*, London, 1936, edited by De Selincourt, pp.589-92). And George Dane's 'dream' is very much a retirement, if temporary, for a writer whose powers of imaginative creation have been obstructed by the 'irrelevant, destructive, brutalising sides of life' and by what James consistently referred to as the great flood of literary production (and on which he often saw his own art, with its principles of stringent selection, as floating), 'a flood of rushing waters, in which bumping and grasping were all'.

The scenario of the tale is neatly constructed with that usual, but nevertheless effective, blurring of the distinctions between the real and the dream worlds. It partly turns around the axis of a mutual I-wish-I-were-you basis between a 'successful' but weary writer and a young man who has yet to stand the test of such success.

George Dane's powers of imaginative creation are restored both by a communion with their source in his own consciousness and by a return as a kind of demiurge to the source of life, to an original inspiration whose projection is the context of this retreat. (The allusions to Wordsworth, Goethe, Plato, and Germany suggest the background of idealism and Romanticism which underpins this fable.) The dream is a moment of transcendence, in Protestant terms (but with Catholic overtones) a seeing of the light. Dane is disembodied — 'nobody talking with nobody' — but finds the self: 'the inner life woke up again, and it was the inner life, for people of his generation, victims of the modern madness, mere maniacal extension and motion, that was returning health'. He is in possession of the essence without the extension, without the 'complication of an identity', of the 'wordless fact', without a language entangled in the world and thus subjected to 'material simplification'. Dane, in fact, is in Ralph Limbert's 'country of the blue' where there is ultimately little worry about the extension of the 'idea' into a literary form analogous to the vulgar form of the modern world.

The whole of this world is initially defined in terms of absences, absences which Dane is quite happy to leave as such until his healing imagination gives him the urge to puzzle and to 'read into the general wealth of his comfort all the particular absences of which it was composed' and to conclude that 'it was a part of the whole impression that, by some extraordinary law, one's vision seemed less from the facts than the facts from one's vision'. The turning point, when the impulse to return impinges, comes (wryly) when Dane begins to consider the cost of this retreat into the consciousness, this exclusive concern with a restored imagination now feeding on itself (and all his interlocutors seem but projections of his self): 'there *must* be a price to anything so awfully sane?'. It is necessary to counteract the dulling effect of the world on the imagination, but total retreat to a world of 'beguiled suppositions' where 'nothing contradicts them' defeats the very object of that retreat. The imperative of the restored imagination is creation. And by definition creation is an embodying, a breathing of the inspirational spirit into some form. Imagination needs to be combined with experience.

This, finally, is where a good many of James' concerns in these tales of the 1890s converge. The writer's is a constant battle to preserve the power of his imagination in a world which values only that work which is immediately accessible. James oscillated between seeing art as an affair purely of the imagination and striving to employ his craft in order to embody it. He delighted in the creative power of his imagination; but any attempt to transform imaginative process into a literary product necessarily brought him into conflict with the market. The lure of a retreat into the imagination within the context of an ordered, perhaps neo-classical and certainly aristocratic world, is strong in 'The Great Good Place'. But the allurement is resisted not least because of the irresistibility of the creative urge.

Not for James, then, was Ralph Limbert's 'country of the blue' nor, as he put it in 'Dumas the Younger' (1895), that choice between 'the roar of the market and the silence of the tomb'. His was a constant struggle to narrow the gap between imaginative intention and its execution in an appropriate and acceptable form. And there was always the rent at Lamb House to pay. Immortality had its cost.

Peter Rawlings

THE NEXT TIME

MRS HIGHMORE'S errand this morning was odd enough to deserve commemoration: she came to ask me to write a notice of her great forthcoming work. Her great works have come forth so frequently without my assistance that I was sufficiently entitled on this occasion to open my eyes; but what really made me stare was the ground on which her request reposed, and what leads me to record the incident is the train of memory lighted by that explanation. Poor Ray Limbert, while we talked, seemed to sit there between us: she reminded me that my acquaintance with him had begun, eighteen years ago, with her having come in precisely as she came in this morning to bespeak my charity for him. If she didn't know then how little my charity was worth she is at least enlightened about it to-day, and this is just the circumstance that makes the drollery of her visit. As I hold up the torch to the dusky years—by which I mean as I cipher up with a pen that stumbles and stops the figured column of my reminiscences—I see that Limbert's public hour, or at least my small apprehension of it, is rounded by those two occasions. It was *finis*, with a little moralising flourish, that Mrs Highmore seemed to trace to-day at the bottom of the page. "One of the most voluminous writers of the time," she has often repeated this sign; but never, I dare say, in spite of her professional command of appropriate emotion, with an equal sense of that mystery and that sadness of things which to people of imagination generally hover over the close of human histories. This romance at any rate is bracketed by her early and her late appeal; and when its melancholy protrusions had caught the declining light again from my half-hour's talk with her I took a private vow to recover while that light still lingers something of the delicate flush, to pick out with a brief patience the perplexing lesson.

It was wonderful to observe how for herself Mrs Highmore had already done so: she wouldn't have hesitated to announce to me what was the matter with Ralph Limbert, or at all events to give me a glimpse of the high admonition she had read in his career. There could have been no better proof of the vividness of this parable, which we were really in our pleasant sympathy quite at one about, than that Mrs Highmore, of all hardened sinners, should have been converted. This indeed was not news to me: she impressed upon me that for the last ten years she had wanted to do something artistic, something as to which she was prepared not to care a rap whether or no it should sell. She brought home to me further that it had been mainly seeing what her brother-in-law did and how he did it that had wedded her to this perversity. As *he* didn't sell dear soul, and as several persons, of whom I was one, thought highly of that, the fancy had taken her—taken her even quite early in her prolific course—of reaching, if only once, the same heroic eminence. She yearned to be, like Limbert, but of course only once, an exquisite failure. There was something a failure was, a failure in the market, that a success somehow wasn't. A success was as prosaic as a good dinner: there was nothing more to be said about it than that you had had it. Who but vulgar people, in such a case, made gloating remarks about the courses? It was often by such vulgar people that a success was attested. It made if you came to look at it nothing but money; that is it made so much that any other result showed small in comparison. A failure now could make—oh, with the aid of immense talent of course, for there were failures and failures—such a reputation! She did me the honour—she had often done it—to intimate that what she meant by reputation was seeing *me* toss a flower. If it took a failure to catch a failure I was by my own admission well qualified to place the laurel. It was because she had made so much money and Mr Highmore had taken such care of it that she could treat herself to an hour of pure glory. She perfectly remembered that as often as I had heard her heave that sigh I had been prompt with my declaration that a book sold might easily be as glorious as a book unsold. Of course she knew this, but she knew also that it was the age of trash triumphant and that she had never heard me speak of anything that had "done well" exactly as she had sometimes heard me speak of something that hadn't—with just two or three words of respect which, when I used them, seemed to convey more than they commonly stood for, seemed to hush up the discussion a little, as if for the very beauty of the secret.

I may declare in regard to these allusions that, whatever I then thought of myself as a holder of the scales I had never scrupled to laugh out at the humour of Mrs Highmore's pursuit of quality at any price. It had never rescued her even for a day from the hard doom of popularity, and though I never gave her my word for it there was no reason at all why it should. The public *would* have her, as her husband used roguishly to remark; not indeed that, making her bargains, standing up to her publishers and even, in his higher flights, to her reviewers, he ever had a glimpse of her attempted conspiracy against her genius, or rather as I may say against mine. It was not that when she tried to be what she called subtle (for wasn't Limbert subtle, and wasn't I?) her fond consumers, bless them, didn't suspect the trick nor show what they thought of it: they straightway rose on the contrary to the morsel she had hoped to hold too high, and, making but a big, cheerful bite of it, wagged their great collective tail artlessly for more. It was not given to her not to please, nor granted even to her best refinements to affright. I have always respected the mystery of those humiliations, but I was fully aware this morning that they were practically the reason why she had come to me. Therefore when she said with the flush of a bold joke in her kind, coarse face, "What I feel is, you know, that *you* could settle me if you only would," I knew quite well what she meant. She meant that of old it had always appeared to be the fine blade, as some one had hyperbolically called it, of my particular opinion that snapped the silken thread by which Limbert's chance in the market was wont to hang. She meant that my favour was compromising, that my praise indeed was fatal. I had made myself a little specialty of seeing nothing in certain celebrities, of seeing overmuch in an occasional nobody, and of judging from a point of view that, say what I would for it (and I had a monstrous deal to say) remained perverse and obscure. Mine was in short the love that killed, for my subtlety, unlike Mrs Highmore's, produced no tremor of the public tail. She had not forgotten how, toward the end, when his case was worst, Limbert would absolutely come to me with a funny, shy pathos in his eyes and say: "My dear fellow, I think I've done it this time, if you'll only keep quiet." If my keeping quiet in those days was to help him to appear to have hit the usual taste, for the want of which he was starving, so now my breaking out was to help Mrs Highmore to appear to have hit the unusual.

The moral of all this was that I had frightened the public too much for our late friend, but that as she was not starving this was exactly what her grosser reputation required. And then, she good-naturedly and delicately intimated, there would always be, if further reasons were wanting, the price of my clever little article. I think she gave that hint with a flattering impression—spoiled child of the booksellers as she is—that the price of my clever little articles is high. Whatever it is, at any rate, she had evidently reflected that poor Limbert's anxiety for his own profit used to involve my sacrificing mine. Any inconvenience that my obliging her might entail would not in fine be pecuniary. Her appeal, her motive, her fantastic thirst for quality and her ingenious theory of my influence struck me all as excellent comedy, and when I consented contingently to oblige her she left me the sheets of her new novel. I could plead no inconvenience and have been looking them over; but I am frankly appalled at what she expects of me. What is she thinking of, poor dear, and what has put it into her head that "quality" has descended upon her? Why does she suppose that she has been "artistic?" She hasn't been anything whatever, I surmise, that she has not inveterately been. What does she imagine she has left out? What does she conceive she has put in? She has neither left out nor put in anything. I shall have to write her an embarrassed note. The book doesn't exist, and there's nothing in life to say about it. How can there be anything but the same old faithful rush for it?

I

THIS rush had already begun when, early in the seventies, in the interest of her prospective brother-in-law, she approached me on the singular ground of the unencouraged sentiment I had entertained for her sister. Pretty pink Maud had cast me out, but I appear to have passed in the flurried little circle for a magnanimous youth. Pretty pink Maud, so lovely then, before her troubles, that dusky Jane was gratefully conscious of all she made up for, Maud Stannace, very literary too, very languishing and extremely bullied by her mother, had yielded, invidiously as it might have struck me, to Ray Limbert's suit, which Mrs Stannace was not the woman to stomach. Mrs Stannace was seldom the woman to do anything: she had been shocked at the way her children, with the grubby taint of their father's blood (he had published pale Remains or flat Conversations of *his* father) breathed the alien air of authorship. If not the daughter, nor even the niece, she was, if I am not mistaken, the second cousin of a hundred earls and a great stickler for relationship, so that she had other views for her brilliant child, especially after her quiet one (such had been her original discreet forecast of the producer of eighty volumes) became the second wife of an ex-army-surgeon, already the father of four children. Mrs Stannace had too manifestly dreamed it would be given to pretty pink Maud to detach some one of the hundred, who wouldn't be missed, from the cluster. It was because she cared only for cousins that I unlearnt the way to her house, which she had once reminded me was one of the few paths of gentility I could hope to tread. Ralph Limbert, who belonged to nobody and had done nothing—nothing even at Cambridge—had only the uncanny spell he had cast upon her younger daughter to recommend him; but if her younger daughter had a spark of filial feeling she wouldn't commit the indecency of deserting for his sake a deeply dependent and intensely aggravated mother.

These things I learned from Jane Highmore, who, as if her books had been babies (they remained her only ones), had waited till after marriage to show what she could do and now bade fair to surround her satisfied spouse (he took, for some mysterious reason, a part of the credit) with a little family, in sets of triplets, which properly handled would be the support of his declining years. The young couple, neither of whom had a penny, were now virtually engaged: the thing was subject to Ralph's putting his hand on some regular employment. People more enamoured couldn't be conceived, and Mrs Highmore, honest woman, who had moreover a professional sense for a love-story, was eager to take them under her wing. What was wanted was a decent opening for Limbert, which it had occurred to her I might assist her to find, though indeed I had not yet found any such matter for myself. But it was well known that I was too particular, whereas poor Ralph, with the easy manners of genius, was ready to accept almost anything to which a salary, even a small one, was attached. If he could only for instance get a place on a newspaper the rest of his maintenance would come freely enough. It was true that his two novels, one of which she had brought to leave with me, had passed unperceived and that to her, Mrs Highmore personally, they didn't irresistibly appeal; but she could all the same assure me that I should have only to spend ten minutes with him (and our encounter must speedily take place) to receive an impression of latent power.

Our encounter took place soon after I had read the volumes Mrs Highmore had left with me, in which I recognised an intention of a sort that I had then pretty well given up the hope of meeting. I daresay that without knowing it I had been looking out rather hungrily for an altar of sacrifice: however that may be I submitted when I came across Ralph Limbert to one of the rarest emotions of my literary life, the sense of an activity in which I could critically rest. The rest was deep and salutary, and it has not been disturbed to this hour. It has been a long, large surrender, the luxury of dropped discriminations. He couldn't trouble me, whatever he did, for I practically enjoyed him as much when he was worse as when he was better. It was a case, I suppose, of natural prearrangement, in which, I hasten to add, I keep excellent company. We are a numerous band, partakers of the same repose, who sit together in the shade of the tree, by the plash of the fountain, with the glare of the desert around us and no great vice that I know of but the habit perhaps of estimating people a little too much by what they think of a certain style. If it had been laid upon these few pages, none the less, to be the history of an enthusiasm, I should not have undertaken them: they are concerned with Ralph Limbert in relations to which I was a stranger or in which I participated only by sympathy. I used to talk about his work, but I seldom talk now: the brotherhood of the faith have become, like the Trappists, a silent order. If to the day of his death, after mortal disenchantments, the impression he first produced always evoked the word "ingenuous," those to whom his face was familiar can easily imagine what it must have been when it still had the light of youth. I had never seen a man of genius look so passive, a man of experience so off his guard. At the period I made his acquaintance this freshness was all unbrushed. His foot had begun to stumble, but he was full of big intentions and of sweet Maud Stannace. Black-haired and pale, deceptively languid, he had the eyes of a clever child and the voice of a bronze bell. He saw more even than I had done in the girl he was engaged to; as time went on I became conscious that we had both, properly enough, seen rather more than there was. Our odd situation, that of the three of us, became perfectly possible from the moment I observed that he had more patience with her than I should have had. I was happy at not having to supply this quantity, and she, on her side, found pleasure in being able to be impertinent to me without incurring the reproach of a bad wife.

Limbert's novels appeared to have brought him no money: they had only brought him, so far as I could then make out, tributes that took up his time. These indeed brought him from several quarters some other things, and on my part at the end of three months *The Blackport Beacon*. I don't to-day remember how I obtained for him the London correspondence of the great northern organ, unless it was through somebody's having obtained it for myself. I seem to recall that I got rid of it in Limbert's interest, persuaded the editor that he was much the better man. The better man was naturally the man who had pledged himself to support a charming wife. We were neither of us good, as the event proved, but he had a finer sort of badness. *The Blackport Beacon* had two London correspondents—one a supposed haunter of political circles, the other a votary of questions sketchily classified as literary. They were both expected to be lively, and what was held out to each was that it was honourably open to him to be livelier than the other. I recollect the political correspondent of that period and how the problem offered to Ray Limbert was to try to be livelier than Pat Moyle. He had not yet seemed to me so candid as when he undertook this exploit, which brought matters to a head with Mrs Stannace, inasmuch as her opposition to the marriage now logically fell to the ground. It's all tears and laughter as I look back upon that admirable time, in which nothing was so romantic as our intense vision of the real. No fool's paradise ever rustled such a cradle-song. It was anything but Bohemia—it was the very temple of Mrs Grundy. We knew we were too critical, and that made us sublimely indulgent; we believed we did our duty or wanted to, and that made us free to dream. But we dreamed over the multiplication-table; we were nothing if not practical. Oh, the long smokes and sudden ideas, the knowing hints and banished scruples! The great thing was for Limbert to bring out his next book, which was just what his delightful engagement with the *Beacon* would give him leisure and liberty to do. The kind of work, all human and elastic and suggestive, was capital experience: in picking up things for his bi-weekly letter he would pick up life as well, he would pick up literature. The new publications, the new pictures, the new people—there would be nothing too novel for us and nobody too sacred. We introduced everything and everybody into Mrs Stannace's drawing-room, of which I again became a familiar.

Mrs Stannace, it was true, thought herself in strange company; she didn't particularly mind the new books, though some of them seemed queer enough, but to the new people she had decided objections. It was notorious however that poor Lady Robeck secretly wrote for one of the papers, and the thing had certainly, in its glance at the doings of the great world, a side that might be made attractive. But we were going to make every side attractive and we had everything to say about the sort of thing a paper like the *Beacon* would want. To give it what it would want and to give it nothing else was not doubtless an inspiring, but it was a perfectly respectable task, especially for a man with an appealing bride and a contentious mother-in-law. I thought Limbert's first letters as charming as the type allowed, though I won't deny that in spite of my sense of the importance of concessions I was just a trifle disconcerted at the way he had caught the tone. The tone was of course to be caught, but need it have been caught so in the act? The creature was even cleverer, as Maud Stannace said, than she had ventured to hope. Verily it was a good thing to have a dose of the wisdom of the serpent. If it had to be journalism—well, it *was* journalism. If he had to be "chatty" —well, he *was* chatty. Now and then he made a hit that—it was stupid of me—brought the blood to my face. I hated him to be so personal; but still, if it would make his fortune——! It wouldn't of course directly, but the book would, practically and in the sense to which our pure ideas of fortune were confined; and these things were all for the book. The daily balm meanwhile was in what one knew of the book—there were exquisite things to know; in the quiet monthly cheques from Blackport and in the deeper rose of Maud's little preparations, which were as dainty, on their tiny scale, as if she had been a humming-bird building a nest. When at the end of three months her betrothed had fairly settled down to his correspondence—in which Mrs Highmore was the only person, so far as we could discover, disappointed, even she moreover being in this particular tortuous and possibly jealous; when the situation had assumed such a comfortable shape it was quite time to prepare. I published at that moment my first volume, mere faded ink to-day, a little collection of literary impressions, odds and ends of criticism contributed to a journal less remunerative but also less chatty than the *Beacon*, small ironies and ecstasies, great phrases and mistakes; and the very week it came out poor Limbert devoted half of one of his letters to it, with the happy sense this time of gratifying both himself and me as well as the Blackport breakfast-tables. I remember his saying it wasn't literature, the stuff, superficial stuff, he had to write about me; but what did that matter if it came back, as we knew, to the making for literature in the round-about way? I sold the thing, I remember, for ten pounds, and with the money I bought in Vigo Street a quaint piece of old silver for Maud Stannace, which I carried to her with my own hand as a wedding-gift. In her mother's small drawing-room, a faded bower of photography fenced in and bedimmed by folding screens out of which sallow persons of fashion with dashing signatures looked at you from retouched eyes and little windows of plush, I was left to wait long enough to feel in the air of the house a hushed vibration of disaster. When our young lady came in she was very pale and her eyes too had been retouched.

"Something horrid has happened," I immediately said; and having really all along but half believed in her mother's meagre permission I risked with an unguarded groan the introduction of Mrs Stannace's name.

"Yes, she has made a dreadful scene; she insists on our putting it off again. We're very unhappy: poor Ray has been turned off." Her tears began to flow again.

I had such a good conscience that I stared. "Turned off what?"

"Why, his paper of course. The *Beacon* has given him what he calls the sack. They don't like his letters: they're not the style of thing they want."

My blankness could only deepen. "Then what style of thing *do* they want?"

"Something more chatty."

"More?" I cried, aghast.

"More gossipy, more personal. They want 'journalism.' They want tremendous trash."

"Why, that's just what his letters have *been!*" I broke out.

This was strong, and I caught myself up, but the girl offered me the pardon of a beautiful wan smile. "So Ray himself declares. He says he has stooped so low."

"Very well—he must stoop lower. He *must* keep the place."

"He can't!" poor Maud wailed. "He says he has tried all he knows, has been abject, has gone on all fours, and that if they don't like that——"

"He accepts his dismissal?" I interposed in dismay.

She gave a tragic shrug. "What other course is open to him? He wrote to them that such work as he has done is the very worst he can do for the money."

"Therefore," I inquired with a flash of hope, "they'll offer him more for worse?"

"No indeed," she answered, "they haven't even offered him to go on at a reduction. He isn't funny enough."

I reflected a moment. "But surely such a thing as his notice of my book——!"

"It was your wretched book that was the last straw! He should have treated it superficially."

"Well, if he didn't't——!" I began. Then I checked myself. "*Je vous porte malheur.*"

She didn't deny this; she only went on: "What on earth is he to do?"

"He's to do better than the monkeys! He's to write!"

"But what on earth are we to marry on?"

I considered once more. "You're to marry on *The Major Key*."

II

The Major Key was the new novel, and the great thing accordingly was to finish it; a consummation for which three months of the *Beacon* had in some degree prepared the way. The action of that journal was indeed a shock, but I didn't know then the worst, didn't know that in addition to being a shock it was also a symptom. It was the first hint of the difficulty to which poor Limbert was eventually to succumb. His state was the happier of a truth for his not immediately seeing all that it meant. Difficulty was the law of life, but one could thank heaven it was exceptionally present in that horrid quarter. There was the difficulty that inspired, the difficulty of *The Major Key* to wit, which it was after all base to sacrifice to the turning of somersaults for pennies. These convictions Ray Limbert beguiled his fresh wait by blandly entertaining: not indeed, I think, that the failure of his attempt to be chatty didn't leave him slightly humiliated. If it was bad enough to have grinned through a horse-collar it was very bad indeed to have grinned in vain. Well, he would try no more grinning or at least no more horse-collars. The only success worth one's powder was success in the line of one's idiosyncrasy. Consistency was in itself distinction, and what was talent but the art of being completely whatever it was that one happened to be? One's things were characteristic or they were nothing. I look back rather fondly on our having exchanged in those days these admirable remarks and many others; on our having been very happy too, in spite of postponements and obscurities, in spite also of such occasional hauntings as could spring from our lurid glimpse of the fact that even twaddle cunningly calculated was far above people's heads. It was easy to wave away spectres by the reflection that all one had to do was not to write for people; it was certainly not for people that Limbert wrote while he hammered at *The Major Key*. The taint of literature was fatal only in a certain kind of air, which was precisely the kind against which we had now closed our window. Mrs Stannace rose from her crumpled cushions as soon as she had obtained an adjournment, and Maud looked pale and proud, quite victorious and superior, at her having obtained nothing more. Maud behaved well, I thought, to her mother, and well indeed for a girl who had mainly been taught to be flowerlike to every one. What she gave Ray Limbert her fine abundant needs made him then and ever pay for; but the gift was liberal, almost wonderful—an assertion I make even while remembering to how many clever women, early and late, his work has been dear. It was not only that the woman he was to marry was in love with him, but that (this was the strangeness) she had really seen almost better than any one what he could do. The greatest strangeness was that she didn't want him to do something different. This boundless belief was indeed the main way of her devotion; and as an act of faith it naturally asked for miracles. She was a rare wife for a poet if she was not perhaps the best who could have been picked out for a poor man.

Well, we were to have the miracles at all events and we were in a perfect state of mind to receive them. There were more of us every day, and we thought highly even of our friend's odd jobs and pot-boilers. The *Beacon* had had no successor, but he found some quiet corners and stray chances. Perpetually poking the fire and looking out of the window, he was certainly not a monster of facility, but he was, thanks perhaps to a certain method in that madness, a monster of certainty. It wasn't every one however who knew him for this: many editors printed him but once. He was getting a small reputation as a man it was well to have the first time; he created obscure apprehensions as to what might happen the second. He was good for making an impression, but no one seemed exactly to know what the impression was good for when made. The reason was simply that they had not seen yet *The Major Key*, that fiery-hearted rose as to which we watched in private the formation of petal after petal and flame after flame. Nothing mattered but this, for it had already elicited a splendid bid, much talked about in Mrs Highmore's drawing-room, where at this point my reminiscences grow particularly thick. *Her* roses bloomed all the year and her sociability increased with her row of prizes. We had an idea that we "met every one" there—so we naturally thought when we met each other.

Between our hostess and Ray Limbert flourished the happiest relation, the only cloud on which was that her husband eyed him rather askance. When he was called clever this personage wanted to know what he had to "show"; and it was certain that he showed nothing that could compare with Jane Highmore. Mr Highmore took his stand on accomplished work and, turning up his coat-tails, warmed his rear with a good conscience at the neat bookcase in which the generations of triplets were chronologically arranged. The harmony between his companions rested on the fact that, as I have already hinted, each would have liked so much to be the other. Limbert couldn't but have a feeling about a woman who in addition to being the best creature and her sister's backer would have made, could she have condescended, such a success with the *Beacon*. On the other hand Mrs Highmore used freely to say: "Do you know, he'll do exactly the thing that *I* want to do? I shall never do it myself, but he'll do it instead. Yes, he'll do *my* thing, and I shall hate him for it—the wretch." Hating him was her pleasant humour, for the wretch was personally to her taste.

She prevailed on her own publisher to promise to take *The Major Key* and to engage to pay a considerable sum down, as the phrase is, on the presumption of its attracting attention. This was good news for the evening's end at Mrs Highmore's when there were only four or five left and cigarettes ran low; but there was better news to come, and I have never forgotten how, as it was I who had the good fortune to bring it, I kept it back on one of those occasions, for the sake of my effect, till only the right people remained. The right people were now more and more numerous, but this was a revelation addressed only to a choice residuum—a residuum including of course Limbert himself, with whom I haggled for another cigarette before I announced that as a consequence of an interview I had had with him that afternoon, and of a subtle argument I had brought to bear, Mrs Highmore's pearl of publishers had agreed to put forth the new book as a serial. He was to "run" it in his magazine and he was to pay ever so much more for the privilege. I produced a fine gasp which presently found a more articulate relief, but poor Limbert's voice failed him once for all (he knew he was to walk away with me) and it was some one else who asked me in what my subtle argument had resided. I forget what florid description I then gave of it: to-day I have no reason not to confess that it had resided in the simple plea that the book was exquisite. I had said: "Come, my dear friend, be original; just risk it for that!" My dear friend seemed to rise to the chance, and I followed up my advantage, permitting him honestly no illusion as to the quality of the work. He clutched interrogatively at two or three attenuations, but I dashed them aside, leaving him face to face with the formidable truth. It was just a pure gem: was he the man not to flinch? His danger appeared to have acted upon him as the anaconda acts upon the rabbit; fascinated and paralysed, he had been engulfed in the long pink throat. When a week before, at my request, Limbert had let me possess for a day the complete manuscript, beautifully copied out by Maud Stannace, I had flushed with indignation at its having to be said of the author of such pages that he hadn't the common means to marry. I had taken the field in a great glow to repair this scandal, and it was therefore quite directly my fault if three months later, when *The Major Key* began to run, Mrs Stannace was driven to the wall. She had made a condition of a fixed income; and at last a fixed income was achieved.

She had to recognise it, and after much prostration among the photographs she recognised it to the extent of accepting some of the convenience of it in the form of a project for a common household, to the expenses of which each party should proportionately contribute. Jane Highmore made a great point of her not being left alone, but Mrs Stannace herself determined the proportion, which on Limbert's side at least and in spite of many other fluctuations was never altered.

His income had been "fixed" with a vengeance: having painfully stooped to the comprehension of it Mrs Stannace rested on this effort to the end and asked no further question on the subject. *The Major Key* in other words ran ever so long, and before it was half out Limbert and Maud had been married and the common household set up. These first months were probably the happiest in the family annals, with wedding-bells and budding laurels, the quiet, assured course of the book and the friendly, familiar note, round the corner, of Mrs Highmore's big guns. They gave Ralph time to block in another picture as well as to let me know after a while that he had the happy prospect of becoming a father. We had at times some dispute as to whether *The Major Key* was making an impression, but our contention could only be futile so long as we were not agreed as to what an impression consisted of. Several persons wrote to the author and several others asked to be introduced to him: wasn't that an impression? One of the lively "weeklies," snapping at the deadly "monthlies," said the whole thing was "grossly inartistic"—wasn't that? It was somewhere else proclaimed "a wonderfully subtle character-study"—wasn't that too? The strongest effect doubtless was produced on the publisher when, in its lemon-coloured volumes, like a little dish of three custards, the book was at last served cold: he never got his money back and so far as I know has never got it back to this day. *The Major Key* was rather a great performance than a great success. It converted readers into friends and friends into lovers; it placed the author, as the phrase is—placed him all too definitely; but it shrank to obscurity in the account of sales eventually rendered. It was in short an exquisite thing, but it was scarcely a thing to have published and certainly not a thing to have married on. I heard all about the matter, for my intervention had much exposed me. Mrs Highmore said the second volume had given her ideas, and the ideas are probably to be found in some of her works, to the circulation of which they have even perhaps contributed. This was not absolutely yet the very thing she wanted to do, but it was on the way to it. So much, she informed me, she particularly perceived in the light of a critical study which I put forth in a little magazine; which the publisher in his advertisements quoted from profusely; and as to which there sprang up some absurd story that Limbert himself had written it. I remember that on my asking some one why such an idiotic thing had been said my interlocutor replied: "Oh, because, you know, it's just the way he *would* have written!" My spirit sank a little perhaps as I reflected that with such analogies in our manner there might prove to be some in our fate.

It was during the next four or five years that our eyes were open to what, unless something could be done, that fate, at least on Limbert's part, might be. The thing to be done was of course to write the book, the book that would make the difference, really justify the burden he had accepted and consummately express his power. For the works that followed upon *The Major Key* he had inevitably to accept conditions the reverse of brilliant, at a time too when the strain upon his resources had begun to show sharpness. With three babies in due course, an ailing wife and a complication still greater than these, it became highly important that a man should do only his best. Whatever Limbert did was his best; so at least each time I thought and so I unfailingly said somewhere, though it was not my saying it, heaven knows, that made the desired difference. Every one else indeed said it, and there was among multiplied worries always the comfort that his position was quite assured. The two books that followed *The Major Key* did more than anything else to assure it, and Jane Highmore was always crying out: "You stand alone, dear Ray; you stand absolutely alone!" Dear Ray used to tell me that he felt the truth of this in feebly-attempted discussions with his bookseller. His sister-in-law gave him good advice into the bargain; she was a repository of knowing hints, of esoteric learning. These things were doubtless not the less valuable to him for bearing wholly on the question of how a reputation might be with a little gumption, as Mrs Highmore said, "worked." Save when she occasionally bore testimony to her desire to do, as Limbert did, something some day for her own very self, I never heard her speak of the literary motive as if it were distinguishable from the pecuniary. She cocked up his hat, she pricked up his prudence for him, reminding him that as one seemed to take one's self so the silly world was ready to take one. It was a fatal mistake to be too candid even with those who were all right—not to look and to talk prosperous, not at least to pretend that one had beautiful sales. To listen to her you would have thought the profession of letters a wonderful game of bluff. Wherever one's idea began it ended somehow in inspired paragraphs in the newspapers. "*I* pretend, I assure you, that you are going off like wildfire—I can at least do that for you!" she often declared, prevented as she was from doing much else by Mr Highmore's insurmountable objection to *their* taking Mrs Stannace.

I couldn't help regarding the presence of this latter lady in Limbert's life as the major complication: whatever he attempted it appeared given to him to achieve as best he could in the mere margin of the space in which she swung her petticoats. I may err in the belief that she practically lived on him, for though it was not in him to follow adequately Mrs Highmore's counsel there were exasperated confessions he never made, scanty domestic curtains he rattled on their rings. I may exaggerate in the retrospect his apparent anxieties, for these after all were the years when his talent was freshest and when as a writer he most laid down his line. It wasn't of Mrs Stannace nor even as time went on of Mrs Limbert that we mainly talked when I got at longer intervals a smokier hour in the little grey den from which we could step out, as we used to say, to the lawn. The lawn was the back-garden, and Limbert's study was behind the dining-room, with folding doors not impervious to the clatter of the children's tea. We sometimes took refuge from it in the depths—a bush and a half deep—of the shrubbery, where was a bench that gave us a view while we gossiped of Mrs Stannace's tiara-like headdress nodding at an upper window. Within doors and without Limbert's life was overhung by an awful region that figured in his conversation, comprehensively and with unpremeditated art, as Upstairs. It was Upstairs that the thunder gathered, that Mrs Stannace kept her accounts and her state, that Mrs Limbert had her babies and her headaches, that the bells for ever jangled at the maids, that everything imperative in short took place—everything that he had somehow, pen in hand, to meet and dispose of in the little room on the garden-level. I don't think he liked to go Upstairs, but no special burst of confidence was needed to make me feel that a terrible deal of service went. It was the habit of the ladies of the Stannace family to be extremely waited on, and I've never been in a house where three maids and a nursery-governess gave such an impression of a retinue. "Oh, they're so deucedly, so hereditarily fine!"—I remember how that dropped from him in some worried hour. Well, it was because Maud was so universally fine that we had both been in love with her. It was not an air moreover for the plaintive note: no private inconvenience could long outweigh for him the great happiness of these years—the happiness that sat with us when we talked and that made it always amusing to talk, the sense of his being on the heels of success, coming closer and closer, touching it at last, knowing that he should touch it again and hold it fast and hold it high. Of course when we said success we didn't mean exactly what Mrs Highmore for instance meant. He used to quote at me as a definition something from a nameless page of my own, some stray dictum to the effect that the man of his craft had achieved it when of a beautiful subject his expression was complete. Well, wasn't Limbert's in all conscience complete?

III

It was bang upon this completeness all the same that the turn arrived, the turn I can't say of his fortune—for what was that? —but of his confidence, of his spirits and, what was more to the point, of his system. The whole occasion on which the first symptom flared out is before me as I write. I had met them both at dinner: they were diners who had reached the penultimate stage—the stage which in theory is a rigid selection and in practice a wan submission. It was late in the season and stronger spirits than theirs were broken; the night was close and the air of the banquet such as to restrict conversation to the refusal of dishes and consumption to the sniffing of a flower. It struck me all the more that Mrs Limbert was flying her flag. As vivid as a page of her husband's prose, she had one of those flickers of freshness that are the miracle of her sex and one of those expensive dresses that are the miracle of ours. She had also a neat brougham in which she had offered to rescue an old lady from the possibilities of a queer cab-horse; so that when she had rolled away with her charge I proposed a walk home with her husband, whom I had overtaken on the doorstep. Before I had gone far with him he told me he had news for me—he had accepted, of all people and of all things, an "editorial position." It had come to pass that very day, from one hour to another, without time for appeals or ponderations: Mr Bousefield, the proprietor of a "high-class monthly," making, as they said, a sudden change, had dropped on him heavily out of the blue. It was all right—there was a salary and an idea, and both of them, as such things went, rather high. We took our way slowly through the vacant streets, and in the explanations and revelations that as we lingered under lamp-posts I drew from him I found with an apprehension that I tried to gulp down a foretaste of the bitter end. He told me more than he had ever told me yet. He couldn't balance accounts—that was the trouble: his expenses were too rising a tide. It was absolutely necessary that he should at last make money, and now he must work only for that. The need this last year had gathered the force of a crusher: it had rolled over him and laid him on his back. He had his scheme; this time he knew what he was about; on some good occasion, with leisure to talk it over, he would tell me the blessed whole. His editorship would help him, and for the rest he must help himself. If he couldn't they would have to do something fundamental—change their life altogether, give up London, move into the country, take a house at thirty pounds a year, send their children to the Board-school. I saw that he was excited, and he admitted that he was: he had waked out of a trance. He had been on the wrong tack; he had piled mistake on mistake. It was the vision of his remedy that now excited him: ineffably, grotesquely simple, it had yet come to him only within a day or two. No, he wouldn't tell me what it was; he would give me the night to guess, and if I shouldn't guess it would be because I was as big an ass as himself. However, a lone man might be an ass: he had room in his life for his ears. Ray had a burden that demanded a back: the back must therefore now be properly instituted. As to the editorship, it was simply heaven-sent, being not at all another case of *The Blackport Beacon* but a case of the very opposite. The proprietor, the great Mr Bousefield, had approached him precisely because his name, which was to be on the cover, *didn't* represent the chatty. The whole thing was to be—oh, on fiddling little lines of course—a protest against the chatty. Bousefield wanted him to be himself; it was for himself Bousefield had picked him out. Wasn't it beautiful and brave of Bousefield? He wanted literature, he saw the great reaction coming, the way the cat was going to jump. "Where will you get literature?" I woefully asked; to which he replied with a laugh that what he had to get was not literature but only what Bousefield would take for it.

In that single phrase without more ado I discovered his famous remedy. What was before him for the future was not to do his work but to do what somebody else would take for it. I had the question out with him on the next opportunity, and of all the lively discussions into which we had been destined to drift it lingers in my mind as the liveliest. This was not, I hasten to add, because I disputed his conclusions: it was an effect of the very force with which, when I had fathomed his wretched premises, I took them to my soul. It was very well to talk with Jane Highmore about his standing alone: the eminent relief of this position had brought him to the verge of ruin. Several persons admired his books—nothing was less contestable; but they appeared to have a mortal objection to acquiring them by subscription or by purchase: they begged or borrowed or stole, they delegated one of the party perhaps to commit the volumes to memory and repeat them, like the bards of old, to listening multitudes. Some ingenious theory was required at any rate to account for the inexorable limits of his circulation. It wasn't a thing for five people to live on; therefore either the objects circulated must change their nature or the organisms to be nourished must. The former change was perhaps the easier to consider first. Limbert considered it with extraordinary ingenuity from that time on, and the ingenuity, greater even than any I had yet had occasion to admire in him, made the whole next stage of his career rich in curiosity and suspense.

"I have been butting my skull against a wall," he had said in those hours of confidence; "and, to be as sublime a blockhead, if you'll allow me the word, you, my dear fellow, have kept sounding the charge. We've sat prating here of 'success,' heaven help us, like chanting monks in a cloister, hugging the sweet delusion that it lies somewhere in the work itself, in the expression, as you said, of one's subject or the intensification, as somebody else somewhere says, of one's note. One has been going on in short as if the only thing to do were to accept the law of one's talent and thinking that if certain consequences didn't follow it was only because one wasn't logical enough. My disaster has served me right—I mean for using that ignoble word at all. It's a mere distributor's, a mere hawker's word. What *is* 'success' anyhow? When a book's right, it's right—shame to it surely if it isn't. When it sells it sells—it brings money like potatoes or beer. If there's dishonour one way and inconvenience the other, it certainly is comfortable, but it as certainly isn't glorious to have escaped them. People of delicacy don't brag either about their probity or about their luck. Success be hanged!—I want to sell. It's a question of life and death. I must study the way. I've studied too much the other way—I know the other way now, every inch of it. I must cultivate the market—it's a science like another. I must go in for an infernal cunning. It will be very amusing, I foresee that; I shall lead a dashing life and drive a roaring trade. I haven't been obvious—I must *be* obvious. I haven't been popular—I must *be* popular. It's another art—or perhaps it isn't an art at all. It's something else; one must find out *what* it is. Is it something awfully queer?—you blush!—something barely decent? All the greater incentive to curiosity! Curiosity's an immense motive; we shall have tremendous sport. They all do it; it's only a question of how. Of course I've everything to unlearn; but what is life, as Jane Highmore says, but a lesson? I must get all I can, all she can give me, from Jane. She can't explain herself much; she's all intuition; her processes are obscure; it's the spirit that swoops down and catches her up. But I must study her reverently in her works. Yes, you've defied me before, but now my loins are girded: I declare I'll read one of them—I really will: I'll put it through if I perish!"

I won't pretend that he made all these remarks at once; but there wasn't one that he didn't make at one time or another, for suggestion and occasion were plentiful enough, his life being now given up altogether to his new necessity. It wasn't a question of his having or not having, as they say, my intellectual sympathy: the brute force of the pressure left no room for judgment; it made all emotion a mere recourse to the spy-glass. I watched him as I should have watched a long race or a long chase, irresistibly siding with him but much occupied with the calculation of odds. I confess indeed that my heart, for the endless stretch that he covered so fast, was often in my throat. I saw him peg away over the sun-dappled plain, I saw him double and wind and gain and lose; and all the while I secretly entertained a conviction. I wanted him to feed his many mouths, but at the bottom of all things was my sense that if he should succeed in doing so in this particular way I should think less well of him. Now I had an absolute terror of that. Meanwhile so far as I could I backed him up, I helped him: all the more that I had warned him immensely at first, smiled with a compassion it was very good of him not to have found exasperating over the complacency of his assumption that a man could escape from himself. Ray Limbert at all events would certainly never escape; but one could make believe for him, make believe very hard—an undertaking in which at first Mr Bousefield was visibly a blessing. Limbert was delightful on the business of this being at last my chance too—my chance, so miraculously vouchsafed, to appear with a certain luxuriance. He didn't care how often he printed me, for wasn't it exactly in my direction Mr Bousefield held that the cat was going to jump? This was the least he could do for me. I might write on anything I liked—on anything at least but Mr Limbert's second manner. He didn't wish attention strikingly called to his second manner; it was to operate insidiously; people were to be left to believe they had discovered it long ago. "Ralph Limbert? Why, when did we ever live without him?"—that's what he wanted them to say. Besides, they hated manners—let sleeping dogs lie. His understanding with Mr Bousefield—on which he had had not at all to insist; it was the excellent man who insisted—was that he should run one of his beautiful stories in the magazine. As to the beauty of his story however Limbert was going to be less admirably straight than as to the beauty of everything else. That was another reason why I mustn't write about his new line: Mr Bousefield was not to be too definitely warned that such a periodical was exposed to prostitution. By the time he should find it out for himself the public—*le gros public*—would have bitten, and then perhaps he would be conciliated and forgive. Everything else would be literary in short, and above all *I* would be; only Ralph Limbert wouldn't—he'd chuck up the whole thing sooner. He'd be vulgar, he'd be rudimentary, he'd be atrocious: he'd be elaborately what he hadn't been before.

I duly noticed that he had more trouble in making "everything else" literary than he had at first allowed for; but this was largely counteracted by the ease with which he was able to obtain that his mark should not be overshot. He had taken well to heart the old lesson of the *Beacon;* he remembered that he was after all there to keep his contributors down much rather than to keep them up. I thought at times that he kept them down a trifle too far, but he assured me that I needn't be nervous: he had his limit—his limit was inexorable. He would reserve pure vulgarity for his serial, over which he was sweating blood and water; elsewhere it should be qualified by the prime qualification, the mediocrity that attaches, that endears. Bousefield, he allowed, was proud, was difficult: nothing was really good enough for him but the middling good; but he himself was prepared for adverse comment, resolute for his noble course. Hadn't Limbert moreover in the event of a charge of laxity from headquarters the great strength of being able to point to my contributions? Therefore I must let myself go, I must abound in my peculiar sense, I must be a resource in case of accidents. Limbert's vision of accidents hovered mainly over the sudden awakening of Mr Bousefield to the stuff that in the department of fiction his editor was palming off. He would then have to confess in all humility that this was not what the good old man wanted, but I should be all the more there as a salutary specimen. I would cross the scent with something showily impossible, splendidly unpopular—I must be sure to have something on hand. I always had plenty on hand—poor Limbert needn't have worried: the magazine was forearmed each month by my care with a retort to any possible accusation of trifling with Mr Bousefield's standard. He had admitted to Limbert, after much consideration indeed, that he was prepared to be perfectly human; but he had added that he was not prepared for an abuse of this admission. The thing in the world I think I least felt myself was an abuse, even though (as I had never mentioned to my friendly editor) I too had my project for a bigger reverberation. I daresay I trusted mine more than I trusted Limbert's; at all events the golden mean in which in the special case he saw his salvation as an editor was something I should be most sure of if I were to exhibit it myself. I exhibited it month after month in the form of a monstrous levity, only praying heaven that my editor might now not tell me, as he had so often told me, that my result was awfully good. I knew what that would signify—it would signify, sketchily speaking, disaster. What he did tell me heartily was that it was just what his game required: his new line had brought with it an earnest assumption—earnest save when we privately laughed about it—of the locutions proper to real bold enterprise. If I tried to keep him in the dark even as he kept Mr Bousefield there was nothing to show that I was not tolerably successful: each case therefore presented a promising analogy for the other. He never noticed my descent, and it was accordingly possible that Mr Bousefield would never notice his. But would nobody notice it at all?—that was a question that added a prospective zest to one's possession of a critical sense. So much depended upon it that I was rather relieved than otherwise not to know the answer too soon. I waited in fact a year—the year for which Limbert had cannily engaged on trial with Mr Bousefield; the year as to which through the same sharpened shrewdness it had been conveyed in the agreement between them that Mr Bousefield was not to intermeddle. It had been Limbert's general prayer that we would during this period let him quite alone. His terror of my direct rays was a droll, dreadful force that always operated: he explained it by the fact that I understood him too well, expressed too much of his intention, saved him too little from himself. The less he was saved the more he didn't sell: I literally interpreted, and that was simply fatal.

I held my breath accordingly; I did more—I closed my eyes, I guarded my treacherous ears. He induced several of us to do that (of such devotions we were capable) so that not even glancing at the thing from month to month, and having nothing but his shamed, anxious silence to go by, I participated only vaguely in the little hum that surrounded his act of sacrifice. It was blown about the town that the public would be surprised; it was hinted, it was printed that he was making a desperate bid. His new work was spoken of as "more calculated for general acceptance." These tidings produced in some quarters much reprobation, and nowhere more, I think, than on the part of certain persons who had never read a word of him, or assuredly had never spent a shilling on him, and who hung for hours over the other attractions of the newspaper that announced his abasement. So much asperity cheered me a little—seemed to signify that he might really be doing something. On the other hand I had a distinct alarm; some one sent me for some alien reason an American journal (containing frankly more than that source of affliction) in which was quoted a passage from our friend's last instalment. The passage—I couldn't for my life help reading it—was simply superb. Ah, he *would* have to move to the country if that was the worst he could do! It gave me a pang to see how little after all he had improved since the days of his competition with Pat Moyle. There was nothing in the passage quoted in the American paper that Pat would for a moment have owned. During the last weeks, as the opportunity of reading the complete thing drew near, one's suspense was barely endurable, and I shall never forget the July evening on which I put it to rout. Coming home to dinner I found the two volumes on my table, and I sat up with them half the night, dazed, bewildered, rubbing my eyes, wondering at the monstrous joke. *Was* it a monstrous joke, his second manner—was *this* the new line, the desperate bid, the scheme for more general acceptance and the remedy for material failure? Had he made a fool of all his following, or had he most injuriously made a still bigger fool of himself? Obvious?—where the deuce was it obvious? Popular?—how on earth could it be popular? The thing was charming with all his charm and powerful with all his power: it was an unscrupulous, an unsparing, a shameless, merciless masterpiece. It was, no doubt, like the old letters to the *Beacon*, the worst he could do; but the perversity of the effort, even though heroic, had been frustrated by the purity of the gift. Under what illusion had he laboured, with what wavering, treacherous compass had he steered? His honour was inviolable, his measurements were all wrong. I was thrilled with the whole impression and with all that came crowding in its train. It was too grand a collapse—it was too hideous a triumph; I exulted almost with tears—I lamented with a strange delight. Indeed as the short night waned and, threshing about in my emotion, I fidgeted to my high-perched window for a glimpse of the summer dawn, I became at last aware that I was staring at it out of eyes that had compassionately and admiringly filled. The eastern sky, over the London housetops, had a wonderful tragic crimson. That was the colour of his magnificent mistake.

IV

If something less had depended on my impression I daresay I should have communicated it as soon as I had swallowed my breakfast; but the case was so embarrassing that I spent the first half of the day in reconsidering it, dipping into the book again, almost feverishly turning its leaves and trying to extract from them, for my friend's benefit, some symptom of re-assurance, some ground for felicitation. This rash challenge had consequences merely dreadful; the wretched volumes, imperturbable and impeccable, with their shyer secrets and their second line of defence, were like a beautiful woman more denuded or a great symphony on a new hearing. There was something quite sinister in the way they stood up to me. I couldn't however be dumb—that was to give the wrong tinge to my disappointment; so that later in the afternoon, taking my courage in both hands, I approached with a vain tortuosity poor Limbert's door. A smart victoria waited before it in which from the bottom of the street I saw that a lady who had apparently just issued from the house was settling herself. I recognised Jane Highmore and instantly paused till she should drive down to me. She presently met me half-way and as soon as she saw me stopped her carriage in agitation. This was a relief—it postponed a moment the sight of that pale, fine face of our friend's fronting me for the right verdict. I gathered from the flushed eagerness with which Mrs Highmore asked me if I had heard the news that a verdict of some sort had already been rendered.

"What news?—about the book?"

"About that horrid magazine. They're shockingly upset. He has lost his position—he has had a fearful flare-up with Mr Bousefield."

I stood there blank, but not unaware in my blankness of how history repeats itself. There came to me across the years Maud's announcement of their ejection from the *Beacon*, and dimly, confusedly the same explanation was in the air. This time however I had been on my guard; I had had my suspicion. "He has made it too flippant?" I found breath after an instant to inquire.

Mrs Highmore's vacuity exceeded my own. "Too 'flippant?' He has made it too oracular. Mr Bousefield says he has killed it." Then perceiving my stupefaction: "Don't you know what has happened?" she pursued; "isn't it because in his trouble, poor love, he has sent for you that you've come? You've heard nothing at all? Then you had better know before you see them. Get in here with me—I'll take you a turn and tell you." We were close to the Park, the Regent's, and when with extreme alacrity I had placed myself beside her and the carriage had begun to enter it she went on: "It was what I feared, you know. It reeked with culture. He keyed it up too high."

I felt myself sinking in the general collapse. "What are you talking about?"

"Why, about that beastly magazine. They're all on the streets. I shall have to take mamma."

I pulled myself together. "What on earth then did Bousefield want? He said he wanted intellectual power."

"Yes, but Ray overdid it."

"Why, Bousefield said it was a thing he *couldn't* overdo."

"Well, Ray managed: he took Mr Bousefield too literally. It appears the thing has been doing dreadfully, but the proprietor couldn't say anything, because he had covenanted to leave the editor quite free. He describes himself as having stood there in a fever and seen his ship go down. A day or two ago the year was up, so he could at last break out. Maud says he did break out quite fearfully; he came to the house and let poor Ray have it. Ray gave it to him back; he reminded him of his own idea of the way the cat was going to jump."

I gasped with dismay. "Has Bousefield abandoned that idea? Isn't the cat going to jump?"

Mrs Highmore hesitated. "It appears that she doesn't seem in a hurry. Ray at any rate has jumped too far ahead of her. He should have temporised a little, Mr Bousefield says; but I'm beginning to think, you know," said my companion, "that Ray *can't* temporise." Fresh from my emotions of the previous twenty-four hours I was scarcely in a position to disagree with her. "He published too much pure thought."

"Pure thought?" I cried. "Why, it struck me so often—certainly in a due proportion of cases—as pure drivel!"

"Oh, you're more keyed up than he! Mr Bousefield says that of course he wanted things that were suggestive and clever, things that he could point to with pride. But he contends that Ray didn't allow for human weakness. He gave everything in too stiff doses."

Sensibly, I fear, to my neighbour I winced at her words; I felt a prick that made me meditate. Then I said: "Is that, by chance, the way he gave *me?*" Mrs Highmore remained silent so long that I had somehow the sense of a fresh pang; and after a minute, turning in my seat, I laid my hand on her arm, fixed my eyes upon her face and pursued pressingly: "Do you suppose it to be to my 'Occasional Remarks' that Mr Bousefield refers?"

At last she met my look. "Can you bear to hear it?"

"I think I can bear anything now."

"Well then, it was really what I wanted to give you an inkling of. It's largely over you that they've quarrelled. Mr Bousefield wants him to chuck you."

I grabbed her arm again. "And Limbert *won't?*"

"He seems to cling to you. Mr Bousefield says no magazine can afford you."

I gave a laugh that agitated the very coachman. "Why, my dear lady, has he any idea of my price?"

"It isn't your price—he says you're dear at any price; you

do so much to sink the ship. Your 'Remarks' are called 'Occasional,' but nothing could be more deadly regular: you're there month after month and you're never anywhere else. And you supply no public want."

"I supply the most delicious irony."

"So Ray appears to have declared. Mr Bousefield says that's not in the least a public want. No one can make out what you're talking about and no one would care if he could. I'm only quoting *him*, mind."

"Quote, quote—if Limbert holds out. I think I must leave you now, please: I must rush back to express to him what I feel."

"I'll drive you to his door. That isn't all," said Mrs Highmore. And on the way, when the carriage had turned, she communicated the rest. "Mr Bousefield really arrived with an ultimatum: it had the form of something or other by Minnie Meadows."

"Minnie Meadows?" I was stupefied.

"The new lady-humourist every one is talking about. It's the first of a series of screaming sketches for which poor Ray was to find a place."

"Is *that* Mr Bousefield's idea of literature?"

"No, but he says it's the public's, and you've got to take *some* account of the public. *Aux grands maux les grands remèdes*. They had a tremendous lot of ground to make up, and no one would make it up like Minnie. She would be the best concession they could make to human weakness; she would strike at least this note of showing that it was not going to be quite all—well, all *you*. Now Ray draws the line at Minnie; he won't stoop to Minnie; he declines to touch, to look at Minnie. When Mr Bousefield—rather imperiously, I believe—made Minnie a *sine quâ non* of his retention of his post he said something rather violent, told him to go to some unmentionable place and take Minnie with him. That of course put the fat on the fire. They had really a considerable scene."

"So had he with the *Beacon* man," I musingly replied. "Poor dear, he seems born for considerable scenes! It's on Minnie, then, that they've really split?" Mrs Highmore exhaled her despair in a sound which I took for an assent, and when we had rolled a little further I rather inconsequently and to her visible surprise broke out of my reverie. "It will never do in the world—he *must* stoop to Minnie!"

"It's too late—and what I've told you still isn't all. Mr Bousefield raises another objection."

"What other, pray?"

"Can't you guess?"

I wondered. "No more of Ray's fiction?"

"Not a line. That's something else no magazine can stand. Now that his novel has run its course Mr Bousefield is distinctly disappointed."

I fairly bounded in my place. "Then it may do?"

Mrs Highmore looked bewildered. "Why so, if he finds it too dull?"

"Dull? Ralph Limbert? He's as fine as a needle!"

"It comes to the same thing—he won't penetrate leather. Mr Bousefield had counted on something that *would*, on something that would have a wider acceptance. Ray says he wants iron pegs." I collapsed again; my flicker of elation dropped to a throb of quieter comfort; and after a moment's silence I asked my neighbour if she had herself read the work our friend had just put forth. "No," she replied, "I gave him my word at the beginning, on his urgent request, that I wouldn't."

"Not even as a book?"

"He begged me never to look at it at all. He said he was trying a low experiment. Of course I knew what he meant and I entreated him to let me just for curiosity take a peep. But he was firm, he declared he couldn't bear the thought that a woman like me should see him in the depths."

"He's only, thank God, in the depths of distress," I replied. "His experiment's nothing worse than a failure."

"Then Bousefield *is* right—his circulation won't budge?"

"It won't move one, as they say in Fleet Street. The book has extraordinary beauty."

"Poor duck—after trying so hard!" Jane Highmore sighed with real tenderness. "What *will* then become of them?"

I was silent an instant. "You must take your mother."

She was silent too. "I must speak of it to Cecil!" she presently said. Cecil is Mr Highmore, who then entertained, I knew, strong views on the inadjustability of circumstances in general to the idiosyncrasies of Mrs Stannace. He held it supremely happy that in an important relation she should have met her match. Her match was Ray Limbert—not much of a writer but a practical man. "The dear things still think, you know," my companion continued, "that the book will be the beginning of their fortune. Their illusion, if you're right, will be rudely dispelled."

"That's what makes me dread to face them. I've just spent with his volumes an unforgettable night. His illusion has lasted because so many of us have been pledged till this moment to turn our faces the other way. We haven't known the truth and have therefore had nothing to say. Now that we do know it indeed we have practically quite as little. I hang back from the threshold. How can I follow up with a burst of enthusiasm such a catastrophe as Mr Bousefield's visit?"

As I turned uneasily about my neighbour more comfortably snuggled. "Well, I'm glad then I haven't read him and have nothing unpleasant to say!" We had come back to Limbert's door, and I made the coachman stop short of it. "But he'll try again, with that determination of his: he'll build his hopes on the next time."

"On what else has he built them from the very first? It's never the present for him that bears the fruit; that's always postponed and for somebody else: there has always to be another try. I admit that his idea of a 'new line' has made him try harder than ever. It makes no difference," I brooded, still timorously lingering; "his achievement of his necessity, his hope of a market will continue to attach themselves to the future. But the next time will disappoint him as each last time has done—and then the next and the next and the next!"

I found myself seeing it all with a clearness almost inspired: it evidently cast a chill on Mrs Highmore. "Then what on earth will become of him?" she plaintively asked.

"I don't think I particularly care what may become of *him*," I returned with a conscious, reckless increase of my exaltation; "I feel it almost enough to be concerned with what may become of one's enjoyment of him. I don't know in short what will become of his circulation; I am only quite at my ease as to what will become of his work. It will simply keep all its quality. He'll try again for the common with what he'll believe to be a still more infernal cunning, and again the common will fatally elude him, for his infernal cunning will have been only his genius in an ineffectual disguise." We sat drawn up by the pavement, facing poor Limbert's future as I saw it. It relieved me in a manner to know the worst, and I prophesied with an assurance which as I look back upon it strikes me as rather remarkable. "*Que voulez-vous?*" I went on; "you can't make a sow's ear of a silk purse! It's grievous indeed if you like—there are people who can't be vulgar for trying. *He* can't—it wouldn't come off, I promise you, even once. It takes more than trying—it comes by grace. It happens not to be given to Limbert to fall. He belongs to the heights—he breathes there, he lives there, and it's accordingly to the heights I must ascend," I said as I took leave of my conductress, "to carry him this wretched news from where *we* move!"

V

A FEW months were sufficient to show how right I had been about his circulation. It didn't move one, as I had said; it stopped short in the same place, fell off in a sheer descent, like some precipice gaped up at by tourists. The public in other words drew the line for him as sharply as he had drawn it for Minnie Meadows. Minnie has skipped with a flouncing caper over his line, however; whereas the mark traced by a lustier cudgel has been a barrier insurmountable to Limbert. Those next times I had spoken of to Jane Highmore, I see them simplified by retrocession. Again and again he made his desperate bid—again and again he tried to. His rupture with Mr Bousefield caused him, I fear, in professional circles to be thought impracticable, and I am perfectly aware, to speak candidly, that no sordid advantage ever accrued to him from such public patronage of my performances as he had occasionally been in a position to offer. I reflect for my comfort that any injury I may have done him by untimely application of a faculty of analysis which could point to no converts gained by honourable exercise was at least equalled by the injury he did himself. More than once, as I have hinted, I held my tongue at his request, but my frequent plea that such favours weren't politic never found him, when in other connections there was an opportunity to give me a lift, anything but indifferent to the danger of the association. He let them have me in a word whenever he could; sometimes in periodicals in which he had credit, sometimes only at dinner. He talked about me when he couldn't get me in, but it was always part of the bargain that I shouldn't make him a topic. "How can I successfully serve you if you do?" he used to ask: he was more afraid than I thought he ought to have been of the charge of tit for tat. I didn't care, for I never could distinguish tat from tit; but as I have intimated I dropped into silence really more than anything else because there was a certain fascinated observation of his course which was quite testimony enough and to which in this huddled conclusion of it he practically reduced me.

I see it all foreshortened, his wonderful remainder—see it from the end backward, with the direction widening toward me as if on a level with the eye. The migration to the country promised him at first great things—smaller expenses, larger leisure, conditions eminently conducive on each occasion to the possible triumph of the next time. Mrs Stannace, who altogether disapproved of it, gave as one of her reasons that her son-in-law, living mainly in a village on the edge of a goose-green, would be deprived of that contact with the great world which was indispensable to the painter of manners. She had the showiest arguments for keeping him in touch, as she called it, with good society; wishing to know with some force where, from the moment he ceased to represent it from observation, the novelist could be said to be. In London fortunately a clever man was just a clever man; there were charming houses in which a person of Ray's undoubted ability, even though without the knack of making the best use of it, could always be sure of a quiet corner for watching decorously the social kaleidoscope. But the kaleidoscope of the goose-green, what in the world was that, and what such delusive thrift as drives about the land (with a fearful account for flys from the inn) to leave cards on the country magnates? This solicitude for Limbert's subject-matter was the specious colour with which, deeply determined not to affront mere tolerance in a cottage, Mrs Stannace overlaid her indisposition to place herself under the heel of Cecil Highmore. She knew that he ruled Upstairs as well as down, and she clung to the fable of the association of interests in the north of London. The Highmores had a better address—they lived now in Stanhope Gardens; but Cecil was fearfully artful—he wouldn't hear of an association of interests nor treat with his mother-in-law save as a visitor. She didn't like false positions; but on the other hand she didn't like the sacrifice of everything she was accustomed to. Her universe at all events was a universe full of card-leavings and charming houses, and it was fortunate that she couldn't Upstairs catch the sound of the doom to which, in his little grey den, describing to me his diplomacy, Limbert consigned alike the country magnates and the opportunities of London. Despoiled of every guarantee she went to Stanhope Gardens like a mere maidservant, with restrictions on her very luggage, while during the year that followed this upheaval Limbert, strolling with me on the goose-green, to which I often ran down, played extravagantly over the theme that with what he was now going in for it was a positive comfort not to have the social kaleidoscope. With a cold-blooded trick in view what had life or manners or the best society or flys from the inn to say to the question? It was as good a place as another to play his new game. He had found a quieter corner than any corner of the great world, and a damp old house at sixpence a year, which, beside leaving him all his margin to educate his children, would allow of the supreme luxury of his frankly presenting himself as a poor man. This was a convenience that *ces dames*, as he called them, had never yet fully permitted him.

It rankled in me at first to see his reward so meagre, his conquest so mean; but the simplification effected had a charm that I finally felt: it was a forcing-house for the three or four other fine miscarriages to which his scheme was evidently condemned. I limited him to three or four, having had my sharp impression, in spite of the perpetual broad joke of the thing, that a spring had really snapped in him on the occasion of that deeply disconcerting sequel to the episode of his editorship. He never lost his sense of the grotesque want, in the difference made, of adequate relation to the effort that had been the intensest of his life. He had from that moment a charge of shot in him, and it slowly worked its way to a vital part. As he met his embarrassments each year with his punctual false remedy I wondered periodically where he found the energy to return to the attack. He did it every time with a rage more blanched, but it was clear to me that the tension must finally snap the cord. We got again and again the irrepressible work of art, but what did *he* get, poor man, who wanted something so different? There were likewise odder questions than this in the matter, phenomena more curious and mysteries more puzzling, which often for sympathy if not for illumination I intimately discussed with Mrs Limbert. She had her burdens, dear lady: after the removal from London and a considerable interval she twice again became a mother. Mrs Stannace too, in a more restricted sense, exhibited afresh, in relation to the home she had abandoned, the same exemplary character. In her poverty of guarantees at Stanhope Gardens there had been least of all, it appeared, a proviso that she shouldn't resentfully revert again from Goneril to Regan. She came down to the goose-green like Lear himself, with fewer knights, or at least baronets, and the joint household was at last patched up. It fell to pieces and was put together on various occasions before Ray Limbert died. He was ridden to the end by the superstition that he had broken up Mrs Stannace's original home on pretences that had proved hollow and that if he hadn't given Maud what she might have had he could at least give her back her mother. I was always sure that a sense of the compensations he owed was half the motive of the dogged pride with which he tried to wake up the libraries. I believed Mrs Stannace still had money, though she pretended that, called upon at every turn to retrieve deficits, she had long since poured it into the general fund. This conviction haunted me; I suspected her of secret hoards, and I said to myself that she couldn't be so infamous as not some day on her deathbed to leave everything to her less opulent daughter. My compassion for the Limberts led me to hover perhaps indiscreetly round that closing scene, to dream of some happy time when such an accession of means would make up a little for their present penury.

This however was crude comfort, as in the first place I had nothing definite to go by and in the second I held it for more and more indicated that Ray wouldn't outlive her. I never ventured to sound him as to what in this particular he hoped or feared, for after the crisis marked by his leaving London I had new scruples about suffering him to be reminded of where he fell short. The poor man was in truth humiliated, and there were things as to which that kept us both silent. In proportion as he tried more fiercely for the market the old plaintive arithmetic, fertile in jokes, dropped from our conversation. We joked immensely still about the process, but our treatment of the results became sparing and superficial. He talked as much as ever, with monstrous arts and borrowed hints, of the traps he kept setting, but we all agreed to take merely for granted that the animal was caught. This propriety had really dawned upon me the day that after Mr Bousefield's visit Mrs Highmore put me down at his door. Mr Bousefield in that juncture had been served up to me anew, but after we had disposed of him we came to the book, which I was obliged to confess I had already rushed through. It was from this moment—the moment at which my terrible impression of it had blinked out at his anxious query—that the image of his scared face was to abide with me. I couldn't attenuate then—the cat was out of the bag; but later, each of the next times, I did, I acknowledge, attenuate. We all did religiously, so far as was possible; we cast ingenious ambiguities over the strong places, the beauties that betrayed him most, and found ourselves in the queer position of admirers banded to mislead a confiding artist. If we stifled our cheers however and dissimulated our joy our fond hypocrisy accomplished little, for Limbert's finger was on a pulse that told a plainer story. It was a satisfaction to have secured a greater freedom with his wife, who at last, much to her honour, entered into the conspiracy and whose sense of responsibility was flattered by the frequency of our united appeal to her for some answer to the marvellous riddle. We had all turned it over till we were tired of it, threshing out the question why the note he strained every chord to pitch for common ears should invariably insist on addressing itself to the angels. Being, as it were, ourselves the angels we had only a limited quarrel in each case with the event; but its inconsequent character, given the forces set in motion, was peculiarly baffling. It was like an interminable sum that wouldn't come straight; nobody had the time to handle so many figures. Limbert gathered, to make his pudding, dry bones and dead husks; how then was one to formulate the law that made the dish prove a feast? What was the cerebral treachery that defied his own vigilance? There was some obscure interference of taste, some obsession of the exquisite. All one could say was that genius was a fatal disturber or that the unhappy man had no effectual *flair*. When he went abroad to gather garlic he came home with heliotrope.

I hasten to add that if Mrs Limbert was not directly illuminating she was yet rich in anecdote and example, having found a refuge from mystification exactly where the rest of us had found it, in a more devoted embrace and the sense of a finer glory. Her disappointments and eventually her privations had been many, her discipline severe; but she had ended by accepting the long grind of life and was now quite willing to take her turn at the mill. She was essentially one of us—she always understood. Touching and admirable at the last, when through the unmistakable change in Limbert's health her troubles were thickest, was the spectacle of the particular pride that she wouldn't have exchanged for prosperity. She had said to me once—only once, in a gloomy hour in London days when things were not going at all—that one really had to think him a very great man because if one didn't one would be rather ashamed of him. She had distinctly felt it at first—and in a very tender place—that almost every one passed him on the road; but I believe that in these final years she would almost have been ashamed of him if he had suddenly gone into editions. It is certain indeed that her complacency was not subjected to that shock. She would have liked the money immensely, but she would have missed something she had taught herself to regard as rather rare. There is another remark I remember her making, a remark to the effect that of course if she could have chosen she would have liked him to be Shakespeare or Scott, but that failing this she was very glad he wasn't—well, she named the two gentlemen, but I won't. I daresay she sometimes laughed out to escape an alternative. She contributed passionately to the capture of the second manner, foraging for him further afield than he could conveniently go, gleaning in the barest stubble, picking up shreds to build the nest and in particular in the study of the great secret of how, as we always said, they all did it laying waste the circulating libraries. If Limbert had a weakness he rather broke down in his reading. It was fortunately not till after the appearance of *The Hidden Heart* that he broke down in everything else. He had had rheumatic fever in the spring, when the book was but half finished, and this ordeal in addition to interrupting his work had enfeebled his powers of resistance and greatly reduced his vitality. He recovered from the fever and was able to take up the book again, but the organ of life was pronounced ominously weak and it was enjoined upon him with some sharpness that he should lend himself to no worries. It might have struck me as on the cards that his worries would now be surmountable, for when he began to mend he expressed to me a conviction almost contagious that he had never yet made so adroit a bid as in the idea of *The Hidden Heart.* It is grimly droll to reflect that this superb little composition, the shortest of his novels but perhaps the loveliest, was planned from the first as an "adventure-story" on approved lines. It was the way they all did the adventure-story that he tried most dauntlessly to emulate. I wonder how many readers ever divined to which of their bookshelves *The Hidden Heart* was so exclusively addressed. High medical advice early in the summer had been quite viciously clear as to the inconvenience that might ensue to him should he neglect to spend the winter in Egypt. He was not a man to neglect anything; but Egypt seemed to us all then as unattainable as a second edition. He finished *The Hidden Heart* with the energy of apprehension and desire, for if the book should happen to do what "books of that class," as the publisher said, sometimes did he might well have a fund to draw on. As soon as I read the deep and delicate thing I knew, as I had known in each case before, exactly how well it would do. Poor Limbert in this long business always figured to me an undiscourageable parent to whom only girls kept being born. A bouncing boy, a son and heir was devoutly prayed for and almanacks and old wives consulted; but the spell was inveterate, incurable, and *The Hidden Heart* proved, so to speak, but another female child. When the winter arrived accordingly Egypt was out of the question. Jane Highmore, to my knowledge, wanted to lend him money, and there were even greater devotees who did their best to induce him to lean on them. There was so marked a "movement" among his friends that a very considerable sum would have been at his disposal; but his stiffness was invincible: it had its root, I think, in his sense, on his own side, of sacrifices already made. He had sacrificed honour and pride, and he had sacrificed them precisely to the question of money. He would evidently, should he be able to go on, have to continue to sacrifice them, but it must be all in the way to which he had now, as he considered, hardened himself. He had spent years in plotting for favour, and since on favour he must live it could only be as a bargain and a price.

He got through the early part of the season better than we feared, and I went down in great elation to spend Christmas on the goose-green. He told me late on Christmas eve, after our simple domestic revels had sunk to rest and we sat together by the fire, that he had been visited the night before in wakeful hours by the finest fancy for a really good thing that he had ever felt descend in the darkness. "It's just the vision of a situation that contains, upon my honour, everything," he said, "and I wonder that I've never thought of it before." He didn't describe it further, contrary to his common practice, and I only knew later, by Mrs Limbert, that he had begun *Derogation* and that he was completely full of his subject. It was a subject however that he was not to live to treat. The work went on for a couple of months in happy mystery, without revelations even to his wife. He had not invited her to help him to get up his case—she had not taken the field with him as on his previous campaigns. We only knew he was at it again but that less even than ever had been said about the impression to be made on the market. I saw him in February and thought him sufficiently at ease. The great thing was that he was immensely interested and was pleased with the omens. I got a strange, stirring sense that he had not consulted the usual ones and indeed that he had floated away into a grand indifference, into a reckless consciousness of art. The voice of the market had suddenly grown faint and far: he had come back at the last, as people so often do, to one of the moods, the sincerities of his prime. Was he really with a blurred sense of the urgent doing something now only for himself? We wondered and waited—we felt that he was a little confused. What had happened, I was afterwards satisfied, was that he had quite forgotten whether he generally sold or not. He had merely waked up one morning again in the country of the blue and had stayed there with a good conscience and a great idea. He stayed till death knocked at the gate, for the pen dropped from his hand only at the moment when from sudden failure of the heart his eyes, as he sank back in his chair, closed for ever. *Derogation* is a splendid fragment; it evidently would have been one of his high successes. I am not prepared to say it would have waked up the libraries.

THE FIGURE IN THE CARPET

I

I HAD done a few things and earned a few pence—I had perhaps even had time to begin to think I was finer than was perceived by the patronising; but when I take the little measure of my course (a fidgety habit, for it's none of the longest yet) I count my real start from the evening George Corvick, breathless and worried, came in to ask me a service. He had done more things than I, and earned more pence, though there were chances for cleverness I thought he sometimes missed. I could only however that evening declare to him that he never missed one for kindness. There was almost rapture in hearing it proposed to me to prepare for *The Middle*, the organ of our lucubrations, so called from the position in the week of its day of appearance, an article for which he had made himself responsible and of which, tied up with a stout string, he laid on my table the subject. I pounced upon my opportunity—that is on the first volume of it—and paid scant attention to my friend's explanation of his appeal. What explanation could be more to the point than my obvious fitness for the task? I had written on Hugh Vereker, but never a word in *The Middle*, where my dealings were mainly with the ladies and the minor poets. This was his new novel, an advance copy, and whatever much or little it should do for his reputation I was clear on the spot as to what it should do for mine. Moreover if I always read him as soon as I could get hold of him I had a particular reason for wishing to read him now: I had accepted an invitation to Bridges for the following Sunday, and it had been mentioned in Lady Jane's note that Mr Vereker was to be there.

I was young enough to have an emotion about meeting a man of his renown and innocent enough to believe the occasion would demand the display of an acquaintance with his "last."

Corvick, who had promised a review of it, had not even had time to read it; he had gone to pieces in consequence of news requiring—as on precipitate reflection he judged—that he should catch the night-mail to Paris. He had had a telegram from Gwendolen Erme in answer to his letter offering to fly to her aid. I knew already about Gwendolen Erme; I had never seen her, but I had my ideas, which were mainly to the effect that Corvick would marry her if her mother would only die. That lady seemed now in a fair way to oblige him; after some dreadful mistake about some climate or some waters she had suddenly collapsed on the return from abroad. Her daughter, unsupported and alarmed, desiring to make a rush for home but hesitating at the risk, had accepted our friend's assistance, and it was my secret belief that at the sight of him Mrs Erme would pull round. His own belief was scarcely to be called secret; it discernibly at any rate differed from mine. He had showed me Gwendolen's photograph with the remark that she wasn't pretty but was awfully interesting; she had published at the age of nineteen a novel in three volumes, "Deep Down," about which, in *The Middle*, he had been really splendid. He appreciated my present eagerness and undertook that the periodical in question should do no less; then at the last, with his hand on the door, he said to me: "Of course you'll be all right, you know." Seeing I was a trifle vague he added: "I mean you won't be silly."

"Silly—about Vereker! Why, what do I ever find him but awfully clever?"

"Well, what's that but silly? What on earth does 'awfully clever' mean? For God's sake try to get *at* him. Don't let him suffer by our arrangement. Speak of him, you know, if you can, as *I* should have spoken of him."

I wondered an instant. "You mean as far and away the biggest of the lot—that sort of thing?"

Corvick almost groaned. "Oh, you know, I don't put them back to back that way; it's the infancy of art! But he gives me a pleasure so rare; the sense of"—he mused a little—"something or other."

I wondered again. "The sense, pray, of what?"

"My dear man, that's just what I want *you* to say!"

Even before Corvick had banged the door I had begun, book in hand, to prepare myself to say it. I sat up with Vereker half the night; Corvick couldn't have done more than that. He was awfully clever—I stuck to that, but he wasn't a bit the biggest of the lot. I didn't allude to the lot, however; I flattered myself that I emerged on this occasion from the infancy of art. "It's all right," they declared vividly at the office; and when the number appeared I felt there was a basis on which I could meet the great man. It gave me confidence for a day or two, and then that confidence dropped. I had fancied him reading it with relish, but if Corvick was not satisfied how could Vereker himself be? I reflected indeed that the heat of the admirer was sometimes grosser even than the appetite of the scribe. Corvick at all events wrote me from Paris a little ill-humouredly. Mrs Erme was pulling round, and I hadn't at all said what Vereker gave him the sense of.

II

THE effect of my visit to Bridges was to turn me out for more profundity. Hugh Vereker, as I saw him there, was of a contact so void of angles that I blushed for the poverty of imagination involved in my small precautions. If he was in spirits it was not because he had read my review; in fact on the Sunday morning I felt sure he hadn't read it, though *The Middle* had been out three days and bloomed, I assured myself, in the stiff garden of periodicals which gave one of the ormolu tables the air of a stand at a station. The impression he made on me personally was such that I wished him to read it, and I corrected to this end with a surreptitious hand what might be wanting in the careless conspicuity of the sheet. I am afraid I even watched the result of my manœuvre, but up to luncheon I watched in vain.

When afterwards, in the course of our gregarious walk, I found myself for half an hour, not perhaps without another manœuvre, at the great man's side, the result of his affability was a still livelier desire that he should not remain in ignorance of the peculiar justice I had done him. It was not that he seemed to thirst for justice; on the contrary I had not yet caught in his talk the faintest grunt of a grudge—a note for which my young experience had already given me an ear. Of late he had had more recognition, and it was pleasant, as we used to say in *The Middle*, to see that it drew him out. He wasn't of course popular, but I judged one of the sources of his good humour to be precisely that his success was independent of that. He had none the less become in a manner the fashion; the critics at least had put on a spurt and caught up with him. We had found out at last how clever he was, and he had had to make the best of the loss of his mystery. I was strongly tempted, as I walked beside him, to let him know how much of that unveiling was my act; and there was a moment when I probably should have done so had not one of the ladies of our party, snatching a place at his other elbow, just then appealed to him in a spirit comparatively selfish. It was very discouraging: I almost felt the liberty had been taken with myself.

I had had on my tongue's end, for my own part, a phrase or two about the right word at the right time; but later on I was glad not to have spoken, for when on our return we clustered at tea I perceived Lady Jane, who had not been out with us, brandishing *The Middle* with her longest arm. She had taken it up at her leisure; she was delighted with what she had found, and I saw that, as a mistake in a man may often be a felicity in a woman, she would practically do for me what I hadn't been able to do for myself. "Some sweet little truths that needed to be spoken," I heard her declare, thrusting the paper at rather a bewildered couple by the fireplace. She grabbed it away from them again on the reappearance of Hugh Vereker, who after our walk had been upstairs to change something. "I know you don't in general look at this kind of thing, but it's an occasion really for doing so. You *haven't* seen it? Then you must. The man has actually got *at* you, at what *I* always feel, you know." Lady Jane threw into her eyes a look evidently intended to give an idea of what she always felt; but she added that she couldn't have expressed it. The man in the paper expressed it in a striking manner. "Just see there, and there, where I've dashed it, how he brings it out." She had literally marked for him the brightest patches of my prose, and if I was a little amused Vereker himself may well have been. He showed how much he was when before us all Lady Jane wanted to read something aloud. I liked at any rate the way he defeated her purpose by jerking the paper affectionately out of her clutch. He would take it upstairs with him, would look at it on going to dress. He did this half an hour later—I saw it in his hand when he repaired to his room. That was the moment at which, thinking to give her pleasure, I mentioned to Lady Jane that I was the author of the review. I did give her pleasure, I judged, but perhaps not quite so much as I had expected. If the author was "only me" the thing didn't seem quite so remarkable. Hadn't I had the effect rather of diminishing the lustre of the article than of adding to my own? Her ladyship was subject to the most extraordinary drops. It didn't matter; the only effect I cared about was the one it would have on Vereker up there by his bedroom fire.

At dinner I watched for the signs of this impression, tried to fancy there was some happier light in his eyes; but to my disappointment Lady Jane gave me no chance to make sure. I had hoped she would call triumphantly down the table, publicly demand if she hadn't been right. The party was large—there were people from outside as well, but I had never seen a table long enough to deprive Lady Jane of a triumph. I was just reflecting in truth that this interminable board would deprive *me* of one when the guest next me, dear woman—she was Miss Poyle, the vicar's sister, a robust, unmodulated person—had the happy inspiration and the unusual courage to address herself across it to Vereker, who was opposite, but not directly, so that when he replied they were both leaning forward. She inquired, artless body, what he thought of Lady Jane's "panegyric," which she had read—not connecting it however with her right-hand neighbour; and while I strained my ear for his reply I heard him, to my stupefaction, call back gaily, with his mouth full of bread: "Oh, it's all right—it's the usual twaddle!"

I had caught Vereker's glance as he spoke, but Miss Poyle's surprise was a fortunate cover for my own. "You mean he doesn't do you justice?" said the excellent woman.

Vereker laughed out, and I was happy to be able to do the same. "It's a charming article," he tossed us.

Miss Poyle thrust her chin half across the cloth. "Oh you're so deep!" she drove home.

"As deep as the ocean! All I pretend is, the author doesn't see——"

A dish was at this point passed over his shoulder, and we had to wait while he helped himself.

"Doesn't see what?" my neighbour continued.

"Doesn't see anything."

"Dear me—how very stupid!"

"Not a bit," Vereker laughed again. "Nobody does."

The lady on his further side appealed to him, and Miss Poyle sank back to me. "Nobody sees anything!" she cheerfully announced; to which I replied that I had often thought so too, but had somehow taken the thought for a proof on my own part of a tremendous eye. I didn't tell her the article was mine; and I observed that Lady Jane, occupied at the end of the table, had not caught Vereker's words.

I rather avoided him after dinner, for I confess he struck me as cruelly conceited, and the revelation was a pain. "The usual twaddle"—my acute little study! That one's admiration should have had a reserve or two could gall him to that point? I had thought him placid, and he was placid enough; such a surface was the hard, polished glass that encased the bauble of his vanity. I was really ruffled, and the only comfort was that if nobody saw anything George Corvick was quite as much out of it as I. This comfort however was not sufficient, after the ladies had dispersed, to carry me in the proper manner—I mean in a spotted jacket and humming an air—into the smoking-room. I took my way in some dejection to bed; but in the passage I encountered Mr Vereker, who had been up once more to change, coming out of his room. *He* was humming an air and had on a spotted jacket, and as soon as he saw me his gaiety gave a start.

"My dear young man," he exclaimed, "I'm so glad to lay hands on you! I'm afraid I most unwittingly wounded you by those words of mine at dinner to Miss Poyle. I learned but half an hour ago from Lady Jane that you wrote the little notice in *The Middle*."

I protested that no bones were broken; but he moved with me to my own door, his hand, on my shoulder, kindly feeling for a fracture; and on hearing that I had come up to bed he asked leave to cross my threshold and just tell me in three words what his qualification of my remarks had represented. It was plain he really feared I was hurt, and the sense of his solicitude suddenly made all the difference to me. My cheap review fluttered off into space, and the best things I had said in it became flat enough beside the brilliancy of his being there. I can see him there still, on my rug, in the firelight and his spotted jacket, his fine, clear face all bright with the desire to be tender to my youth. I don't know what he had at first meant to say, but I think the sight of my relief touched him, excited him, brought up words to his lips from far within. It was so these words presently conveyed to me something that, as I afterwards knew, he had never uttered to any one. I have always done justice to the generous impulse that made him speak; it was simply compunction for a snub unconsciously administered to a man of letters in a position inferior to his own, a man of letters moreover in the very act of praising him. To make the thing right he talked to me exactly as an equal and on the ground of what we both loved best. The hour, the place, the unexpectedness deepened the impression: he couldn't have done anything more exquisitely successful.

III

"I DON'T quite know how to explain it to you," he said, "but it was the very fact that your notice of my book had a spice of intelligence, it was just your exceptional sharpness that produced the feeling—a very old story with me, I beg you to believe—under the momentary influence of which I used in speaking to that good lady the words you so naturally resent. I don't read the things in the newspapers unless they're thrust upon me as that one was—it's always one's best friend that does it! But I used to read them sometimes—ten years ago. I daresay they were in general rather stupider then; at any rate it always seemed to me that they missed my little point with a perfection exactly as admirable when they patted me on the back as when they kicked me in the shins. Whenever since I've happened to have a glimpse of them they were still blazing away—still missing it, I mean, deliciously. *You* miss it, my dear fellow, with inimitable assurance; the fact of your being awfully clever and your article's being awfully nice doesn't make a hair's breadth of difference. It's quite with you rising young men," Vereker laughed, "that I feel most what a failure I am!"

I listened with intense interest; it grew intenser as he talked. "*You* a failure—heavens! What then may your 'little point' happen to be?"

"Have I got to *tell* you, after all these years and labours?" There was something in the friendly reproach of this—jocosely exaggerated—that made me, as an ardent young seeker for truth, blush to the roots of my hair. I'm as much in the dark as ever, though I've grown used in a sense to my obtuseness; at that moment, however, Vereker's happy accent made me appear to myself, and probably to him, a rare donkey. I was on the point of exclaiming "Ah, yes, don't tell me: for my honour, for that of the craft, don't!" when he went on in a manner that showed he had read my thought and had his own idea of the probability of our some day redeeming ourselves. "By my little point I mean—what shall I call it?—the particular thing I've written my books most *for*. Isn't there for every writer a particular thing of that sort, the thing that most makes him apply himself, the thing without the effort to achieve which he wouldn't write at all, the very passion of his passion, the part of the business in which, for him, the flame of art burns most intensely? Well, it's *that!*"

I considered a moment. I was fascinated—easily, you'll say; but I wasn't going after all to be put off my guard. "Your description's certainly beautiful, but it doesn't make what you describe very distinct."

"I promise you it would be distinct if it should dawn on you at all." I saw that the charm of our topic overflowed for my companion into an emotion as lively as my own. "At any rate," he went on, "I can speak for myself: there's an idea in my work without which I wouldn't have given a straw for the whole job. It's the finest, fullest intention of the lot, and the application of it has been, I think, a triumph of patience, of ingenuity. I ought to leave that to somebody else to say; but that nobody does say it is precisely what we're talking about. It stretches, this little trick of mine, from book to book, and everything else, comparatively, plays over the surface of it. The order, the form, the texture of my books will perhaps some day constitute for the initiated a complete representation of it. So it's naturally the thing for the critic to look for. It strikes me," my visitor added, smiling, "even as the thing for the critic to find."

This seemed a responsibility indeed. "You call it a little trick?"

"That's only my little modesty. It's really an exquisite scheme."

"And you hold that you've carried the scheme out?"

"The way I've carried it out is the thing in life I think a bit well of myself for."

I was silent a moment. "Don't you think you ought—just a trifle—to assist the critic?"

"Assist him? What else have I done with every stroke of my pen? I've shouted my intention in his great blank face!" At this, laughing out again, Vereker laid his hand on my shoulder to show that the allusion was not to my personal appearance.

"But you talk about the initiated. There must therefore, you see, be initiation."

"What else in heaven's name is criticism supposed to be?" I'm afraid I coloured at this too; but I took refuge in repeating that his account of his silver lining was poor in something or other that a plain man knows things by. "That's only because you've never had a glimpse of it," he replied. "If you had had one the element in question would soon have become practically all you'd see. To me it's exactly as palpable as the marble of this chimney. Besides, the critic just *isn't* a plain man: if he were, pray, what would he be doing in his neighbour's garden? You're anything but a plain man yourself, and the very *raison d'être* of you all is that you're little demons of subtlety. If my great affair's a secret, that's only because it's a secret in spite of itself—the amazing event has made it one. I not only never took the smallest precaution to do so, but never dreamed of any such accident. If I had I shouldn't in advance have had the heart to go on. As it was I only became aware little by little, and meanwhile I had done my work."

"And now you quite like it?" I risked.

"My work?"

"Your secret. It's the same thing."

"Your guessing that," Vereker replied, "is a proof that you're as clever as I say!" I was encouraged by this to remark that he would clearly be pained to part with it, and he confessed that it was indeed with him now the great amusement of life. "I live almost to see if it will ever be detected." He looked at me for a jesting challenge; something at the back of his eyes seemed to peep out. "But I needn't worry—it won't!"

"You fire me as I've never been fired," I returned; "you make me determined to do or die." Then I asked: "Is it a kind of esoteric message?"

His countenance fell at this—he put out his hand as if to bid me good-night. "Ah, my dear fellow, it can't be described in cheap journalese!"

I knew of course he would be awfully fastidious, but our talk had made me feel how much his nerves were exposed. I was unsatisfied—I kept hold of his hand. "I won't make use of the expression then," I said, "in the article in which I shall eventually announce my discovery, though I daresay I shall have hard work to do without it. But meanwhile, just to hasten that difficult birth, can't you give a fellow a clue?" I felt much more at my ease.

"My whole lucid effort gives him the clue—every page and line and letter. The thing's as concrete there as a bird in a cage, a bait on a hook, a piece of cheese in a mouse-trap. It's stuck into every volume as your foot is stuck into your shoe. It governs every line, it chooses every word, it dots every i, it places every comma."

I scratched my head. "Is it something in the style or something in the thought? An element of form or an element of feeling?"

He indulgently shook my hand again, and I felt my questions to be crude and my distinctions pitiful. "Good-night, my dear boy—don't bother about it. After all, you do like a fellow."

"And a little intelligence might spoil it?" I still detained him.

He hesitated. "Well, you've got a heart in your body. Is that an element of form or an element of feeling? What I contend that nobody has ever mentioned in my work is the organ of life."

"I see—it's some idea about life, some sort of philosophy. Unless it be," I added with the eagerness of a thought perhaps still happier, "some kind of game you're up to with your style, something you're after in the language. Perhaps it's a preference for the letter P!" I ventured profanely to break out. "Papa, potatoes, prunes—that sort of thing?" He was suitably indulgent: he only said I hadn't got the right letter. But his amusement was over; I could see he was bored. There was nevertheless something else I had absolutely to learn. "Should you be able, pen in hand, to state it clearly yourself—to name it, phrase it, formulate it?"

"Oh," he almost passionately sighed, "if I were only, pen in hand, one of *you* chaps!"

"That would be a great chance for you of course. But why should you despise us chaps for not doing what you can't do yourself?"

"Can't do?" He opened his eyes. "Haven't I done it in twenty volumes? I do it in my way," he continued. "You don't do it in yours."

"Ours is so devilish difficult," I weakly observed.

"So is mine. We each choose our own. There's no compulsion. You won't come down and smoke?"

"No. I want to think this thing out."

"You'll tell me then in the morning that you've laid me bare?"

"I'll see what I can do; I'll sleep on it. But just one word more," I added. We had left the room—I walked again with him a few steps along the passage. "This extraordinary 'general intention,' as you call it—for that's the most vivid description I can induce you to make of it—is then generally a sort of buried treasure?"

His face lighted. "Yes, call it that, though it's perhaps not for me to do so."

"Nonsense!" I laughed. "You know you're hugely proud of it."

"Well, I didn't propose to tell you so; but it *is* the joy of my soul!"

"You mean it's a beauty so rare, so great?"

He hesitated a moment. "The loveliest thing in the world!" We had stopped, and on these words he left me; but at the end of the corridor, while I looked after him rather yearningly, he turned and caught sight of my puzzled face. It made him earnestly, indeed I thought quite anxiously, shake his head and wave his finger. "Give it up—give it up!"

This wasn't a challenge—it was fatherly advice. If I had had one of his books at hand I would have repeated my recent act of faith—I would have spent half the night with him. At three o'clock in the morning, not sleeping, remembering moreover how indispensable he was to Lady Jane, I stole down to the library with a candle. There wasn't, so far as I could discover, a line of his writing in the house.

IV

RETURNING to town I feverishly collected them all; I picked out each in its order and held it up to the light. This gave me a maddening month, in the course of which several things took place. One of these, the last, I may as well immediately mention, was that I acted on Vereker's advice: I renounced my ridiculous attempt. I could really make nothing of the business; it proved a dead loss. After all, before, as he had himself observed, I liked him; and what now occurred was simply that my new intelligence and vain preoccupation damaged my liking. I not only failed to find his general intention—I found myself missing the subordinate intentions I had formerly found. His books didn't even remain the charming things they had been for me; the exasperation of my search put me out of conceit of them. Instead of being a pleasure the more they became a resource the less; for from the moment I was unable to follow up the author's hint I of course felt it a point of honour not to make use professionally of my knowledge of them. I *had* no knowledge—nobody had any. It was humiliating, but I could bear it—they only annoyed me now. At last they even bored me, and I accounted for my confusion—perversely, I confess—by the idea that Vereker had made a fool of me. The buried treasure was a bad joke, the general intention a monstrous *pose*.

The great incident of the time however was that I told George Corvick all about the matter and that my information had an immense effect upon him. He had at last come back, but so, unfortunately, had Mrs Erme, and there was as yet, I could see, no question of his nuptials. He was immensely stirred up by the anecdote I had brought from Bridges; it fell in so completely with the sense he had had from the first that there was more in Vereker than met the eye. When I remarked that the eye seemed what the printed page had been expressly invented to meet he immediately accused me of being spiteful because I had been foiled. Our commerce had always that pleasant latitude. The thing Vereker had mentioned to me was exactly the thing he, Corvick, had wanted me to speak of in my review. On my suggesting at last that with the assistance I had now given him he would doubtless be prepared to speak of it himself he admitted freely that before doing this there was more he must understand. What he would have said, had he reviewed the new book, was that there was evidently in the writer's inmost art something to *be* understood. I hadn't so much as hinted at that: no wonder the writer hadn't been flattered! I asked Corvick what he really considered he meant by his own supersubtlety, and, unmistakably kindled, he replied: "It isn't for the vulgar—it isn't for the vulgar!" He had hold of the tail of something; he would pull hard, pull it right out. He pumped me dry on Vereker's strange confidence and, pronouncing me the luckiest of mortals, mentioned half a dozen questions he wished to goodness I had had the gumption to put. Yet on the other hand he didn't want to be told too much—it would spoil the fun of seeing what would come. The failure of my fun was at the moment of our meeting not complete, but I saw it ahead, and Corvick saw that I saw it. I, on my side, saw likewise that one of the first things he would do would be to rush off with my story to Gwendolen.

On the very day after my talk with him I was surprised by the receipt of a note from Hugh Vereker, to whom our encounter at Bridges had been recalled, as he mentioned, by his falling, in a magazine, on some article to which my signature was appended. "I read it with great pleasure," he wrote, "and remembered under its influence our lively conversation by your bedroom fire. The consequence of this has been that I begin to measure the temerity of my having saddled you with a knowledge that you may find something of a burden.

Now that the fit's over I can't imagine how I came to be moved so much beyond my wont. I had never before related, no matter in what expansion, the history of my little secret, and I shall never speak of the business again. I was accidentally so much more explicit with you than it had ever entered into my game to be, that I find this game—I mean the pleasure of playing it—suffers considerably. In short, if you can understand it, I've spoiled a part of my fun. I really don't want to give anybody what I believe you clever young men call the tip. That's of course a selfish solicitude, and I name it to you for what it may be worth to you. If you're disposed to humour me don't repeat my revelation. Think me demented—it's your right; but don't tell anybody why."

The sequel to this communication was that as early on the morrow as I dared I drove straight to Mr Vereker's door. He occupied in those years one of the honest old houses in Kensington-square. He received me immediately, and as soon as I came in I saw I had not lost my power to minister to his mirth. He laughed out at the sight of my face, which doubtless expressed my perturbation. I had been indiscreet—my compunction was great. "I *have* told somebody," I panted, "and I'm sure that person will by this time have told somebody else! It's a woman, into the bargain."

"The person you've told?"

"No, the other person. I'm quite sure he must have told her."

"For all the good it will do her—or do *me!* A woman will never find out."

"No, but she'll talk all over the place: she'll do just what you don't want."

Vereker thought a moment, but he was not so disconcerted as I had feared: he felt that if the harm was done it only served him right. "It doesn't matter—don't worry."

"I'll do my best, I promise you, that your talk with me shall go no further."

"Very good; do what you can."

"In the meantime," I pursued, "George Corvick's possession of the tip may, on his part, really lead to something."

"That will be a brave day."

I told him about Corvick's cleverness, his admiration, the intensity of his interest in my anecdote; and without making too much of the divergence of our respective estimates mentioned that my friend was already of opinion that he saw much further into a certain affair than most people. He was quite as fired as I had been at Bridges. He was moreover in love with the young lady: perhaps the two together would puzzle something out.

Vereker seemed struck with this. "Do you mean they're to be married?"

"I daresay that's what it will come to."

"That may help them," he conceded, "but we must give them time!"

I spoke of my own renewed assault and confessed my difficulties; whereupon he repeated his former advice: "Give it up, give it up!" He evidently didn't think me intellectually equipped for the adventure. I stayed half an hour, and he was most good-natured, but I couldn't help pronouncing him a man of shifting moods. He had been free with me in a mood, he had repented in a mood, and now in a mood he had turned indifferent. This general levity helped me to believe that, so far as the subject of the tip went, there wasn't much in it. I contrived however to make him answer a few more questions about it, though he did so with visible impatience. For himself, beyond doubt, the thing we were all so blank about was vividly there. It was something, I guessed, in the primal plan, something like a complex figure in a Persian carpet. He highly approved of this image when I used it, and he used another himself. "It's the very string," he said, "that my pearls are strung on!" The reason of his note to me had been that he really didn't want to give us a grain of succour—our density was a thing too perfect in its way to touch. He had formed the habit of depending upon it, and if the spell was to break it must break by some force of its own. He comes back to me from that last occasion—for I was never to speak to him again—as a man with some safe secret for enjoyment. I wondered as I walked away where he had got *his* tip.

V

WHEN I spoke to George Corvick of the caution I had received he made me feel that any doubt of his delicacy would be almost an insult. He had instantly told Gwendolen, but Gwendolen's ardent response was in itself a pledge of discretion. The question would now absorb them, and they would enjoy their fun too much to wish to share it with the crowd. They appeared to have caught instinctively Vereker's peculiar notion of fun. Their intellectual pride, however, was not such as to make them indifferent to any further light I might throw on the affair they had in hand. They were indeed of the "artistic temperament," and I was freshly struck with my colleague's power to excite himself over a question of art. He called it letters, he called it life—it was all one thing. In what he said I now seemed to understand that he spoke equally for Gwendolen, to whom, as soon as Mrs Erme was sufficiently better to allow her a little leisure, he made a point of introducing me. I remember our calling together one Sunday in August at a huddled house in Chelsea, and my renewed envy of Corvick's possession of a friend who had some light to mingle with his own. He could say things to her that I could never say to him. She had indeed no sense of humour and, with her pretty way of holding her head on one side, was one of those persons whom you want, as the phrase is, to shake, but who have learnt Hungarian by themselves. She conversed perhaps in Hungarian with Corvick; she had remarkably little English for his friend. Corvick afterwards told me that I had chilled her by my apparent indisposition to oblige her with the detail of what Vereker had said to me. I admitted that I felt I had given thought enough to this exposure: hadn't I even made up my mind that it was hollow, wouldn't stand the test? The importance they attached to it was irritating—it rather envenomed my dissent.

That statement looks unamiable, and what probably happened was that I felt humiliated at seeing other persons derive a daily joy from an experiment which had brought me only chagrin. I was out in the cold while, by the evening fire, under the lamp, they followed the chase for which I myself had sounded the horn. They did as I had done, only more deliberately and sociably—they went over their author from the beginning. There was no hurry, Corvick said—the future was before them and the fascination could only grow; they would take him page by page, as they would take one of the classics, inhale him in slow draughts and let him sink deep in. I doubt whether they would have got so wound up if they had not been in love: poor Vereker's secret gave them endless occasion to put their young heads together. None the less it represented the kind of problem for which Corvick had a special aptitude, drew out the particular pointed patience of which, had he lived, he would have given more striking and, it is to be hoped, more fruitful examples. He at least was, in Vereker's words, a little demon of subtlety. We had begun by disputing, but I soon saw that without my stirring a finger his infatuation would have its bad hours. He would bound off on false scents as I had done—he would clap his hands over new lights and see them blown out by the wind of the turned page. He was like nothing, I told him, but the maniacs who embrace some bedlamitical theory of the cryptic character of Shakespeare. To this he replied that if we had had Shakespeare's own word for his being cryptic he would immediately have accepted it. The case there was altogether different—we had nothing but the word of Mr Snooks. I rejoined that I was stupefied to see him attach such importance even to the word of Mr Vereker. He inquired thereupon whether I treated Mr Vereker's word as a lie. I wasn't perhaps prepared, in my unhappy rebound, to go as far as that, but I insisted that till the contrary was proved I should view it as too fond an imagination. I didn't, I confess, say—I didn't at that time quite know—all I felt. Deep down, as Miss Erme would have said, I was uneasy, I was expectant. At the core of my personal confusion—for my curiosity lived in its ashes—was the sharpness of a sense that Corvick would at last probably come out somewhere. He made, in defence of his credulity, a great point of the fact that from of old, in his study of this genius, he had caught whiffs and hints of he didn't know what, faint wandering notes of a hidden music. That was just the rarity, that was the charm: it fitted so perfectly into what I reported.

If I returned on several occasions to the little house in Chelsea I daresay it was as much for news of Vereker as for news of Miss Erme's mamma. The hours spent there by Corvick were present to my fancy as those of a chessplayer bent with a silent scowl, all the lamplit winter, over his board and his moves. As my imagination filled it out the picture held me fast. On the other side of the table was a ghostlier form, the faint figure of an antagonist good-humouredly but a little wearily secure—an antagonist who leaned back in his chair with his hands in his pockets and a smile on his fine clear face. Close to Corvick, behind him, was a girl who had begun to strike me as pale and wasted and even, on more familiar view, as rather handsome, and who rested on his shoulder and hung upon his moves. He would take up a chessman and hold it poised a while over one of the little squares, and then he would put it back in its place with a long sigh of disappointment. The young lady, at this, would slightly but uneasily shift her position and look across, very hard, very long, very strangely, at their dim participant. I had asked them at an early stage of the business if it mightn't contribute to their success to have some closer communication with him. The special circumstances would surely be held to have given me a right to introduce them. Corvick immediately replied that he had no wish to approach the altar before he had prepared the sacrifice. He quite agreed with our friend both as to the sport and as to the honour—he would bring down the animal with his own rifle. When I asked him if Miss Erme were as keen a shot he said after an hesitation: "No; I'm ashamed to say she wants to set a trap. She'd give anything to see him; she says she requires another tip. She's really quite morbid about it. But she must play fair—she *shan't* see him!" he emphatically added. I had a suspicion that they had even quarrelled a little on the subject—a suspicion not corrected by the way he more than once exclaimed to me: "She's quite incredibly literary, you know—quite fantastically!" I remember his saying of her that she felt in italics and thought in capitals. "Oh, when I've run him to earth," he also said, "then, you know, I shall knock at his door. Rather—I beg you to believe. I'll have it from his own lips: 'Right you are, my boy; you've done it this time!' He shall crown me victor—with the critical laurel."

Meanwhile he really avoided the chances London life might have given him of meeting the distinguished novelist; a danger however that disappeared with Vereker's leaving England for an indefinite absence, as the newspapers announced—going to the south for motives connected with the health of his wife, which had long kept her in retirement. A year—more than a year—had elapsed since the incident at Bridges, but I had not encountered him again. I think at bottom I was rather ashamed—I hated to remind him that though I had irremediably missed his point a reputation for acuteness was rapidly overtaking me. This scruple led me a dance; kept me out of Lady Jane's house, made me even decline, when in spite of my bad manners she was a second time so good as to make me a sign, an invitation to her beautiful seat. I once saw her with Vereker at a concert and was sure I was seen by them, but I slipped out without being caught. I felt, as on that occasion I splashed along in the rain, that I couldn't have done anything else; and yet I remember saying to myself that it was hard, was even cruel. Not only had I lost the books, but I had lost the man himself: they and their author had been alike spoiled for me. I knew too which was the loss I most regretted. I had liked the man still better than I had liked the books.

VI

SIX months after Vereker had left England George Corvick, who made his living by his pen, contracted for a piece of work which imposed on him an absence of some length and a journey of some difficulty, and his undertaking of which was much of a surprise to me. His brother-in-law had become editor of a great provincial paper, and the great provincial paper, in a fine flight of fancy, had conceived the idea of sending a "special commissioner" to India. Special commissioners had begun, in the "metropolitan press," to be the fashion, and the journal in question felt that it had passed too long for a mere country cousin. Corvick had no hand, I knew, for the big brush of the correspondent, but that was his brother-in-law's affair, and the fact that a particular task was not in his line was apt to be with himself exactly a reason for accepting it. He was prepared to out-Herod the metropolitan press; he took solemn precautions against priggishness, he exquisitely outraged taste. Nobody ever knew it—the taste was all his own. In addition to his expenses he was to be conveniently paid, and I found myself able to help him, for the usual fat book, to a plausible arrangement with the usual fat publisher. I naturally inferred that his obvious desire to make a little money was not unconnected with the prospect of a union with Gwendolen Erme. I was aware that her mother's opposition was largely addressed to his want of means and of lucrative abilities, but it so happened that, on my saying the last time I saw him something that bore on the question of his separation from our young lady, he exclaimed with an emphasis that startled me: "Ah, I'm not a bit engaged to her, you know!"

"Not overtly," I answered, "because her mother doesn't like you. But I've always taken for granted a private understanding."

"Well, there *was* one. But there isn't now." That was all he said, except something about Mrs Erme's having got on her feet again in the most extraordinary way—a remark from which I gathered he wished me to think he meant that private understandings were of little use when the doctor didn't share them. What I took the liberty of really thinking was that the girl might in some way have estranged him. Well, if he had taken the turn of jealousy for instance it could scarcely be jealousy of me. In that case (besides the absurdity of it) he wouldn't have gone away to leave us together. For some time before his departure we had indulged in no allusion to the buried treasure, and from his silence, of which mine was the consequence, I had drawn a sharp conclusion. His courage had dropped, his ardour had gone the way of mine—this inference at least he left me to enjoy. More than that he couldn't do; he couldn't face the triumph with which I might have greeted an explicit admission. He needn't have been afraid, poor dear, for I had by this time lost all need to triumph. In fact I considered that I showed magnanimity in not reproaching him with his collapse, for the sense of his having thrown up the game made me feel more than ever how much I at last depended on him. If Corvick had broken down I should never know; no one would be of any use if *he* wasn't. It wasn't a bit true that I had ceased to care for knowledge; little by little my curiosity had not only begun to ache again, but had become the familiar torment of my consciousness. There are doubtless people to whom torments of such an order appear hardly more natural than the contortions of disease; but I don't know after all why I should in this connection so much as mention them. For the few persons, at any rate, abnormal or not, with whom my anecdote is concerned, literature was a game of skill, and skill meant courage, and courage meant honour, and honour meant passion, meant life. The stake on the table was of a different substance, and our roulette was the revolving mind, but we sat round the green board as intently as the grim gamblers at Monte Carlo. Gwendolen Erme, for that matter, with her white face and her fixed eyes, was of the very type of the lean ladies one had met in the temples of chance. I recognised in Corvick's absence that she made this analogy vivid. It was extravagant, I admit, the way she lived for the art of the pen. Her passion visibly preyed upon her, and in her presence I felt almost tepid. I got hold of "Deep Down" again: it was a desert in which she had lost herself, but in which too she had dug a wonderful hole in the sand—a cavity out of which Corvick had still more remarkably pulled her.

Early in March I had a telegram from her, in consequence of which I repaired immediately to Chelsea, where the first thing she said to me was: "He has got it, he has got it!"

She was moved, as I could see, to such depths that she must mean the great thing. "Vereker's idea?"

"His general intention. George has cabled from Bombay."

She had the missive open there; it was emphatic, but it was brief. "Eureka. Immense." That was all—he had saved the money of the signature. I shared her emotion, but I was disappointed. "He doesn't say what it is."

"How could he—in a telegram? He'll write it."

"But how does he know?"

"Know it's the real thing? Oh, I'm sure when you see it you do know. *Vera incessu patuit dea!*"

"It's you, Miss Erme, who are a dear for bringing me such news!"—I went all lengths in my high spirits. "But fancy finding our goddess in the temple of Vishnu! How strange of George to have been able to go into the thing again in the midst of such different and such powerful solicitations!"

"He hasn't gone into it, I know; it's the thing itself, let severely alone for six months, that has simply sprung out at him like a tigress out of the jungle. He didn't take a book with him—on purpose; indeed he wouldn't have needed to—he knows every page, as I do, by heart. They all worked in him together, and some day somewhere, when he wasn't thinking, they fell, in all their superb intricacy, into the one right combination. The figure in the carpet came out. That's the way he knew it would come and the real reason—you didn't in the least understand, but I suppose I may tell you now—why he went and why I consented to his going. We knew the change would do it, the difference of thought, of scene, would give the needed touch, the magic shake. We had perfectly, we had admirably calculated. The elements were all in his mind, and in the *secousse* of a new and intense experience they just struck light." She positively struck light herself—she was literally, facially luminous. I stammered something about unconscious cerebration, and she continued: "He'll come right home—this will bring him."

"To see Vereker, you mean?"

"To see Vereker—and to see *me*. Think what he'll have to tell me!"

I hesitated. "About India?"

"About fiddlesticks! About Vereker—about the figure in the carpet."

"But, as you say, we shall surely have that in a letter."

She thought like one inspired, and I remembered how Corvick had told me long before that her face was interesting. "Perhaps it won't go in a letter if it's 'immense.'"

"Perhaps not if it's immense bosh. If he has got something

that won't go in a letter he hasn't got *the* thing. Vereker's own statement to me was exactly that the 'figure' *would* go in a letter."

"Well, I cabled to George an hour ago—two words," said Gwendolen.

"Is it indiscreet of me to inquire what they were?"

She hung fire, but at last she brought them out. "'Angel, write.'"

"Good!" I exclaimed. "I'll make it sure—I'll send him the same."

VII

My words however were not absolutely the same—I put something instead of "angel"; and in the sequel my epithet seemed the more apt, for when eventually we heard from Corvick it was merely, it was thoroughly to be tantalised. He was magnificent in his triumph, he described his discovery as stupendous; but his ecstasy only obscured it—there were to be no particulars till he should have submitted his conception to the supreme authority. He had thrown up his commission, he had thrown up his book, he had thrown up everything but the instant need to hurry to Rapallo, on the Genoese shore, where Vereker was making a stay. I wrote him a letter which was to await him at Aden—I besought him to relieve my suspense. That he found my letter was indicated by a telegram which, reaching me after weary days and without my having received an answer to my laconic dispatch at Bombay, was evidently intended as a reply to both communications. Those few words were in familiar French, the French of the day, which Corvick often made use of to show he wasn't a prig. It had for some persons the opposite effect, but his message may fairly be paraphrased. "Have patience; I want to see, as it breaks on you, the face you'll make!" "*Tellement envie de voir ta tête!*"—that was what I had to sit down with. I can certainly not be said to have sat down, for I seem to remember myself at this time as rushing constantly between the little house in Chelsea and my own. Our impatience, Gwendolen's and mine, was equal, but I kept hoping her light would be greater. We all spent during this episode, for people of our means, a great deal of money in telegrams, and I counted on the receipt of news from Rapallo immediately after the junction of the discoverer with the discovered. The interval seemed an age, but late one day I heard a hansom rattle up to my door with the crash engendered by a hint of liberality. I lived with my heart in my mouth and I bounded to the window—a movement which gave me a view of a young lady erect on the footboard of the vehicle and eagerly looking up at my house. At sight of me she flourished a paper with a movement that brought me straight down, the movement with which, in melodramas, handkerchiefs and reprieves are flourished at the foot of the scaffold.

"Just seen Vereker—not a note wrong. Pressed me to bosom—keeps me a month." So much I read on her paper while the cabby dropped a grin from his perch. In my excitement I paid him profusely and in hers she suffered it; then as he drove away we started to walk about and talk. We had talked, heaven knows, enough before, but this was a wondrous lift. We pictured the whole scene at Rapallo, where he would have written, mentioning my name, for permission to call; that is *I* pictured it, having more material than my companion, whom I felt hang on my lips as we stopped on purpose before shop-windows we didn't look into. About one thing we were clear: if he was staying on for fuller communication we should at least have a letter from him that would help us through the dregs of delay. We understood his staying on, and yet each of us saw, I think, that the other hated it. The letter we were clear about arrived; it was for Gwendolen, and I called upon her in time to save her the trouble of bringing it to me. She didn't read it out, as was natural enough; but she repeated to me what it chiefly embodied. This consisted of the remarkable statement that he would tell her when they were married exactly what she wanted to know.

"Only when we're married—not before," she explained. "It's tantamount to saying—isn't it?—that I must marry him straight off!" She smiled at me while I flushed with disappointment, a vision of fresh delay that made me at first unconscious of my surprise. It seemed more than a hint that on me as well he would impose some tiresome condition. Suddenly, while she reported several more things from his letter, I remembered what he had told me before going away. He found Mr Vereker deliriously interesting and his own possession of the secret a kind of intoxication. The buried treasure was all gold and gems. Now that it was there it seemed to grow and grow before him; it was in all time, in all tongues, one of the most wonderful flowers of art. Nothing, above all, when once one was face to face with it, had been more consummately done. When once it came out it came out, was there with a splendour that made you ashamed; and there had not been, save in the bottomless vulgarity of the age, with every one tasteless and tainted, every sense stopped, the smallest reason why it should have been overlooked. It was immense, but it was simple—it was simple, but it was immense, and the final knowledge of it was an experience quite apart. He intimated that the charm of such an experience, the desire to drain it, in its freshness, to the last drop, was what kept him there close to the source. Gwendolen, frankly radiant as she tossed me these fragments, showed the elation of a prospect more assured than my own. That brought me back to the question of her marriage, prompted me to ask her if what she meant by what she had just surprised me with was that she was under an engagement.

"Of course I am!" she answered. "Didn't you know it?" She appeared astonished; but I was still more so, for Corvick had told me the exact contrary. I didn't mention this, however; I only reminded her that I had not been to that degree in her confidence, or even in Corvick's, and that moreover I was not in ignorance of her mother's interdict. At bottom I was troubled by the disparity of the two assertions; but after a moment I felt that Corvick's was the one I least doubted. This simply reduced me to asking myself if the girl had on the spot improvised an engagement—vamped up an old one or dashed off a new—in order to arrive at the satisfaction she desired. I reflected that she had resources of which I was destitute; but she made her case slightly more intelligible by rejoining presently: "What the state of things has been is that we felt of course bound to do nothing in mamma's lifetime."

"But now you think you'll just dispense with your mother's consent?"

"Ah, it may not come to that!" I wondered what it might come to, and she went on: "Poor dear, she may swallow the dose. In fact, you know," she added with a laugh, "she really *must!*"—a proposition of which, on behalf of every one concerned, I fully acknowledged the force.

VIII

Nothing more annoying had ever happened to me than to become aware before Corvick's arrival in England that I should not be there to put him through. I found myself abruptly called to Germany by the alarming illness of my younger brother, who, against my advice, had gone to Munich to study, at the feet indeed of a great master, the art of portraiture in oils. The near relative who made him an allowance had threatened to withdraw it if he should, under specious pretexts, turn for superior truth to Paris—Paris being somehow, for a Cheltenham aunt, the school of evil, the abyss. I deplored this prejudice at the time, and the deep injury of it was now visible—first in the fact that it had not saved the poor boy, who was clever, frail and foolish, from congestion of the lungs, and second in the greater remoteness from London to which the event condemned me. I am afraid that what was uppermost in my mind during several anxious weeks was the sense that if we had only been in Paris I might have run over to see Corvick. This was actually out of the question from every point of view: my brother, whose recovery gave us both plenty to do, was ill for three months, during which I never left him and at the end of which we had to face the absolute prohibition of a return to England. The consideration of climate imposed itself, and he was in no state to meet it alone. I took him to Meran and there spent the summer with him, trying to show him by example how to get back to work and nursing a rage of another sort that I tried not to show him.

The whole business proved the first of a series of phenomena so strangely combined that, taken together (which was how I had to take them) they form as good an illustration as I can recall of the manner in which, for the good of his soul doubtless, fate sometimes deals with a man's avidity. These incidents certainly had larger bearings than the comparatively meagre consequence we are here concerned with—though I feel that consequence also to be a thing to speak of with some respect. It's mainly in such a light, I confess, at any rate, that at this hour the ugly fruit of my exile is present to me. Even at first indeed the spirit in which my avidity, as I have called it, made me regard this term owed no element of ease to the fact that before coming back from Rapallo George Corvick addressed me in a way I didn't like. His letter had none of the sedative action that I must to-day profess myself sure he had wished to give it, and the march of occurrences was not so ordered as to make up for what it lacked. He had begun on the spot, for one of the quarterlies, a great last word on Vereker's writings, and this exhaustive study, the only one that would have counted, have existed, was to turn on the new light, to utter—oh, so quietly!—the unimagined truth. It was in other words to trace the figure in the carpet through every convolution, to reproduce it in every tint. The result, said Corvick, was to be the greatest literary portrait ever painted, and what he asked of me was just to be so good as not to trouble him with questions till he should hang up his masterpiece before me. He did me the honour to declare that, putting aside the great sitter himself, all aloft in his indifference, I was individually the connoisseur he was most working for. I was therefore to be a good boy and not try to peep under the curtain before the show was ready: I should enjoy it all the more if I sat very still.

I did my best to sit very still, but I couldn't help giving a jump on seeing in *The Times*, after I had been a week or two in Munich and before, as I knew, Corvick had reached London, the announcement of the sudden death of poor Mrs Erme. I instantly wrote to Gwendolen for particulars, and she replied that her mother had succumbed to long-threatened failure of the heart. She didn't say, but I took the liberty of reading into her words, that from the point of view of her marriage and also of her eagerness, which was quite a match for mine, this was a solution more prompt than could have been expected and more radical than waiting for the old lady to swallow the dose. I candidly admit indeed that at the time—for I heard from her repeatedly—I read some singular things into Gwendolen's words and some still more extraordinary ones into her silences. Pen in hand, this way, I live the time over, and it brings back the oddest sense of my having been for months and in spite of myself a kind of coerced spectator. All my life had taken refuge in my eyes, which the procession of events appeared to have committed itself to keep astare. There were days when I thought of writing to Hugh Vereker and simply throwing myself on his charity. But I felt more deeply that I hadn't fallen quite so low, besides which, quite properly, he would send me about my business. Mrs Erme's death brought Corvick straight home, and within the month he was united "very quietly"—as quietly I suppose as he meant in his article to bring out his *trouvaille*—to the young lady he had loved and quitted. I use this last term, I may parenthetically say, because I subsequently grew sure that at the time he went to India, at the time of his great news from Bombay, there was no engagement whatever. There was none at the moment she affirmed the opposite. On the other hand he certainly became engaged the day he returned. The happy pair went down to Torquay for their honeymoon, and there, in a reckless hour, it occurred to poor Corvick to take his young bride a drive. He had no command of that business: this had been brought home to me of old in a little tour we had once made together in a dogcart. In a dogcart he perched his companion for a rattle over Devonshire hills, on one of the likeliest of which he brought his horse, who, it was true, had bolted, down with such violence that the occupants of the cart were hurled forward and that he fell horribly on his head. He was killed on the spot; Gwendolen escaped unhurt.

I pass rapidly over the question of this unmitigated tragedy, of what the loss of my best friend meant for me, and I complete my little history of my patience and my pain by the frank statement of my having, in a postscript to my very first letter to her after the receipt of the hideous news, asked Mrs Corvick whether her husband had not at least finished the great article on Vereker. Her answer was as prompt as my inquiry: the article, which had been barely begun, was a mere heartbreaking scrap. She explained that Corvick had just settled down to it when he was interrupted by her mother's death; then, on his return, he had been kept from work by the engrossments into which that calamity plunged them. The opening pages were all that existed; they were striking, they were promising, but they didn't unveil the idol. That great intellectual feat was obviously to have formed his climax. She said nothing more, nothing to enlighten me as to the state of her own knowledge—the knowledge for the acquisition of which I had conceived her doing prodigious things. This was above all what I wanted to know: had *she* seen the idol unveiled? Had there been a private ceremony for a palpitating audience of one? For what else but that ceremony had the previous ceremony been enacted? I didn't like as yet to press her, though when I thought of what had passed between us on the subject in Corvick's absence her reticence surprised me. It was therefore not till much later, from Meran, that I risked another appeal, risked it in some trepidation, for she continued to tell me nothing. "Did you hear in those few days of your blighted bliss," I wrote, "what we desired so to hear?" I said, "we" as a little hint; and she showed me she could take a little hint. "I heard everything," she replied, "and I mean to keep it to myself!"

IX

It was impossible not to be moved with the strongest sympathy for her, and on my return to England I showed her every kindness in my power. Her mother's death had made her means sufficient, and she had gone to live in a more convenient quarter. But her loss had been great and her visitation cruel; it never would have occurred to me moreover to suppose she could come to regard the enjoyment of a technical tip, of a piece of literary experience, as a counterpoise to her grief. Strange to say, none the less, I couldn't help fancying after I had seen her a few times that I caught a glimpse of some such oddity. I hasten to add that there had been other things I couldn't help fancying; and as I never felt I was really clear about these, so, as to the point I here touch on, I give her memory the benefit of every doubt. Stricken and solitary, highly accomplished and now, in her deep mourning, her maturer grace and her uncomplaining sorrow incontestably handsome, she presented herself as leading a life of singular dignity and beauty. I had at first found a way to believe that I should soon get the better of the reserve formulated the week after the catastrophe in her reply to an appeal as to which I was not unconscious that it might strike her as mistimed. Certainly that reserve was something of a shock to me—certainly it puzzled me the more I thought of it, though I tried to explain it, with moments of success, by the supposition of exalted sentiments, of superstitious scruples, of a refinement of loyalty. Certainly it added at the same time hugely to the price of Vereker's secret, precious as that mystery already appeared. I may as well confess abjectly that Mrs Corvick's unexpected attitude was the final tap on the nail that was to fix, as they say, my luckless idea, convert it into the obsession of which I am for ever conscious.

But this only helped me the more to be artful, to be adroit, to allow time to elapse before renewing my suit. There were plenty of speculations for the interval, and one of them was deeply absorbing. Corvick had kept his information from his young friend till after the removal of the last barriers to their intimacy; then he had let the cat out of the bag. Was it Gwendolen's idea, taking a hint from him, to liberate this animal only on the basis of the renewal of such a relation? Was the figure in the carpet traceable or describable only for husbands and wives—for lovers supremely united? It came back to me in a mystifying manner that in Kensington Square, when I told him that Corvick would have told the girl he loved, some word had dropped from Vereker that gave colour to this possibility. There might be little in it, but there was enough to make me wonder if I should have to marry Mrs Corvick to get what I wanted. Was I prepared to offer her this price for the blessing of her knowledge? Ah! that way madness lay—so I said to myself at least in bewildered hours. I could see meanwhile the torch she refused to pass on flame away in her chamber of memory—pour through her eyes a light that made a glow in her lonely house. At the end of six months I was fully sure of what this warm presence made up to her for. We had talked again and again of the man who had brought us together, of his talent, his character, his personal charm, his certain career, his dreadful doom, and even of his clear purpose in that great study which was to have been a supreme literary portrait, a kind of critical Vandyke or Velasquez. She had conveyed to me in abundance that she was tongue-tied by her perversity, by her piety, that she would never break the silence it had not been given to the "right person," as she said, to break. The hour however finally arrived. One evening when I had been sitting with her longer than usual I laid my hand firmly on her arm.

"Now, at last, what *is* it?"

She had been expecting me; she was ready. She gave a long, slow, soundless headshake, merciful only in being inarticulate. This mercy didn't prevent its hurling at me the largest, finest, coldest "Never!" I had yet, in the course of a life that had known denials, had to take full in the face. I took it and was aware that with the hard blow the tears had come into my eyes. So for a while we sat and looked at each other; after which I slowly rose. I was wondering if some day she would accept me; but this was not what I brought out. I said as I smoothed down my hat: "I know what to think then; it's nothing!"

A remote, disdainful pity for me shone out of her dim smile; then she exclaimed in a voice that I hear at this moment: "It's my *life!*" As I stood at the door she added: "You've insulted him!"

"Do you mean Vereker?"

"I mean—the Dead!"

I recognised when I reached the street the justice of her charge. Yes, it was her life—I recognised that too; but her life none the less made room with the lapse of time for another interest. A year and a half after Corvick's death she published in a single volume her second novel, "Overmastered," which I pounced on in the hope of finding in it some tell-tale echo or some peeping face. All I found was a much better book than her younger performance, showing I thought the better company she had kept. As a tissue tolerably intricate it was a carpet with a figure of its own; but the figure was not the figure I was looking for. On sending a review of it to *The Middle* I was surprised to learn from the office that a notice was already in type. When the paper came out I had no hesitation in attributing this article, which I thought rather vulgarly overdone, to Drayton Deane, who in the old days had been something of a friend of Corvick's, yet had only within a few weeks made the acquaintance of his widow. I had had an early copy of the book, but Deane had evidently had an earlier. He lacked all the same the light hand with which Corvick had gilded the gingerbread—he laid on the tinsel in splotches.

X

SIX months later appeared "The Right of Way," the last chance, though we didn't know it, that we were to have to redeem ourselves. Written wholly during Vereker's absence, the book had been heralded, in a hundred paragraphs, by the usual ineptitudes. I carried it, as early a copy as any, I this time flattered myself, straightway to Mrs Corvick. This was the only use I had for it; I left the inevitable tribute of *The Middle* to some more ingenious mind and some less irritated temper. "But I already have it," Gwendolen said. "Drayton Deane was so good as to bring it to me yesterday, and I've just finished it."

"Yesterday? How did he get it so soon?"

"He gets everything soon. He's to review it in *The Middle*."

"He—Drayton Deane—review Vereker?" I couldn't believe my ears.

"Why not? One fine ignorance is as good as another."

I winced, but I presently said: "You ought to review him yourself!"

"I don't 'review,'" she laughed. "I'm reviewed!"

Just then the door was thrown open. "Ah yes, here's your reviewer!" Drayton Deane was there with his long legs and his tall forehead: he had come to see what she thought of "The Right of Way," and to bring news which was singularly relevant. The evening papers were just out with a telegram on the author of that work, who, in Rome, had been ill for some days with an attack of malarial fever. It had at first not been thought grave, but had taken in consequence of complications a turn that might give rise to anxiety. Anxiety had indeed at the latest hour begun to be felt.

I was struck in the presence of these tidings with the fundamental detachment that Mrs Corvick's public regret quite failed to conceal: it gave me the measure of her consummate independence. That independence rested on her knowledge, the knowledge which nothing now could destroy and which nothing could make different. The figure in the carpet might take on another twist or two, but the sentence had virtually been written. The writer might go down to his grave: she was the person in the world to whom—as if she had been his favoured heir—his continued existence was least of a need. This reminded me how I had observed at a particular moment—after Corvick's death—the drop of her desire to see him face to face. She had got what she wanted without that. I had been sure that if she hadn't got it she wouldn't have been restrained from the endeavour to sound him personally by those superior reflections, more conceivable on a man's part than on a woman's, which in my case had served as a deterrent. It wasn't however, I hasten to add, that my case, in spite of this invidious comparison, wasn't ambiguous enough. At the thought that Vereker was perhaps at that moment dying there rolled over me a wave of anguish—a poignant sense of how inconsistently I still depended on him. A delicacy that it was my one compensation to suffer to rule me had left the Alps and the Apennines between us, but the vision of the waning opportunity made me feel as if I might in my despair at last have gone to him. Of course I would really have done nothing of the sort. I remained five minutes, while my companions talked of the new book, and when Drayton Deane appealed to me for my opinion of it I replied, getting up, that I detested Hugh Vereker—simply couldn't read him. I went away with the moral certainty that as the door closed behind me Deane would remark that I was awfully superficial. His hostess wouldn't contradict him.

I continue to trace with a briefer touch our intensely odd concatenation. Three weeks after this came Vereker's death, and before the year was out the death of his wife. That poor lady I had never seen, but I had had a futile theory that, should she survive him long enough to be decorously accessible, I might approach her with the feeble flicker of my petition. Did she know and if she knew would she speak? It was much to be presumed that for more reasons than one she would have nothing to say; but when she passed out of all reach I felt that renouncement was indeed my appointed lot. I was shut up in my obsession for ever—my gaolers had gone off with the key. I find myself quite as vague as a captive in a dungeon about the time that further elapsed before Mrs Corvick became the wife of Drayton Deane. I had foreseen, through my bars, this end of the business, though there was no indecent haste and our friendship had rather fallen off. They were both so "awfully intellectual" that it struck people as a suitable match, but I knew better than any one the wealth of understanding the bride would contribute to the partnership. Never, for a marriage in literary circles—so the newspapers described the alliance—had a bride been so handsomely dowered. I began with due promptness to look for the fruit of their union—that fruit, I mean, of which the premonitory symptoms would be peculiarly visible in the husband. Taking for granted the splendour of the lady's nuptial gift, I expected to see him make a show commensurate with his increase of means. I knew what his means had been—his article on "The Right of Way" had distinctly given one the figure. As he was now exactly in the position in which still more exactly I was not I watched from month to month, in the likely periodicals, for the heavy message poor Corvick had been unable to deliver and the responsibility of which would have fallen on his successor. The widow and wife would have broken by the rekindled hearth the silence that only a widow and wife might break, and Deane would be as aflame with the knowledge as Corvick in his own hour, as Gwendolen in hers had been. Well, he was aflame doubtless, but the fire was apparently not to become a public blaze. I scanned the periodicals in vain: Drayton Deane filled them with exuberant pages, but he withheld the page I most feverishly sought. He wrote on a thousand subjects, but never on the subject of Vereker. His special line was to tell truths that other people either "funked," as he said, or overlooked, but he never told the only truth that seemed to me in these days to signify. I met the couple in those literary circles referred to in the papers: I have sufficiently intimated that it was only in such circles we were all constructed to revolve. Gwendolen was more than ever committed to them by the publication of her third novel, and I myself definitely classed by holding the opinion that this work was inferior to its immediate predecessor. Was it worse because she had been keeping worse company? If her secret was, as she had told me, her life—a fact discernible in her increasing bloom, an air of conscious privilege that, cleverly corrected by pretty charities, gave distinction to her appearance—it had yet not a direct influence on her work. That only made—everything only made—one yearn the more for it, rounded it off with a mystery finer and subtler.

XI

It was therefore from her husband I could never remove my eyes: I hovered about him in a manner that might have made him uneasy. I went even so far as to engage him in conversation. *Didn't* he know, hadn't he come into it as a matter of course?—that question hummed in my brain. Of course he knew; otherwise he wouldn't return my stare so queerly. His wife had told him what I wanted, and he was amiably amused at my impotence. He didn't laugh—he was not a laugher: his system was to present to my irritation, so that I should crudely expose myself, a conversational blank as vast as his big bare brow. It always happened that I turned away with a settled conviction from these unpeopled expanses, which seemed to complete each other geographically and to symbolise together Drayton Deane's want of voice, want of form. He simply hadn't the art to use what he knew; he literally was incompetent to take up the duty where Corvick had left it. I went still further—it was the only glimpse of happiness I had. I made up my mind that the duty didn't appeal to him. He wasn't interested, he didn't care. Yes, it quite comforted me to believe him too stupid to have joy of the thing I lacked. He was as stupid after as before, and that deepened for me the golden glory in which the mystery was wrapped. I had of course however to recollect that his wife might have imposed her conditions and exactions. I had above all to recollect that with Vereker's death the major incentive dropped. He was still there to be honoured by what might be done—he was no longer there to give it his sanction. Who, alas, but he had the authority?

Two children were born to the pair, but the second cost the mother her life. After this calamity I seemed to see another ghost of a chance. I jumped at it in thought, but I waited a certain time for manners, and at last my opportunity arrived in a remunerative way. His wife had been dead a year when I met Drayton Deane in the smoking-room of a small club of which we both were members, but where for months—perhaps because I rarely entered it—I had not seen him. The room was empty and the occasion propitious. I deliberately offered him, to have done with the matter for ever, that advantage for which I felt he had long been looking.

"As an older acquaintance of your late wife's than even you were," I began, "you must let me say to you something I have on my mind. I shall be glad to make any terms with you that you see fit to name for the information she had from George Corvick—the information, you know, that he, poor fellow, in one of the happiest hours of his life, had straight from Hugh Vereker."

He looked at me like a dim phrenological bust. "The information——?"

"Vereker's secret, my dear man—the general intention of his books: the string the pearls were strung on, the buried treasure, the figure in the carpet."

He began to flush—the numbers on his bumps to come out. "Vereker's books had a general intention?"

I stared in my turn. "You don't mean to say you don't know it?" I thought for a moment he was playing with me. "Mrs Deane knew it; she had it, as I say, straight from Corvick, who had, after infinite search and to Vereker's own delight, found the very mouth of the cave. Where *is* the mouth? He told after their marriage—and told alone—the person who, when the circumstances were reproduced, must have told you. Have I been wrong in taking for granted that she admitted you, as one of the highest privileges of the relation in which you stood to her, to the knowledge of which she was after Corvick's death the sole depositary? All *I* know is that that knowledge is infinitely precious, and what I want you to understand is that if you will in your turn admit *me* to it you will do me a kindness for which I shall be everlastingly grateful."

He had turned at last very red; I daresay he had begun by thinking I had lost my wits. Little by little he followed me; on my own side I stared with a livelier surprise. "I don't know what you're talking about," he said.

He wasn't acting—it was the absurd truth. "She *didn't* tell you——?"

"Nothing about Hugh Vereker."

I was stupefied; the room went round. It had been too good even for that! "Upon your honour?"

"Upon my honour. What the devil's the matter with you?" he demanded.

"I'm astounded—I'm disappointed. I wanted to get it out of you."

"It isn't *in* me!" he awkwardly laughed. "And even if it were——"

"If it were you'd let me have it—oh yes, in common humanity. But I believe you. I see—I see!" I went on, conscious, with the full turn of the wheel, of my great delusion, my false view of the poor man's attitude. What I saw, though I couldn't say it, was that his wife hadn't thought him worth enlightening. This struck me as strange for a woman who had thought him worth marrying. At last I explained it by the reflection that she couldn't possibly have married him for his understanding. She had married him for something else. He was to some extent enlightened now, but he was even more astonished, more disconcerted: he took a moment to compare my story with his quickened memories. The result of his meditation was his presently saying with a good deal of rather feeble form:

"This is the first I hear of what you allude to. I think you must be mistaken as to Mrs Drayton Deane's having had any unmentioned, and still less any unmentionable, knowledge about Hugh Vereker. She would certainly have wished it—if it bore on his literary character—to be used."

"It *was* used. She used it herself. She told me with her own lips that she 'lived' on it."

I had no sooner spoken than I repented of my words; he grew so pale that I felt as if I had struck him. "Ah, 'lived'——!" he murmured, turning short away from me.

My compunction was real; I laid my hand on his shoulder. "I beg you to forgive me—I've made a mistake. You *don't* know what I thought you knew. You could, if I had been right, have rendered me a service; and I had my reasons for assuming that you would be in a position to meet me."

"Your reasons?" he asked. "What were your reasons?"

I looked at him well; I hesitated; I considered. "Come and sit down with me here, and I'll tell you." I drew him to a sofa, I lighted another cigarette and, beginning with the anecdote of Vereker's one descent from the clouds, I gave him an account of the extraordinary chain of accidents that had in spite of it kept me till that hour in the dark. I told him in a word just what I've written out here. He listened with deepening attention, and I became aware, to my surprise, by his ejaculations, by his questions, that he would have been after all not unworthy to have been trusted by his wife. So abrupt an experience of her want of trust had an agitating effect on him, but I saw that immediate shock throb away little by little and then gather again into waves of wonder and curiosity—waves that promised, I could perfectly judge, to break in the end with the fury of my own highest tides. I may say that to-day as victims of unappeased desire there isn't a pin to choose between us. The poor man's state is almost my consolation; there are indeed moments when I feel it to be almost my revenge.

THE WAY IT CAME

I FIND, as you prophesied, much that's interesting, but little that helps the delicate question—the possibility of publication. Her diaries are less systematic than I hoped; she only had a blessed habit of noting and narrating. She summarised, she saved; she appears seldom indeed to have let a good story pass without catching it on the wing. I allude of course not so much to things she heard as to things she saw and felt. She writes sometimes of herself, sometimes of others, sometimes of the combination. It's under this last rubric that she's usually most vivid. But it's not, you will understand, when she's most vivid that she's always most publishable. To tell the truth she's fearfully indiscreet, or has at least all the material for making *me* so. Take as an instance the fragment I send you, after dividing it for your convenience into several small chapters. It is the contents of a thin blank-book which I have had copied out and which has the merit of being nearly enough a rounded thing, an intelligible whole. These pages evidently date from years ago. I've read with the liveliest wonder the statement they so circumstantially make and done my best to swallow the prodigy they leave to be inferred. These things would be striking, wouldn't they? to any reader; but can you imagine for a moment my placing such a document before the world, even though, as if she herself had desired the world should have the benefit of it, she has given her friends neither name nor initials? Have you any sort of clue to their identity? I leave her the floor.

I

I KNOW perfectly of course that I brought it upon myself; but that doesn't make it any better. I was the first to speak of her to him—he had never even heard her mentioned. Even if I had happened not to speak some one else would have made up for it: I tried afterwards to find comfort in that reflection. But the comfort of reflections is thin: the only comfort that counts in life is not to have been a fool. That's a beatitude I shall doubtless never enjoy. "Why, you ought to meet her and talk it over," is what I immediately said. "Birds of a feather flock together." I told him who she was and that they were birds of a feather because if he had had in youth a strange adventure she had had about the same time just such another. It was well known to her friends—an incident she was constantly called on to describe. She was charming, clever, pretty, unhappy; but it was none the less the thing to which she had originally owed her reputation.

Being at the age of eighteen somewhere abroad with an aunt she had had a vision of one of her parents at the moment of death. The parent was in England, hundreds of miles away and so far as she knew neither dying nor dead. It was by day, in the museum of some great foreign town. She had passed alone, in advance of her companions, into a small room containing some famous work of art and occupied at that moment by two other persons. One of these was an old custodian; the second, before observing him, she took for a stranger, a tourist. She was merely conscious that he was bareheaded and seated on a bench. The instant her eyes rested on him however she beheld to her amazement her father, who, as if he had long waited for her, looked at her in singular distress, with an impatience that was akin to reproach. She rushed to him with a bewildered cry, "Papa, what *is* it?" but this was followed by an exhibition of still livelier feeling when on her movement he simply vanished, leaving the custodian and her relations, who were at her heels, to gather round her in dismay. These persons, the official, the aunt, the cousins were therefore in a manner witnesses of the fact—the fact at least of the impression made on her; and there was the further testimony of a doctor who was attending one of the party and to whom it was immediately afterwards communicated. He gave her a remedy for hysterics but said to the aunt privately: "Wait and see if something doesn't happen at home." Something *had* happened—the poor father, suddenly and violently seized, had died that morning. The aunt, the mother's sister, received before the day was out a telegram announcing the event and requesting her to prepare her niece for it. Her niece was already prepared, and the girl's sense of this visitation remained of course indelible. We had all as her friends had it conveyed to us and had conveyed it creepily to each other. Twelve years had elapsed and as a woman who had made an unhappy marriage and lived apart from her husband she had become interesting from other sources; but since the name she now bore was a name frequently borne, and since moreover her judicial separation, as things were going, could hardly count as a distinction, it was usual to qualify her as "the one, you know, who saw her father's ghost."

As for him, dear man, he had seen his mother's. I had never heard of that till this occasion on which our closer, our pleasanter acquaintance led him, through some turn of the subject of our talk, to mention it and to inspire me in so doing with the impulse to let him know that he had a rival in the field—a person with whom he could compare notes. Later on his story became for him, perhaps because of my unduly repeating it, likewise a convenient worldly label; but it had not a year before been the ground on which he was introduced to me. He had other merits, just as she, poor thing! had others. I can honestly say that I was quite aware of them from the first —I discovered them sooner than he discovered mine. I remember how it struck me even at the time that his sense of mine was quickened by my having been able to match, though not indeed straight from my own experience, his curious anecdote. It dated, this anecdote, as hers did, from some dozen years before—a year in which, at Oxford, he had for some reason of his own been staying on into the "Long." He had been in the August afternoon on the river. Coming back into his room while it was still distinct daylight he found his mother standing there as if her eyes had been fixed on the door. He had had a letter from her that morning out of Wales, where she was staying with her father. At the sight of him she smiled with extraordinary radiance and extended her arms to him, and then as he sprang forward and joyfully opened his own she vanished from the place. He wrote to her that night, telling her what had happened; the letter had been carefully preserved. The next morning he heard of her death. He was through this chance of our talk extremely struck with the little prodigy I was able to produce for him. He had never encountered another case. Certainly they ought to meet, my friend and he; certainly they would have something in common. I would arrange this, wouldn't I?—if *she* didn't mind; for himself he didn't mind in the least. I had promised to speak to her of the matter as soon as possible, and within the week I was able to do so. She "minded" as little as he; she was perfectly willing to see him. And yet no meeting was to occur—as meetings are commonly understood.

II

THAT's just half my tale—the extraordinary way it was hindered. This was the fault of a series of accidents; but the accidents continued for years and became, for me and for others, a subject of hilarity with either party. They were droll enough at first; then they grew rather a bore. The odd thing was that both parties were amenable: it wasn't a case of their being indifferent, much less of their being indisposed. It was one of the caprices of chance, aided I suppose by some opposition of their interests and habits. His were centred in his office, his eternal inspectorship, which left him small leisure, constantly calling him away and making him break engagements. He liked society, but he found it everywhere and took it at a run. I never knew at a given moment where he was, and there were times when for months together I never saw him. She was on her side practically suburban: she lived at Richmond and never went "out." She was a woman of distinction, but not of fashion, and felt, as people said, her situation. Decidedly proud and rather whimsical she lived her life as she had planned it. There were things one could do with her, but one couldn't make her come to one's parties. One went indeed a little more than seemed quite convenient to hers, which consisted of her cousin, a cup of tea and the view. The tea was good; but the view was familiar, though perhaps not, like the cousin—a disagreeable old maid who had been of the group at the museum and with whom she now lived—offensively so. This connection with an inferior relative, which had partly an economical motive—she proclaimed her companion a marvellous manager—was one of the little perversities we had to forgive her. Another was her estimate of the proprieties created by her rupture with her husband. That was extreme—many persons called it even morbid. She made no advances; she cultivated scruples; she suspected, or I should perhaps rather say she remembered slights: she was one of the few women I have known whom that particular predicament had rendered modest rather than bold. Dear thing! she had some delicacy. Especially marked were the limits she had set to possible attentions from men: it was always her thought that her husband was waiting to pounce on her. She discouraged if she didn't forbid the visits of male persons not senile: she said she could never be too careful.

When I first mentioned to her that I had a friend whom fate had distinguished in the same weird way as herself I put her quite at liberty to say "Oh, bring him out to see me!" I should probably have been able to bring him, and a situation perfectly innocent or at any rate comparatively simple would have been created. But she uttered no such word; she only said: "I must meet him certainly; yes, I shall look out for him!" That caused the first delay, and meanwhile various things happened. One of them was that as time went on she made, charming as she was, more and more friends, and that it regularly befell that these friends were sufficiently also friends of his to bring him up in conversation. It was odd that without belonging, as it were, to the same world or, according to the horrid term, the same set, my baffled pair should have happened in so many cases to fall in with the same people and make them join in the funny chorus. She had friends who didn't know each other but who inevitably and punctually recommended *him*. She had also the sort of originality, the intrinsic interest that led her to be kept by each of us as a kind of private resource, cultivated jealously, more or less in secret, as a person whom one didn't meet in society, whom it was not for every one—whom it was not for the vulgar—to approach, and with whom therefore acquaintance was particularly difficult and particularly precious. We saw her separately, with appointments and conditions, and found it made on the whole for harmony not to tell each other. Somebody had always had a note from her still later than somebody else. There was some silly woman who for a long time, among the unprivileged, owed to three simple visits to Richmond a reputation for being intimate with "lots of awfully clever out-of-the-way people."

Every one has had friends it has seemed a happy thought to bring together, and every one remembers that his happiest thoughts have not been his greatest successes; but I doubt if there was ever a case in which the failure was in such direct proportion to the quantity of influence set in motion. It is really perhaps here the quantity of influence that was most remarkable. My lady and gentleman each declared to me and others that it was like the subject of a roaring farce. The reason first given had with time dropped out of sight and fifty better ones flourished on top of it. They were so awfully alike: they had the same ideas and tricks and tastes, the same prejudices and superstitions and heresies; they said the same things and sometimes did them; they liked and disliked the same persons and places, the same books, authors and styles; any one could see a certain identity even in their looks and their features. It established much of a propriety that they were in common parlance equally "nice" and almost equally handsome. But the great sameness, for wonder and chatter, was their rare perversity in regard to being photographed. They were the only persons ever heard of who had never been "taken" and who had a passionate objection to it. They just *wouldn't* be, for anything any one could say. I had loudly complained of this; him in particular I had so vainly desired to be able to show on my drawing-room chimney-piece in a Bond Street frame. It was at any rate the very liveliest of all the reasons why they ought to know each other—all the lively reasons reduced to naught by the strange law that had made them bang so many doors in each other's face, made them the buckets in the well, the two ends of the see-saw, the two parties in the state, so that when one was up the other was down, when one was out the other was in; neither by any possibility entering a house till the other had left it, or leaving it, all unawares, till the other was at hand. They only arrived when they had been given up, which was precisely also when they departed. They were in a word alternate and incompatible; they missed each other with an inveteracy that could be explained only by its being preconcerted. It was however so far from preconcerted that it had ended—literally after several years—by disappointing and annoying them. I don't think their curiosity was lively till it had been proved utterly vain. A great deal was of course done to help them, but it merely laid wires for them to trip. To give examples I should have to have taken notes; but I happen to remember that neither had ever been able to dine on the right occasion. The right occasion for each was the occasion that would be wrong for the other. On the wrong one they were most punctual, and there were never any but wrong ones. The very elements conspired and the constitution of man reinforced them. A cold, a headache, a bereavement, a storm, a fog, an earthquake, a cataclysm infallibly intervened. The whole business was beyond a joke.

Yet as a joke it had still to be taken, though one couldn't help feeling that the joke had made the situation serious, had produced on the part of each a consciousness, an awkwardness, a positive dread of the last accident of all, the only one with any freshness left, the accident that would bring them face to face. The final effect of its predecessors had been to kindle this instinct. They were quite ashamed—perhaps even a little of each other. So much preparation, so much frustration: what indeed could be good enough for it all to lead up to? A mere meeting would be mere flatness. Did I see them at the end of years, they often asked, just stupidly confronted? If they were bored by the joke they might be worse bored by something else. They made exactly the same reflections, and each in some manner was sure to hear of the other's. I really think it was this peculiar diffidence that finally controlled the situation. I mean that if they had failed for the first year or two because they couldn't help it they kept up the habit because they had—what shall I call it?—grown nervous. It really took some lurking volition to account for anything so absurd.

III

WHEN to crown our long acquaintance I accepted his renewed offer of marriage it was humorously said, I know, that I had made the gift of his photograph a condition. This was so far true that I had refused to give him mine without it. At any rate I had him at last, in his high distinction, on the chimney-piece, where the day she called to congratulate me she came nearer than she had ever done to seeing him. He had set her in being taken an example which I invited her to follow; he had sacrificed his perversity—wouldn't she sacrifice hers? She too must give me something on my engagement—wouldn't she give me the companion-piece? She laughed and shook her head; she had headshakes whose impulse seemed to come from as far away as the breeze that stirs a flower. The companion-piece to the portrait of my future husband was the portrait of his future wife. She had taken her stand—she could depart from it as little as she could explain it. It was a prejudice, an *entêtement*, a vow—she would live and die unphotographed. Now too she was alone in that state: this was what she liked; it made her so much more original. She rejoiced in the fall of her late associate and looked a long time at his picture, about which she made no memorable remark, though she even turned it over to see the back. About our engagement she was charming—full of cordiality and sympathy. "You've known him even longer than I've *not*," she said, "and that seems a very long time." She understood how we had jogged together over hill and dale and how inevitable it was that we should now rest together. I'm definite about all this because what followed is so strange that it's a kind of relief to me to mark the point up to which our relations were as natural as ever. It was I myself who in a sudden madness altered and destroyed them. I see now that she gave me no pretext and that I only found one in the way she looked at the fine face in the Bond Street frame. How then would I have had her look at it? What I had wanted from the first was to make her care for him. Well, that was what I still wanted—up to the moment of her having promised me that he would on this occasion really aid me to break the silly spell that had kept them asunder. I had arranged with him to do his part if she would as triumphantly do hers. I was on a different footing now—I was on a footing to answer for him. I would positively engage that at five on the following Saturday he would be on that spot. He was out of town on pressing business; but pledged to keep his promise to the letter he would return on purpose and in abundant time. "Are you perfectly sure?" I remember she asked, looking grave and considering: I thought she had turned a little pale. She was tired, she was indisposed: it was a pity he was to see her after all at so poor a moment. If he only *could* have seen her five years before! However, I replied that this time I was sure and that success therefore depended simply on herself. At five o'clock on the Saturday she would find him in a particular chair I pointed out, the one in which he usually sat and in which—though this I didn't mention—he had been sitting when, the week before, he put the question of our future to me in the way that had brought me round. She looked at it in silence, just as she had looked at the photograph, while I repeated for the twentieth time that it was too preposterous it shouldn't somehow be feasible to introduce to one's dearest friend one's second self. "*Am* I your dearest friend?" she asked with a smile that for a moment brought back her beauty. I replied by pressing her to my bosom; after which she said: "Well, I'll come. I'm extraordinarily afraid, but you may count on me."

When she had left me I began to wonder what she was afraid of, for she had spoken as if she fully meant it. The next day, late in the afternoon, I had three lines from her: she had found on getting home the announcement of her husband's death. She had not seen him for seven years, but she wished me to know it in this way before I should hear of it in another. It made however in her life, strange and sad to say, so little difference that she would scrupulously keep her appointment. I rejoiced for her—I supposed it would make at least the difference of her having more money; but even in this diversion, far from forgetting that she had said she was afraid, I seemed to catch sight of a reason for her being so. Her fear as the evening went on became contagious, and the contagion took in my breast the form of a sudden panic. It wasn't jealousy—it was the dread of jealousy. I called myself a fool for not having been quiet till we were man and wife. After that I should somehow feel secure. It was only a question of waiting another month—a trifle surely for people who had waited so long. It had been plain enough she was nervous, and now that she was free she naturally wouldn't be less so. What was her nervousness therefore but a presentiment? She had been hitherto the victim of interference, but it was quite possible she would henceforth be the source of it. The victim in that case would be my simple self. What had the interference been but the finger of providence pointing out a danger? The danger was of course for poor *me*. It had been kept at bay by a series of accidents unexampled in their frequency; but the reign of accident was now visibly at an end. I had an intimate conviction that both parties would keep the tryst. It was more and more impressed upon me that they were approaching, converging. We had talked about breaking the spell; well, it would be effectually broken—unless indeed it should merely take another form and overdo their encounters as it had overdone their escapes. This was something I couldn't sit still for thinking of; it kept me awake—at midnight I was full of unrest. At last I felt there was only one way of laying the ghost. If the reign of accident was over I must just take up the succession. I sat down and wrote a hurried note which would meet him on his return and which as the servants had gone to bed I sallied forth bareheaded into the empty, gusty street to drop into the nearest pillar-box. It was to tell him that I shouldn't be able to be at home in the afternoon as I had hoped and that he must postpone his visit till dinner-time. This was an implication that he would find me alone.

IV

WHEN accordingly at five she presented herself I naturally felt false and base. My act had been a momentary madness, but I had at least to be consistent. She remained an hour; he of course never came; and I could only persist in my perfidy. I had thought it best to let her come; singular as this now seems to me I thought it diminished my guilt. Yet as she sat there so visibly white and weary, stricken with a sense of everything her husband's death had opened up, I felt an almost intolerable pang of pity and remorse. If I didn't tell her on the spot what I had done it was because I was too ashamed. I feigned astonishment—I feigned it to the end; I protested that if ever I had had confidence I had had it that day. I blush as I tell my story—I take it as my penance. There was nothing indignant I didn't say about him; I invented suppositions, attenuations; I admitted in stupefaction, as the hands of the clock travelled, that their luck hadn't turned. She smiled at this vision of their "luck," but she looked anxious—she looked unusual: the only thing that kept me up was the fact that, oddly enough, she wore mourning—no great depths of crape, but simple and scrupulous black. She had in her bonnet three small black feathers. She carried a little muff of astrachan. This put me by the aid of some acute reflection a little in the right. She had written to me that the sudden event made no difference for her, but apparently it made as much difference as that. If she was inclined to the usual forms why didn't she observe that of not going the first day or two out to tea? There was some one she wanted so much to see that she couldn't wait till her husband was buried. Such a betrayal of eagerness made me hard and cruel enough to practise my odious deceit, though at the same time, as the hour waxed and waned, I suspected in her something deeper still than disappointment and somewhat less successfully concealed. I mean a strange underlying relief, the soft, low emission of the breath that comes when a danger is past. What happened as she spent her barren hour with me was that at last she gave him up. She let him go for ever. She made the most graceful joke of it that I've ever seen made of anything; but it was for all that a great date in her life. She spoke with her mild gaiety of all the other vain times, the long game of hide-and-seek, the unprecedented queerness of such a relation. For it *was*, or had been, a relation, wasn't it, hadn't it? That was just the absurd part of it. When she got up to go I said to her that it was more a relation than ever, but that I hadn't the face after what had occurred to propose to her for the present another opportunity. It was plain that the only valid opportunity would be my accomplished marriage. Of course she would be at my wedding? It was even to be hoped that *he* would.

"If *I* am, he won't be!" she declared with a laugh. I admitted there might be something in that. The thing was therefore to get us safely married first. "That won't help us. Nothing will help us!" she said as she kissed me farewell. "I shall never, never see him!" It was with those words she left me.

I could bear her disappointment as I've called it; but when a couple of hours later I received him at dinner I found that I couldn't bear his. The way my manœuvre might have affected him had not been particularly present to me; but the result of it was the first word of reproach that had ever yet dropped from him. I say "reproach" because that expression is scarcely too strong for the terms in which he conveyed to me his surprise that under the extraordinary circumstances I should not have found some means not to deprive him of such an occasion. I might really have managed either not to be obliged to go out or to let their meeting take place all the same. They would probably have got on in my drawing-room without me. At this I quite broke down—I confessed my iniquity and the miserable reason of it. I had not put her off and I had not gone out; she had been there and after waiting for him an hour had departed in the belief that he had been absent by his own fault.

"She must think me a precious brute!" he exclaimed. "Did she say of me—what she had a right to say?"

"I assure you she said nothing that showed the least feeling. She looked at your photograph, she even turned round the back of it, on which your address happens to be inscribed. Yet it provoked her to no demonstration. She doesn't care so much as all that."

"Then why are you afraid of her?"

"It was not of her I was afraid. It was of you."

"Did you think I would fall in love with her? You never alluded to such a possibility before," he went on as I remained silent. "Admirable person as you pronounced her, that wasn't the light in which you showed her to me."

"Do you mean that if it *had* been you would have managed by this time to catch a glimpse of her? I didn't fear things then," I added. "I hadn't the same reason."

He kissed me at this, and when I remembered that she had done so an hour or two before I felt for an instant as if he were taking from my lips the very pressure of hers. In spite of kisses the incident had shed a certain chill, and I suffered horribly from the sense that he had seen me guilty of a fraud. He had seen it only through my frank avowal, but I was as unhappy as if I had a stain to efface. I couldn't get over the manner of his looking at me when I spoke of her apparent indifference to his not having come. For the first time since I had known him he seemed to have expressed a doubt of my word. Before we parted I told him that I would undeceive her, start the first thing in the morning for Richmond and there let her know that he had been blameless. At this he kissed me again. I would expiate my sin, I said; I would humble myself in the dust; I would confess and ask to be forgiven. At this he kissed me once more.

V

In the train the next day this struck me as a good deal for him to have consented to; but my purpose was firm enough to carry me on. I mounted the long hill to where the view begins, and then I knocked at her door. I was a trifle mystified by the fact that her blinds were still drawn, reflecting that if in the stress of my compunction I had come early I had certainly yet allowed people time to get up.

"At home, mum? She has left home for ever."

I was extraordinarily startled by this announcement of the elderly parlour-maid. "She has gone away?"

"She's dead, mum, please." Then as I gasped at the horrible word: "She died last night."

The loud cry that escaped me sounded even in my own ears like some harsh violation of the hour. I felt for the moment as if I had killed her; I turned faint and saw through a vagueness the woman hold out her arms to me. Of what next happened I have no recollection, nor of anything but my friend's poor stupid cousin, in a darkened room, after an interval that I suppose very brief, sobbing at me in a smothered accusatory way. I can't say how long it took me to understand, to believe and then to press back with an immense effort that pang of responsibility which, superstitiously, insanely, had been at first almost all I was conscious of. The doctor, after the fact, had been superlatively wise and clear: he was satisfied of a long-latent weakness of the heart, determined probably years before by the agitations and terrors to which her marriage had introduced her. She had had in those days cruel scenes with her husband, she had been in fear of her life. All emotion, everything in the nature of anxiety and suspense had been after that to be strongly deprecated, as in her marked cultivation of a quiet life she was evidently well aware; but who could say that any one, especially a "real lady," could be successfully protected from every little rub? She had had one a day or two before in the news of her husband's death; for there were shocks of all kinds, not only those of grief and surprise. For that matter she had never dreamed of so near a release: it had looked uncommonly as if he would live as long as herself. Then in the evening, in town, she had manifestly had another: something must have happened there which it would be indispensable to clear up. She had come back very late—it was past eleven o'clock, and on being met in the hall by her cousin, who was extremely anxious, had said that she was tired and must rest a moment before mounting the stairs. They had passed together into the dining-room, her companion proposing a glass of wine and bustling to the sideboard to pour it out. This took but a moment, and when my informant turned round our poor friend had not had time to seat herself. Suddenly, with a little moan that was barely audible, she dropped upon the sofa. She was dead. What unknown "little rub" had dealt her the blow? What shock, in the name of wonder, *had* she had in town? I mentioned immediately the only one I could imagine—her having failed to meet at my house, to which by invitation for the purpose she had come at five o'clock, the gentleman I was to be married to, who had been accidentally kept away and with whom she had no acquaintance whatever. This obviously counted for little; but something else might easily have occurred: nothing in the London streets was more possible than an accident, especially an accident in those desperate cabs. What had she done, where had she gone on leaving my house? I had taken for granted she had gone straight home.

We both presently remembered that in her excursions to town she sometimes, for convenience, for refreshment, spent an hour or two at the "Gentlewomen," the quiet little ladies' club, and I promised that it should be my first care to make at that establishment thorough inquiry. Then we entered the dim and dreadful chamber where she lay locked up in death and where, asking after a little to be left alone with her, I remained for half an hour. Death had made her, had kept her beautiful; but I felt above all, as I kneeled at her bed, that it had made her, had kept her silent. It had turned the key on something I was concerned to know.

On my return from Richmond and after another duty had been performed I drove to his chambers. It was the first time, but I had often wanted to see them. On the staircase, which, as the house contained twenty sets of rooms, was unrestrictedly public, I met his servant, who went back with me and ushered me in. At the sound of my entrance he appeared in the doorway of a further room, and the instant we were alone I produced my news: "She's dead!"

"Dead?"

He was tremendously struck, and I observed that he had no need to ask whom, in this abruptness, I meant.

"She died last evening—just after leaving me."

He stared with the strangest expression, his eyes searching mine as if they were looking for a trap. "Last evening—after leaving you?" He repeated my words in stupefaction. Then he brought out so that it was in stupefaction I heard: "Impossible! I saw her."

"You 'saw' her?"

"On that spot—where you stand."

This called back to me after an instant, as if to help me to take it in, the great wonder of the warning of his youth. "In the hour of death—I understand: as you so beautifully saw your mother."

"Ah! *not* as I saw my mother—not that way, not that way!"

He was deeply moved by my news—far more moved, I perceived, than he would have been the day before: it gave me a vivid sense that, as I had then said to myself, there was indeed a relation between them and that he had actually been face to face with her. Such an idea, by its reassertion of his extraordinary privilege, would have suddenly presented him as painfully abnormal had he not so vehemently insisted on the difference. "I saw her living—I saw her to speak to her—I saw her as I see you now!"

It is remarkable that for a moment, though only for a moment, I found relief in the more personal, as it were, but also the more natural of the two odd facts. The next, as I embraced this image of her having come to him on leaving me and of just what it accounted for in the disposal of her time, I demanded with a shade of harshness of which I was aware—

"What on earth did she come for?"

He had now had a minute to think—to recover himself and judge of effects, so that if it was still with excited eyes he spoke he showed a conscious redness and made an inconsequent attempt to smile away the gravity of his words.

"She came just to see me. She came—after what had passed at your house—so that we *should*, after all, at last meet. The impulse seemed to me exquisite, and that was the way I took it."

I looked round the room where she had been—where she had been and I never had been.

"And was the way you took it the way she expressed it?"

"She only expressed it by being here and by letting me look at her. That was enough!" he exclaimed with a singular laugh.

I wondered more and more. "You mean she didn't speak to you?"

"She said nothing. She only looked at me as I looked at her."

"And you didn't speak either?"

He gave me again his painful smile. "I thought of *you.* The situation was every way delicate. I used the finest tact. But she saw she had pleased me." He even repeated his dissonant laugh.

"She evidently pleased you!" Then I thought a moment. "How long did she stay?"

"How can I say? It seemed twenty minutes, but it was probably a good deal less."

"Twenty minutes of silence!" I began to have my definite view and now in fact quite to clutch at it. "Do you know you're telling me a story positively monstrous?"

He had been standing with his back to the fire; at this, with a pleading look, he came to me. "I beseech you, dearest, to take it kindly."

I could take it kindly, and I signified as much; but I couldn't somehow, as he rather awkwardly opened his arms, let him draw me to him. So there fell between us for an appreciable time the discomfort of a great silence.

VI

He broke it presently by saying: "There's absolutely no doubt of her death?"

"Unfortunately none. I've just risen from my knees by the bed where they've laid her out."

He fixed his eyes hard on the floor; then he raised them to mine. "How does she look?"

"She looks—at peace."

He turned away again, while I watched him; but after a moment he began: "At what hour, then——?"

"It must have been near midnight. She dropped as she reached her house—from an affection of the heart which she knew herself and her physician knew her to have, but of which, patiently, bravely she had never spoken to me."

He listened intently and for a minute he was unable to speak. At last he broke out with an accent of which the almost boyish confidence, the really sublime simplicity rings in my ears as I write: "Wasn't she *wonderful!*" Even at the time I was able to do it justice enough to remark in reply that I had always told him so; but the next minute, as if after speaking he had caught a glimpse of what he might have made me feel, he went on quickly: "You see that if she didn't get home till midnight——"

I instantly took him up. "There was plenty of time for you to have seen her? How so," I inquired, "when you didn't leave my house till late? I don't remember the very moment—I was preoccupied. But you know that though you said you had lots to do you sat for some time after dinner. She, on her side, was all the evening at the 'Gentlewomen.' I've just come from there—I've ascertained. She had tea there; she remained a long, long time."

"What was she doing all the long, long time?"

I saw that he was eager to challenge at every step my account of the matter; and the more he showed this the more I found myself disposed to insist on that account, to prefer with apparent perversity an explanation which only deepened the marvel and the mystery, but which, of the two prodigies it had to choose from, my reviving jealousy found easiest to accept. He stood there pleading with a candour that now seems to me beautiful for the privilege of having in spite of supreme defeat known the living woman; while I, with a passion I wonder at to-day, though it still smoulders in a manner in its ashes, could only reply that, through a strange gift shared by her with his mother and on her own side likewise hereditary, the miracle of his youth had been renewed for him, the miracle of hers for her. She had been to him—yes, and by an impulse as charming as he liked; but oh! she had not been in the body. It was a simple question of evidence. I had had, I assured him, a definite statement of what she had done—most of the time—at the little club. The place was almost empty, but the servants had noticed her. She had sat motionless in a deep chair by the drawing-room fire; she had leaned back her head, she had closed her eyes, she had seemed softly to sleep.

"I see. But till what o'clock?"

"There," I was obliged to answer, "the servants fail me a little. The portress in particular is unfortunately a fool, though even she too is supposed to be a Gentlewoman. She was evidently at that period of the evening, without a substitute and against regulations, absent for some little time from the cage in which it's her business to watch the comings and goings. She's muddled, she palpably prevaricates; so I can't positively, from her observation, give you an hour. But it was remarked toward half-past ten that our poor friend was no longer in the club."

"She came straight here; and from here she went straight to the train."

"She couldn't have run it so close," I declared. "That was a thing she particularly never did."

"There was no need of running it close, my dear—she had plenty of time. Your memory is at fault about my having left you late: I left you, as it happens, unusually early. I'm sorry my stay with you seemed long; for I was back here by ten."

"To put yourself into your slippers," I rejoined, "and fall asleep in your chair. You slept till morning—you saw her in a dream!" He looked at me in silence and with sombre eyes—eyes that showed me he had some irritation to repress. Presently I went on: "You had a visit, at an extraordinary hour, from a lady—*soit:* nothing in the world is more probable. But there are ladies and ladies. How in the name of goodness, if she was unannounced and dumb and you had into the bargain never seen the least portrait of her—how could you identify the person we're talking of?"

"Haven't I to absolute satiety heard her described? I'll describe her for you in every particular."

"Don't!" I exclaimed with a promptness that made him laugh once more. I coloured at this, but I continued: "Did your servant introduce her?"

"He wasn't here—he's always away when he's wanted. One of the features of this big house is that from the street-door the different floors are accessible practically without challenge. My servant makes love to a young person employed in the rooms above these, and he had a long bout of it last evening. When he's out on that job he leaves my outer door, on the staircase, so much ajar as to enable him to slip back without a sound. The door then only requires a push. She pushed it—that simply took a little courage."

"A little? It took tons! And it took all sorts of impossible calculations."

"Well, she had them—she made them. Mind you, I don't deny for a moment," he added, "that it was very, very wonderful!"

Something in his tone prevented me for a while from trusting myself to speak. At last I said: "How did she come to know where you live?"

"By remembering the address on the little label the shop-people happily left sticking to the frame I had had made for my photograph."

"And how was she dressed?"

"In mourning, my own dear. No great depths of crape, but simple and scrupulous black. She had in her bonnet three small black feathers. She carried a little muff of astrachan. She has near the left eye," he continued, "a tiny vertical scar——"

I stopped him short. "The mark of a caress from her husband." Then I added: "How close you must have been to her!" He made no answer to this, and I thought he blushed, observing which I broke straight off. "Well, good-bye."

"You won't stay a little?" He came to me again tenderly,

and this time I suffered him. "Her visit had its beauty," he murmured as he held me, "but yours has a greater one."

I let him kiss me, but I remembered, as I had remembered the day before, that the last kiss she had given, as I supposed, in this world had been for the lips he touched.

"I'm life, you see," I answered. "What you saw last night was death."

"It was life—it was life!"

He spoke with a kind of soft stubbornness, and I disengaged myself. We stood looking at each other hard.

"You describe the scene—so far as you describe it at all—in terms that are incomprehensible. She was in the room before you knew it?"

"I looked up from my letter-writing—at that table under the lamp I had been wholly absorbed in it—and she stood before me."

"Then what did you do?"

"I sprang up with an ejaculation, and she, with a smile, laid her finger, ever so warningly, yet with a sort of delicate dignity, to her lips. I knew it meant silence, but the strange thing was that it seemed immediately to explain and to justify her. We at any rate stood for a time that, as I've told you, I can't calculate, face to face. It was just as you and I stand now."

"Simply staring?"

He impatiently protested. "Ah! *we're* not staring!"

"Yes, but we're talking."

"Well, *we* were—after a fashion." He lost himself in the memory of it. "It was as friendly as this." I had on my tongue's point to ask if that were saying much for it, but I remarked instead that what they had evidently done was to gaze in mutual admiration. Then I inquired whether his recognition of her had been immediate. "Not quite," he replied, "for of course I didn't expect her; but it came to me long before she went who she was—who she could only be."

I thought a little. "And how did she at last go?"

"Just as she arrived. The door was open behind her, and she passed out."

"Was she rapid—slow?"

"Rather quick. But looking behind her," he added, with a smile. "I let her go, for I perfectly understood that I was to take it as she wished."

I was conscious of exhaling a long, vague sigh. "Well, you must take it now as *I* wish—you must let *me* go."

At this he drew near me again, detaining and persuading me, declaring with all due gallantry that I was a very different matter. I would have given anything to have been able to ask him if he had touched her, but the words refused to form themselves: I knew well enough how horrid and vulgar they would sound. I said something else—I forget exactly what; it was feebly tortuous and intended to make him tell me without my putting the question. But he didn't tell me; he only repeated, as if from a glimpse of the propriety of soothing and consoling me, the sense his of declaration of some minutes before—the assurance that she was indeed exquisite, as I had always insisted, but that I was his "real" friend and his very own for ever. This led me to reassert, in the spirit of my previous rejoinder, that I had at least the merit of being alive; which in turn drew from him again the flash of contradiction I dreaded. "Oh, *she* was alive! she was, she was!"

"She was dead! she was dead!" I asseverated with an energy, a determination that it should *be* so, which comes back to me now almost as grotesque. But the sound of the word as it rang out filled me suddenly with horror, and all the natural emotion the meaning of it might have evoked in other conditions gathered and broke in a flood. It rolled over me that here was a great affection quenched and how much I had loved and trusted her. I had a vision at the same time of the lonely beauty of her end. "She's gone—she's lost to us for ever!" I burst into sobs.

"That's exactly what I feel," he exclaimed, speaking with extreme kindness and pressing me to him for comfort. "She's gone; she's lost to us for ever: so what does it matter now?" He bent over me, and when his face had touched mine I scarcely knew if it were wet with my tears or with his own.

VII

It was my theory, my conviction, it became, as I may say, my attitude, that they had still never "met;" and it was just on this ground that I said to myself it would be generous to ask him to stand with me beside her grave. He did so, very modestly and tenderly, and I assumed, though he himself clearly cared nothing for the danger, that the solemnity of the occasion, largely made up of persons who had known them both and had a sense of the long joke, would sufficiently deprive his presence of all light association. On the question of what had happened the evening of her death little more passed between us; I had been overtaken by a horror of the element of evidence. It seemed gross and prying on either hypothesis. He on his side had none to produce, none at least but a statement of his house-porter—on his own admission a most casual and intermittent personage—that between the hours of ten o'clock and midnight no less than three ladies in deep black had flitted in and out of the place. This proved far too much; we had neither of us any use for three. He knew that I considered I had accounted for every fragment of her time, and we dropped the matter as settled; we abstained from further discussion. What *I* knew however was that he abstained to please me rather than because he yielded to my reasons. He didn't yield—he was only indulgent; he clung to his interpretation because he liked it better. He liked it better, I held, because it had more to say to his vanity. That, in a similar position, would not have been its effect on me, though I had doubtless quite as much; but these are things of individual humour, as to which no person can judge for another. I should have supposed it more gratifying to be the subject of one of those inexplicable occurrences that are chronicled in thrilling books and disputed about at learned meetings; I could conceive, on the part of a being just engulfed in the infinite and still vibrating with human emotion, of nothing more fine and pure, more high and august than such an impulse of reparation, of admonition or even of curiosity. *That* was beautiful, if one would, and I should in his place have thought more of myself for being so distinguished. It was public that he had already, that he had long been distinguished, and what was this in itself but almost a proof? Each of the strange visitations contributed to establish the other. He had a different feeling; but he had also, I hasten to add, an unmistakable desire not to make a stand or, as they say, a fuss about it. I might believe what I liked—the more so that the whole thing was in a manner a mystery of my producing. It was an event of my history, a puzzle of my consciousness, not of his; therefore he would take about it any tone that struck me as convenient. We had both at all events other business on hand; we were pressed with preparations for our marriage.

Mine were assuredly urgent, but I found as the days went on that to believe what I "liked" was to believe what I was more and more intimately convinced of. I found also that I didn't like it so much as that came to, or that the pleasure at all events was far from being the cause of my conviction. My obsession, as I may really call it and as I began to perceive, refused to be elbowed away, as I had hoped, by my sense of paramount duties. If I had a great deal to do I had still more to think about, and the moment came when my occupations were gravely menaced by my thoughts. I see it all now, I feel it, I live it over. It's terribly void of joy, it's full indeed to overflowing of bitterness; and yet I must do myself justice—I couldn't possibly be other than I was. The same strange impressions, had I to meet them again, would produce the same deep anguish, the same sharp doubts, the same still sharper certainties. Oh, it's all easier to remember than to write, but even if I could retrace the business hour by hour, could find terms for the inexpressible, the ugliness and the pain would quickly stay my hand. Let me then note very simply and briefly that a week before our wedding-day, three weeks after her death, I became fully aware that I had something very serious to look in the face and that if I was to make this effort I must make it on the spot and before another hour should elapse. My unextinguished jealousy—that was the Medusa-mask. It hadn't died with her death, it had lividly survived, and it was fed by suspicions unspeakable. They *would* be unspeakable to-day, that is, if I hadn't felt the sharp need of uttering them at the time. This need took possession of me—to save me, as it appeared, from my fate. When once it had done so I saw—in the urgency of the case, the diminishing hours and shrinking interval—only one issue, that of absolute promptness and frankness. I could at least not do him the wrong of delaying another day; I could at least treat my difficulty as too fine for a subterfuge. Therefore very quietly, but none the less abruptly and hideously, I put it before him on a certain evening that we must reconsider our situation and recognise that it had completely altered.

He stared bravely. "How has it altered?"

"Another person has come between us."

He hesitated a moment. "I won't pretend not to know whom you mean." He smiled in pity for my aberration, but he meant to be kind. "A woman dead and buried!"

"She's buried, but she's not dead. She's dead for the world—she's dead for me. But she's not dead for *you*."

"You hark back to the different construction we put on her appearance that evening?"

"No," I answered, "I hark back to nothing. I've no need of it. I've more than enough with what's before me."

"And pray, darling, what is that?"

"You're completely changed."

"By that absurdity?" he laughed.

"Not so much by that one as by other absurdities that have followed it."

"And what may they have been?"

We had faced each other fairly, with eyes that didn't flinch; but his had a dim, strange light, and my certitude triumphed in his perceptible paleness. "Do you really pretend," I asked, "not to know what they are?"

"My dear child," he replied, "you describe them too sketchily!"

I considered a moment. "One may well be embarrassed to finish the picture! But from that point of view—and from the beginning—what was ever more embarrassing than your idiosyncrasy?"

He was extremely vague. "My idiosyncrasy?"

"Your notorious, your peculiar power."

He gave a great shrug of impatience, a groan of overdone disdain. "Oh, my peculiar power!"

"Your accessibility to forms of life," I coldly went on, "your command of impressions, appearances, contacts closed—for our gain or our loss—to the rest of us. That was originally a part of the deep interest with which you inspired me—one of the reasons I was amused, I was indeed positively proud to know you. It was a magnificent distinction; it's a magnificent distinction still. But of course I had no prevision then of the way it would operate now; and even had that been the case I should have had none of the extraordinary way in which its action would affect me."

"To what in the name of goodness," he pleadingly inquired, "are you fantastically alluding?" Then as I remained silent, gathering a tone for my charge, "How in the world *does* it operate?" he went on; "and how in the world are you affected?"

"She missed you for five years," I said, "but she never misses you now. You're making it up!"

"Making it up?" He had begun to turn from white to red.

"You see her—you see her: you see her every night!" He gave a loud sound of derision, but it was not a genuine one. "She comes to you as she came that evening," I declared; "having tried it she found she liked it!" I was able, with God's help, to speak without blind passion or vulgar violence; but those were the exact words—and far from "sketchy" they then appeared to me—that I uttered. He had turned away in his laughter, clapping his hands at my folly, but in an instant he faced me again with a change of expression that struck me. "Do you dare to deny," I asked, "that you habitually see her?"

He had taken the line of indulgence, of meeting me halfway and kindly humouring me. At all events to my astonishment he suddenly said: "Well, my dear, what if I do?"

"It's your natural right; it belongs to your constitution and to your wonderful if not perhaps quite enviable fortune. But you will easily understand that it separates us. I unconditionally release you."

"Release me?"

"You must choose between me and her."

He looked at me hard. "I see." Then he walked away a little, as if grasping what I had said and thinking how he had best treat it. At last he turned upon me afresh. "How on earth do you know such an awfully private thing?"

"You mean because you've tried so hard to hide it? It *is* awfully private, and you may believe I shall never betray you. You've done your best, you've acted your part, you've behaved, poor dear! loyally and admirably. Therefore I've watched you in silence, playing my part too; I've noted every drop in your voice, every absence in your eyes, every effort in your indifferent hand: I've waited till I was utterly sure and miserably unhappy. How *can* you hide it when you're abjectly in love with her, when you're sick almost to death with the joy of what she gives you?" I checked his quick protest with a quicker gesture. "You love her as you've *never* loved, and, passion for passion, she gives it straight back! She rules you, she holds you, she has you all! A woman, in such a case as mine, divines and feels and sees; she's not an idiot who has to be credibly informed. You come to me mechanically, compunctiously, with the dregs of your tenderness and the remnant of your life. I can renounce you, but I can't share you; the best of you is hers; I know what it is and I freely give you up to her for ever!"

He made a gallant fight, but it couldn't be patched up; he repeated his denial, he retracted his admission, he ridiculed my charge, of which I freely granted him moreover the indefensible extravagance. I didn't pretend for a moment that we were talking of common things; I didn't pretend for a moment that he and she were common people. Pray, if they *had* been, how should I ever have cared for them? They had enjoyed a rare extension of being and they had caught me up in their flight; only I couldn't breathe in such an air and I promptly asked to be set down. Everything in the facts was monstrous, and most of all my lucid perception of them; the only thing allied to nature and truth was my having to act on that perception. I felt after I had spoken in this sense that my assurance was complete; nothing had been wanting to it but the sight of my effect on him. He disguised indeed the effect in a cloud of chaff, a diversion that gained him time and covered his retreat. He challenged my sincerity, my sanity, almost my humanity, and that of course widened our breach and confirmed our rupture. He did everything in short but convince me either that I was wrong or that he was unhappy: we separated and I left him to his inconceivable communion.

He never married, any more than I've done. When six years

later, in solitude and silence, I heard of his death I hailed it as a direct contribution to my theory. It was sudden, it was never properly accounted for, it was surrounded by circumstances in which—for oh, I took them to pieces!—I distinctly read an intention, the mark of his own hidden hand. It was the result of a long necessity, of an unquenchable desire. To say exactly what I mean, it was a response to an irresistible call.

JOHN DELAVOY

I

THE friend who kindly took me to the first night of poor Windon's first—which was also poor Windon's last: it was removed as fast as, at an unlucky dinner, a dish of too perceptible a presence—also obligingly pointed out to me the notabilities in the house. So it was that we came round, just opposite, to a young lady in the front row of the balcony—a young lady in mourning so marked that I rather wondered to see her at a place of pleasure. I dare say my surprise was partly produced by my thinking her face, as I made it out at the distance, refined enough to aid a little the contradiction. I remember at all events dropping a word about the manners and morals of London—a word to the effect that, for the most part, elsewhere, people so bereaved as to be so becraped were bereaved enough to stay at home. We recognised of course, however, during the wait, that nobody ever did stay at home; and, as my companion proved vague about my young lady, who was yet somehow more interesting than any other as directly in range, we took refuge in the several theories that might explain her behaviour. One of these was that she had a sentiment for Windon which could override superstitions; another was that her scruples had been mastered by an influence discernible on the spot. This was nothing less than the spell of a gentleman beside her, whom I had at first mentally disconnected from her on account of some visibility of difference. He was not, as it were, quite good enough to have come with her; and yet he was strikingly handsome, whereas she, on the contrary, would in all likelihood have been pronounced almost occultly so. That was what, doubtless, had led me to put a question about her; the fact of her having the kind of distinction that is quite independent of beauty. Her friend, on the other hand, whose clustering curls were fair, whose moustache and whose fixed monocular glass particularly, if indescribably, matched them, and whose expanse of white shirt and waistcoat had the air of carrying out and balancing the scheme of his large white forehead—her friend had the kind of beauty that is quite independent of distinction. That he was her friend—and very much—was clear from his easy imagination of all her curiosities. He began to show her the company, and to do much better in this line than my own companion did for me, inasmuch as he appeared even to know who we ourselves were. That gave a propriety to my finding, on the return from a dip into the lobby in the first entr'acte, that the lady beside me was at last prepared to identify him. I, for my part, knew too few people to have picked up anything. She mentioned a friend who had edged in to speak to her and who had named the gentleman opposite as Lord Yarracome.

Somehow I questioned the news. "It sounds like the sort of thing that's too good to be true."

"Too good?"

"I mean he's too much like it."

"Like what? Like a lord?"

"Well, like the name, which is expressive, and—yes—even like the dignity. Isn't that just what lords are usually not?" I didn't, however, pause for a reply, but inquired further if his lordship's companion might be regarded as his wife.

"Dear, no. She's Miss Delavoy."

I forget how my friend had gathered this—not from the informant who had just been with her; but on the spot I accepted it, and the young lady became vividly interesting. "The daughter of the great man?"

"What great man?"

"Why, the wonderful writer, the immense novelist: the one

who died last year." My friend gave me a look that led me to add: "Did you never hear of him?" and, though she professed inadvertence, I could see her to be really so vague that—perhaps a trifle too sharply—I afterwards had the matter out with her. Her immediate refuge was in the question of Miss Delavoy's mourning. It was for *him*, then, her illustrious father; though that only deepened the oddity of her coming so soon to the theatre, and coming with a lord. My companion spoke as if the lord made it worse, and, after watching the pair a moment with her glass, observed that it was easy to see he could do anything he liked with his young lady. I permitted her, I confess, but little benefit from this diversion, insisting on giving it to her plainly that I didn't know what we were coming to and that there was in the air a gross indifference to which perhaps more almost than anything else the general density on the subject of Delavoy's genius testified. I even let her know, I am afraid, how scant, for a supposedly clever woman, I thought the grace of these *lacunæ*; and I may as well immediately mention that, as I have had time to see, we were not again to be just the same allies as before my explosion. This was a brief, thin flare, but it expressed a feeling, and the feeling led me to concern myself for the rest of the evening, perhaps a trifle too markedly, with Lord Yarracome's victim. She was the image of a nearer approach, of a personal view: I mean in respect to my great artist, on whose consistent aloofness from the crowd I needn't touch, any more than on his patience in going his way and attending to his work, the most unadvertised, unreported, uninterviewed, unphotographed, uncriticised of all originals. Was he not the man of the time about whose private life we delightfully knew least? The young lady in the balcony, with the stamp of her close relation to him in her very dress, was a sudden opening into that region. I borrowed my companion's glass; I treated myself, in this direction—yes, I was momentarily gross—to an excursion of some minutes. I came back from it with the sense of something gained; I felt as if I had been studying Delavoy's own face, no portrait of which I had ever met. The result of it all, I easily recognised, would be to add greatly to my impatience for the finished book he had left behind, which had not yet seen the light, which was announced for a near date, and as to which rumour—I mean of course only in the particular warm air in which it lived at all—had already been sharp. I went out after the second act to make room for another visitor—they buzzed all over the place—and when I rejoined my friend she was primed with rectifications.

"He isn't Lord Yarracome at all. He's only Mr Beston."

I fairly jumped; I see, as I now think, that it was as if I had read the future in a flash of lightning. "Only——? The mighty editor?"

"Yes, of the celebrated *Cynosure*." My interlocutress was determined this time not to be at fault. "He's always at first nights."

"What a chance for me, then," I replied, "to judge of my particular fate!"

"Does that depend on Mr Beston?" she inquired; on which I again borrowed her glass and went deeper into the subject.

"Well, my literary fortune does. I sent him a fortnight ago the best thing I've ever done. I've not as yet had a sign from him, but I can perhaps make out in his face, in the light of his type and expression, some little portent or promise." I did my best, but when after a minute my companion asked what I discovered I was obliged to answer "Nothing!" The next moment I added: "He won't take it."

"Oh, I hope so!"

"That's just what I've been doing." I gave back the glass. "Such a face is an abyss."

"Don't you think it handsome?"

"Glorious. Gorgeous. Immense. Oh, I'm lost! What does Miss Delavoy think of it?" I then articulated.

"Can't you see?" My companion used her glass. "She's

under the charm—she has succumbed. How else can he have dragged her here in her state?" I wondered much, and indeed her state seemed happy enough, though somehow, at the same time, the pair struck me as not in the least matching. It was only for half a minute that my friend made them do so by going on: "It's perfectly evident. She's not a daughter, I should have told you, by the way—she's only a sister. They've struck up an intimacy in the glow of his having engaged to publish from month to month the wonderful book that, as I understand you, her brother has left behind."

That was plausible, but it didn't bear another look. "Never!" I at last returned. "Daughter or sister, that fellow won't touch him."

"Why in the world——?"

"Well, for the same reason that, as you'll see, he won't touch *me*. It's wretched, but we're too good for him." My explanation did as well as another, though it had the drawback of leaving me to find another for Miss Delavoy's enslavement. I was not to find it that evening, for as poor Windon's play went on we had other problems to meet, and at the end our objects of interest were lost to sight in the general blinding blizzard. The affair was a bitter "frost," and if we were all in our places to the last everything else had disappeared. When I got home it was to be met by a note from Mr Beston accepting my article almost with enthusiasm, and it is a proof of the rapidity of my fond revulsion that before I went to sleep, which was not till ever so late, I had excitedly embraced the prospect of letting him have, on the occasion of Delavoy's new thing, my peculiar view of the great man. I must add that I was not a little ashamed to feel I had made a fortune the very night Windon had lost one.

II

Mr Beston really proved, in the event, most kind, though his appeal, which promised to become frequent, was for two or three quite different things before it came round to my peculiar view of Delavoy. It in fact never addressed itself at all to that altar, and we met on the question only when, the posthumous volume having come out, I had found myself wound up enough to risk indiscretions. By this time I had twice been with him and had had three or four of his notes. They were the barest bones, but they phrased, in a manner, a connection. This was not a triumph, however, to bring me so near to him as to judge of the origin and nature of his relations with Miss Delavoy. That his magazine would, after all, publish no specimens was proved by the final appearance of the new book at a single splendid bound. The impression it made was of the deepest—it remains the author's highest mark; but I heard, in spite of this, of no emptying of table-drawers for Mr Beston's benefit. What the book is we know still better to-day, and perhaps even Mr Beston does; but there was no approach at the time to a general rush, and I therefore of course saw that if he was thick with the great man's literary legatee—as I, at least, supposed her—it was on some basis independent of his bringing anything out. Nevertheless he quite rose to the idea of my study, as I called it, which I put before him in a brief interview.

"You ought to have something. That thing has brought him to the front with a leap——!"

"The front? What do you call the front?"

He had laughed so good-humouredly that I could do the same. "Well, the front is where you and I are." I told him my paper was already finished.

"Ah then, you must write it again."

"Oh, but look at it first——!"

"You must write it again," Mr Beston only repeated. Before I left him, however, he had explained a little. "You must see his sister."

"I shall be delighted to do that."

"She's a great friend of mine, and my having something may please her—which, though my first, my only duty is to please my subscribers and shareholders, is a thing I should rather like to do. I'll take from you something of the kind you mention, but only if she's favourably impressed by it."

I just hesitated, and it was not without a grain of hypocrisy that I artfully replied: "I would much rather *you* were!"

"Well, I shall be if she is." Mr Beston spoke with gravity. "She can give you a good deal, don't you know?—all sorts of leads and glimpses. She naturally knows more about him than anyone. Besides, she's charming herself."

To dip so deep could only be an enticement; yet I already felt so saturated, felt my cup so full, that I almost wondered what was left to me to learn, almost feared to lose, in greater waters, my feet and my courage. At the same time I welcomed without reserve the opportunity my patron offered, making as my one condition that if Miss Delavoy assented he would print my article as it stood. It was arranged that he should tell her that I would, with her leave, call upon her, and I begged him to let her know in advance that I was prostrate before her brother. He had all the air of thinking that he should have put us in a relation by which *The Cynosure* would largely profit, and I left him with the peaceful consciousness that if I had baited my biggest hook he had opened his widest mouth. I wondered a little, in truth, how he could care enough for Delavoy without caring more than enough, but I may at once say that I was, in respect to Mr Beston, now virtually in possession of my point of view. This had revealed to me an intellectual economy of the rarest kind. There was not a thing in the world—with a single exception, on which I shall presently touch—that he valued for itself, and not a scrap he knew about anything save whether or no it would do. To "do" with Mr Beston, was to do for *The Cynosure*. The wonder was that he could know that of things of which he knew nothing else whatever.

There are a hundred reasons, even in this most private record, which, from a turn of mind so unlike Mr Beston's, I keep exactly for a love of the fact in itself: there are a hundred confused delicacies, operating however late, that hold my hand from any motion to treat the question of the effect produced on me by first meeting with Miss Delavoy. I say there are a hundred, but it would better express my sense perhaps to speak of them all in the singular. Certain it is that one of them embraces and displaces the others. It was not the first time, and I dare say it was not even the second, that I grew sure of a shyness on the part of this young lady greater than any exhibition in such a line that my kindred constitution had ever allowed me to be clear about. My own diffidence, I may say, kept me in the dark so long that my perception of hers had to be retroactive—to go back and put together and, with an element of relief, interpret and fill out. It failed, inevitably, to operate in respect to a person in whom the infirmity of which I speak had none of the awkwardness, the tell-tale anguish, that makes it as a rule either ridiculous or tragic. It was too deep, too still, too general—it was perhaps even too proud. I must content myself, however, with saying that I have in all my life known nothing more beautiful than the faint, cool morning-mist of confidence less and less embarrassed in which it slowly evaporated. We have made the thing all out since, and we understand it all now. It took her longer than I measured to believe that a man without her particular knowledge could make such an approach to her particular love. The approach was made in my paper, which I left with her on my first visit and in which, on my second, she told me she had not an alteration to suggest. She said of it what I had occasionally, to an artist, heard said, or said myself, of a likeness happily caught: that to touch it again would spoil it, that it had "come" and must only be left. It may be imagined that after such a speech I was willing to wait for anything; unless indeed it be suggested that there could be then nothing more to wait for. A great deal more, at any rate, seemed to arrive, and it was all in conversation about Delavoy that we ceased to be hindered and hushed. The place was still full of him, and in everything there that spoke to me I heard the sound of his voice. I read his style into everything—I read it into his sister. She was surrounded by his relics, his possessions, his books; all of which were not many, for he had worked without material reward: this only, however, made each more charged, somehow, and more personal. He had been her only devotion, and there were moments when she might have been taken for the guardian of a temple or a tomb. That was what brought me nearer than I had got even in my paper; the sense that it was he, in a manner, who had made her, and that to be with her was still to be with himself. It was not only that I could talk to him so; it was that he listened and that he also talked. Little by little and touch by touch she built him up to me; and then it was, I confess, that I felt, in comparison, the shrinkage of what I had written. It grew faint and small—though indeed only for myself; it had from the first, for the witness who counted so much more, a merit that I have ever since reckoned the great good fortune of my life, and even, I will go so far as to say, a fine case of inspiration. I hasten to add that this case had been preceded by a still finer. Miss Delavoy had made of her brother the year before his death a portrait in pencil that was precious for two rare reasons. It was the only representation of the sort in existence, and it was a work of curious distinction. Conventional but sincere, highly finished and smaller than life, it had a quality that, in any collection, would have caused it to be scanned for some signature known to the initiated. It was a thing of real vision, yet it was a thing of taste, and as soon as I learned that our hero, sole of his species, had succeeded in never, save on this occasion, sitting, least of all to a photographer, I took the full measure of what the studied strokes of a pious hand would some day represent for generations more aware of John Delavoy than, on the whole, his own had been. My feeling for them was not diminished, moreover, by learning from my young lady that Mr Beston, who had given them some attention, had signified that, in the event of his publishing an article, he would like a reproduction of the drawing to accompany it. The "pictures" in *The Cynosure* were in general a marked chill to my sympathy: I had always held that, like good wine, honest prose needed, as it were, no bush. I took them as a sign that if good wine, as we know, is more and more hard to meet, the other commodity was becoming as scarce. The bushes, at all events, in *The Cynosure*, quite planted out the text; but my objection fell in the presence of Miss Delavoy's sketch, which already, in the forefront of my study, I saw as a flower in the coat of a bridegroom.

I was obliged just after my visit to leave town for three weeks and was, in the country, surprised at their elapsing without bringing me a proof from Mr Beston. I finally wrote to ask of him an explanation of the delay; for which in turn I had again to wait so long that before I heard from him I received a letter from Miss Delavoy, who, thanking me as for a good office, let me know that our friend had asked her for the portrait. She appeared to suppose that I must have put in with him some word for it that availed more expertly than what had passed on the subject between themselves. This gave me occasion, on my return to town, to call on her for the purpose of explaining how little as yet, unfortunately, she owed me. I am not indeed sure that it didn't quicken my return. I knocked at her door with rather a vivid sense that if Mr Beston had her drawing I was yet still without my proof. My privation was the next moment to feel a sharper pinch, for on entering her apartment I found Mr Beston in possession. Then it was that I was fairly confronted with the problem given me from this time to solve. I began at that hour to look it straight in the face. What I in the first place saw was that Mr Beston was "making up" to our hostess; what I saw in the second—what at any rate I believed I saw—was that she had come a certain distance to meet him; all of which would have been simple and usual enough had not the very things that gave it such a character been exactly the things I should least have expected. Even this first time, as my patron sat there, I made out somehow that in that position at least he was sincere and sound. Why should this have surprised me? Why should I immediately have asked myself how he would make it pay? He was there because he liked to be, and where was the wonder of his liking? There was no wonder in my own, I felt, so that my state of mind must have been already a sign of how little I supposed we could like the same things. This even strikes me, on looking back, as an implication sufficiently ungraceful of the absence on Miss Delavoy's part of direct and designed attraction. I dare say indeed that Mr Beston's subjection would have seemed to me a clearer thing if I had not had by the same stroke to account for his friend's. She liked him, and I grudged her that, though with the actual limits of my knowledge of both parties I had literally to invent reasons for its being a perversity, I could only in private treat it as one, and this in spite of Mr Beston's notorious power to please. He was the handsomest man in "literary" London, and, controlling the biggest circulation—a body of subscribers as vast as a conscript army—he represented in a manner the modern poetry of numbers. He was in love moreover, or he thought he was; that flushed with a general glow the large surface he presented. This surface, from my quiet corner, struck me as a huge tract, a sort of particoloured map, a great spotted social chart. He abounded in the names of things, and his mind was like a great staircase at a party—you heard them bawled at the top. He ought to have liked Miss Delavoy because *her* name, so announced, sounded well, and I grudged him, as I grudged the young lady, the higher motive of an intelligence of her charm. It was a charm so fine and so veiled that if she had been a piece of prose or of verse I was sure he would never have discovered it. The oddity was that, as the case stood, he had seen she would "do." I too had seen it, but then I was a critic: these remarks will sadly have miscarried if they fail to show the reader how much of one.

III

I MENTIONED my paper and my disappointment, but I think it was only in the light of subsequent events that I could fix an impression of his having, at the moment, looked a trifle embarrassed. He smote his brow and took out his tablets; he deplored the accident of which I complained, and promised to look straight into it. An accident it could only have been, the result of a particular pressure, a congestion of work. Of course he had had my letter and had fully supposed it had been answered and acted on. My spirits revived at this, and I almost thought the incident happy when I heard Miss Delavoy herself put a clear question.

"It won't be for April, then, which was what I had hoped?"

It was what *I* had hoped, goodness knew, but if I had had no anxiety I should not have caught the low, sweet ring of her own. It made Mr Beston's eyes fix her a moment, and, though the thing has as I write it a fatuous air, I remember thinking that he must at this instant have seen in her face almost all his contributor saw. If he did he couldn't wholly have enjoyed it; yet he replied genially enough: "I'll put it into June."

"Oh, June!" our companion murmured in a manner that I took as plaintive—even as exquisite.

Mr Beston had got up. I had not promised myself to sit him

out, much less to drive him away; and at this sign of his retirement I had a sense still dim, but much deeper, of being literally lifted by my check. Even before it was set up my article was somehow operative, so that I could look from one of my companions to the other and quite magnanimously smile. "June will do very well."

"Oh, if *you* say so——!" Miss Delavoy sighed and turned away.

"We must have time for the portrait; it will require great care," Mr Beston said.

"Oh, please be sure it has the greatest!" I eagerly returned.

But Miss Delavoy took this up, speaking straight to Mr Beston. "I attach no importance to the portrait. My impatience is all for the article."

"The article's very neat. It's very neat," Mr Beston repeated. "But your drawing's our great prize."

"Your great prize," our young lady replied, "can only be the thing that tells most about my brother."

"Well, that's the case with your picture," Mr Beston protested.

"How can you say that? My picture tells nothing in the world but that he never sat for another."

"Which is precisely the enormous and final fact!" I laughingly exclaimed.

Mr Beston looked at me as if in uncertainty and just the least bit in disapproval; then he found his tone. "It's the big fact for *The Cynosure*. I shall leave you in no doubt of *that*!" he added, to Miss Delavoy, as he went away.

I was surprised at his going, but I inferred that, from the pressure at the office, he had no choice; and I was at least not too much surprised to guess the meaning of his last remark to have been that our hostess must expect a handsome draft. This allusion had so odd a grace on a lover's lips that, even after the door had closed, it seemed still to hang there between Miss Delavoy and her second visitor. Naturally, however, we let it gradually drop; she only said with a kind of conscious quickness: "I'm really very sorry for the delay." I thought her beautiful as she spoke, and I felt that I had taken with her a longer step than the visible facts explained. "Yes, it's a great bore. But to an editor—one doesn't show it."

She seemed amused. "Are they such queer fish?"

I considered. "You know the great type."

"Oh, I don't know Mr Beston as an editor."

"As what, then?"

"Well, as what you call, I suppose, a man of the world. A very kind, clever one."

"Of course *I* see him mainly in the saddle and in the charge—at the head of his hundreds of thousands. But I mustn't undermine him," I added, smiling, "when he's doing so much for me."

She appeared to wonder about it. "Is it really a great deal?"

"To publish a thing like that? Yes—as editors go. They're all tarred with the same brush."

"Ah, but he has immense ideas. He goes in for the best in all departments. That's his own phrase. He has often assured me that he'll never stoop."

"He wants none but 'first-class stuff.' That's the way he has expressed it to *me*; but it comes to the same thing. It's our great comfort. He's charming."

"He's charming," my friend replied; and I thought for the moment we had done with Mr Beston. A rich reference to him, none the less, struck me as flashing from her very next words—words that she uttered without appearing to have noticed any I had pronounced in the interval. "Does no one, then, really care for my brother?"

I was startled by the length of her flight. "Really care?"

"No one but you? Every month your study doesn't appear is at this time a kind of slight."

"I see what you mean. But of course *we're* serious."

"Whom do you mean by 'we'?"

"Well, you and me."

She seemed to look us all over and not to be struck with our mass. "And no one else? No one else is serious?"

"What I should say is that no one *feels* the whole thing, don't you know? as much."

Miss Delavoy hesitated. "Not even so much as Mr Beston?" And her eyes, as she named him, waited, to my surprise, for my answer.

I couldn't quite see why she returned to him, so that my answer was rather lame. "Don't ask me too many things; else there are some *I* shall have to ask."

She continued to look at me; after which she turned away. "Then I won't—for I don't understand him." She turned away, I say, but the next moment had faced about with a fresh, inconsequent question. "Then why in the world has he cooled off?"

"About my paper? *Has* he cooled? Has he shown you that otherwise?" I asked.

"Than by his delay? Yes, by silence—and by worse."

"What do you call worse?"

"Well, to say of it—and twice over—what he said just now."

"That it's very 'neat'? You don't think it *is*?" I laughed.

"I don't say it"; and with that she smiled. "My brother might hear!"

Her tone was such that, while it lingered in the air, it deepened, prolonging the interval, whatever point there was in this; unspoken things therefore had passed between us by the time I at last brought out: "He hasn't read me! It doesn't matter," I quickly went on; "his relation to what I may do or not do is, for his own purposes, quite complete enough without that."

She seemed struck with this. "Yes, his relation to almost anything is extraordinary."

"His relation to everything!" It rose visibly before us and, as we felt, filled the room with its innumerable, indistinguishable objects. "Oh, it's the making of him!"

She evidently recognised all this, but after a minute she again broke out: "You say he hasn't read you and that it doesn't matter. But has he read my brother? Doesn't *that* matter?"

I waved away the thought. "For what do you take him, and why in the world should it? He knows perfectly what he wants to do, and his postponement is quite in your interest. The reproduction of the drawing——"

She took me up. "I hate the drawing!"

"So do I," I laughed, "and I rejoice in there being something on which we can feel so together!"

IV

WHAT may further have passed between us on this occasion loses, as I try to recall it, all colour in the light of a communication that I had from her four days later. It consisted of a note in which she announced to me that she had heard from Mr Beston in terms that troubled her: a letter from Paris—he had dashed over on business—abruptly proposing that she herself should, as she quoted, give him something; something that her intimate knowledge of the subject—which was of course John Delavoy—her rare opportunities for observation and study would make precious, would make as unique as the work of her pencil. He appealed to her to gratify him in this particular, exhorted her to sit right down to her task, reminded her that to tell a loving sister's tale was her obvious, her highest duty. She confessed to mystification and invited me to explain. Was this sudden perception of her duty a result on Mr Beston's part of any difference with myself? Did he want two papers? Did he want an alternative to mine? Did he want hers as a supplement or as a substitute? She begged instantly to be informed if anything had happened to mine. To meet her request I had first to make sure, and I repaired on the morrow to Mr Beston's office in the eager hope that he was back from Paris. This hope was crowned; he had crossed in the night and was in his room; so that on sending up my card I was introduced to his presence, where I promptly broke ground by letting him know that I had had even yet no proof.

"Oh, yes! about Delavoy. Well, I've rather expected you, but you must excuse me if I'm brief. My absence has put me back; I've returned to arrears. Then from Paris I meant to write to you, but even there I was up to my neck. I think, too, I've instinctively held off a little. You won't like what I have to say—you *can't*!" He spoke almost as if I might wish to prove I could. "The fact is, you see, your thing won't do. No—not even a little."

Even after Miss Delavoy's note it was a blow, and I felt myself turn pale. "Not even a little? Why, I thought you wanted it so!"

Mr Beston just perceptibly braced himself. "My dear man, we didn't want *that*! We couldn't do it. I've every desire to be agreeable to you, but we really couldn't."

I sat staring. "What in the world's the matter with it?"

"Well, it's impossible. That's what's the matter with it."

"Impossible?" There rolled over me the ardent hours and a great wave of the feeling that I had put into it.

He hung back but an instant—he faced the music. "It's indecent."

I could only wildly echo him. "Indecent? Why, it's absolutely, it's almost to the point of a regular chill, expository. What in the world is it but critical?"

Mr Beston's retort was prompt. "Too critical by half! That's just where it is. It says too much."

"But what it says is all about its subject."

"I dare say, but I don't think we want quite so much about its subject."

I seemed to swing in the void and I clutched, fallaciously, at the nearest thing. "What you do want, then—what is *that* to be about?"

"That's for you to find out—it's not my business to tell you."

It was dreadful, this snub to my happy sense that I *had* found out. "I thought you wanted John Delavoy. I've simply stuck to him."

Mr Beston gave a dry laugh. "I should think you had!" Then after an instant he turned oracular. "Perhaps we wanted him—perhaps we didn't. We didn't at any rate want indelicacy."

"Indelicacy?" I almost shrieked. "Why it's pure portraiture."

"'Pure,' my dear fellow, just begs the question. It's most objectionable—that's what it is. For portraiture of *such* things, at all events, there's no place in our scheme."

I speculated. "Your scheme for an account of Delavoy?"

Mr Beston looked as if I trifled. "Our scheme for a successful magazine."

"No place, do I understand you, for criticism? No place for the great figures——? If you don't want too much detail," I went on, "I recall perfectly that I was careful not to go into it. What I tried for was a general vivid picture—which I really supposed I arrived at. I boiled the man down—I gave the three or four leading notes. *Them* I did try to give with some intensity."

Mr Beston, while I spoke, had turned about and, with a movement that confessed to impatience and even not a little, I thought, to irritation, fumbled on his table among a mass of papers and other objects; after which he had pulled out a couple of drawers. Finally he fronted me anew with my copy in his hand, and I had meanwhile added a word about the disadvantage at which he placed me. To have made me wait was unkind; but to have made me wait for such news——! I ought at least to have been told it earlier. He replied to this that he had not at first had time to read me, and, on the evidence of my other things, had taken me pleasantly for granted: he had only been enlightened by the revelation of the proof. What he had fished out of his drawer was, in effect, not my manuscript, but the "galleys" that had never been sent me. The thing was all set up there, and my companion, with eyeglass and thumb, dashed back the sheets and looked up and down for places. The proof-reader, he mentioned, had so waked him up with the blue pencil that he had no difficulty in finding them. They were all in his face when he again looked at me. "Did you candidly think that we were going to print this?"

All my silly young pride in my performance quivered as if under the lash. "Why the devil else should I have taken the trouble to write it? If you're not going to print it, why the devil did you ask me for it?"

"I didn't ask you. You proposed it yourself."

"You jumped at it; you quite agreed you ought to have it: it comes to the same thing. So indeed you ought to have it. It's too ignoble, your not taking up such a man."

He looked at me hard. "I *have* taken him up. I do want something about him, and I've got his portrait there—coming out beautifully."

"Do you mean you've taken him up," I inquired, "by asking for something of his sister? Why, in that case, do you speak as if I had forced on you the question of a paper? If you want one you want one."

Mr Beston continued to sound me. "How do you know what I've asked of his sister?"

"I know what Miss Delavoy tells me. She let me know it as soon as she had heard from you."

"Do you mean that you've just seen her?"

"I've not seen her since the time I met you at her house; but I had a note from her yesterday. She couldn't understand your appeal—in the face of knowing what I've done myself."

Something seemed to tell me at this instant that she had not yet communicated with Mr Beston, but that he wished me not to know she hadn't. It came out still more in the temper with which he presently said: "I want what Miss Delavoy can do, but I don't want this kind of thing!" And he shook my proof at me as if for a preliminary to hurling it.

I took it from him, to show I anticipated his violence, and, profoundly bewildered, I turned over the challenged pages. They grinned up at me with the proof-reader's shocks, but the shocks, as my eye caught them, bloomed on the spot like flowers. I didn't feel abased—so many of my good things came back to me. "What on earth do you seriously mean? This thing isn't bad. It's awfully good—it's beautiful."

With an odd movement he plucked it back again, though not indeed as if from any new conviction. He had had after all a kind of contact with it that had made it a part of his stock. "I dare say it's clever. For the kind of thing it is, it's as beautiful as you like. It's simply not *our* kind." He seemed to break out afresh. "Didn't you know more——?"

I waited. "More what?"

He in turn did the same. "More everything. More about Delavoy. The whole point was that I thought you did."

I fell back in my chair. "You think my article shows ignorance? I sat down to it with the sense that I knew more than any one."

Mr Beston restored it again to my hands. "You've kept that pretty well out of sight then. Didn't you get anything out of *her*? It was simply for that I addressed you to her."

I took from him with this, as well, a silent statement of what it had not been for. "I got everything in the wide world I could. We almost worked together, but what appeared was that all her own knowledge, all her own view, quite fell in with what I had already said. There appeared nothing to subtract or to add."

He looked hard again, not this time at me, but at the

document in my hands. "You mean she has gone into all that—seen it just as it stands there?"

"If I've still," I replied, "any surprise left, it's for the surprise your question implies. You put our heads together, and you've surely known all along that they've remained so. She told me a month ago that she had immediately let you know the good she thought of what I had done."

Mr Beston very candidly remembered, and I could make out that if he flushed as he did so it was because what most came back to him was his own simplicity. "I see. That must have been why I trusted you—sent you, without control, straight off to be set up. But now that I see you——!" he went on.

"You're surprised at her indulgence?"

Once more he snatched at the record of my rashness—once more he turned it over. Then he read out two or three paragraphs. "Do you mean she has gone into all that?"

"My dear sir, what do you take her for? There wasn't a line we didn't thresh out, and our talk wouldn't for either of us have been a bit interesting if it hadn't been really frank. Have you to learn at this time of day," I continued, "what her feeling is about her brother's work? She's not a bit stupid. She has a kind of worship for it."

Mr Beston kept his eyes on one of my pages. "She passed her life with him and was extremely fond of him."

"Yes, and she has the point of view and no end of ideas. She's tremendously intelligent."

Our friend at last looked up at me, but I scarce knew what to make of his expression. "Then she'll do me exactly what I want."

"Another article, you mean, to replace mine?"

"Of a totally different sort. Something the public *will* stand." His attention reverted to my proof, and he suddenly reached out for a pencil. He made a great dash against a block of my prose and placed the page before me. "Do you pretend to me they'll stand *that*?"

"That" proved, as I looked at it, a summary of the subject, deeply interesting and treated, as I thought, with extraordinary art, of the work to which I gave the highest place in my author's array. I took it in, sounding it hard for some hidden vice, but with a frank relish, in effect, of its lucidity; then I answered: "If they won't stand it, what will they stand?"

Mr Beston looked about and put a few objects on his table to rights. "They won't stand anything." He spoke with such pregnant brevity as to make his climax stronger. "And quite right too! *I'm* right, at any rate; I can't plead ignorance. I know where I am, and I want to stay there. That single page would have cost me five thousand subscribers."

"Why, that single page is a statement of the very essence ——!"

He turned sharp round at me. "Very essence of what?"

"Of my very topic, damn it."

"Your very topic is John Delavoy."

"And what's *his* very topic? Am I not to attempt to utter it? What under the sun else am I writing about?"

"You're not writing in *The Cynosure* about the relations of the sexes. With those relations, with the question of sex in any degree, I should suppose you would already have seen that we have nothing whatever to do. If you want to know what our public won't stand, there you have it."

I seem to recall that I smiled sweetly as I took it. "I don't know, I think, what you mean by those phrases, which strike me as too empty and too silly, and of a nature therefore to be more deplored than any, I'm positive, that I use in my analysis. I don't use a single one that even remotely resembles them. I simply try to express my author, and if your public won't stand his being expressed, mention to me kindly the source of its interest in him."

Mr Beston was perfectly ready. "He's all the rage with the clever people—that's the source. The interest of the public is whatever a clever article may make it."

"I don't understand you. How can an article be clever, to begin with, and how can it make anything of anything, if it doesn't avail itself of material?"

"There *is* material, which I'd hoped you'd use. Miss Delavoy has lots of material. I don't know what she has told you, but I know what she has told *me*." He hung fire but an instant. "Quite lovely things."

"And have you told *her*——?"

"Told her what?" he asked as I paused.

"The lovely things you've just told me."

Mr Beston got up; folding the rest of my proof together, he made the final surrender with more dignity than I had looked for. "You can do with this what you like." Then as he reached the door with me: "Do you suppose that I talk with Miss Delavoy on such subjects?" I answered that he could leave that to me—I shouldn't mind so doing; and I recall that before I quitted him something again passed between us on the question of her drawing. "What we want," he said, "is just the really nice thing, the pleasant, right thing to go with it. That drawing's going to take!"

V

A FEW minutes later I had wired to our young lady that, should I hear nothing from her to the contrary, I would come to her that evening. I had other affairs that kept me out; and on going home I found a word to the effect that though she should not be free after dinner she hoped for my presence at five o'clock: a notification betraying to me that the evening would, by arrangement, be Mr Beston's hour and that she wished to see me first. At five o'clock I was there, and as soon as I entered the room I perceived two things. One of these was that she had been highly impatient; the other was that she had not heard, since my call on him, from Mr Beston, and that her arrangement with him therefore dated from earlier. The tea-service was by the fire—she herself was at the window; and I am at a loss to name the particular revelation that I drew from this fact of her being restless on general grounds. My telegram had fallen in with complications at which I could only guess; it had not found her quiet; she was living in a troubled air. But her wonder leaped from her lips. "He does want two?"

I had brought in my proof with me, putting it in my hat and my hat on a chair. "Oh, no—he wants only one, only yours."

Her wonder deepened. "He won't print——?"

"My poor old stuff! He returns it with thanks."

"Returns it? When he had accepted it!"

"Oh, that doesn't prevent—when he doesn't like it."

"But he does; he did. He liked it to *me*. He called it 'sympathetic.'"

"He only meant that *you* are—perhaps even that I myself am. He hadn't read it then. He read it but a day or two ago, and horror seized him."

Miss Delavoy dropped into a chair. "Horror?"

"I don't know how to express to you the fault he finds with it." I had gone to the fire, and I looked to where it peeped out of my hat; my companion did the same, and her face showed the pain she might have felt, in the street, at sight of the victim of an accident. "It appears it's indecent."

She sprang from her chair. "To describe my brother?"

"As *I've* described him. That, at any rate, is how my account sins. What I've said is unprintable." I leaned against the chimney-piece with a serenity of which, I admit, I was conscious; I rubbed it in and felt a private joy in watching my influence.

"Then what *have* you said?"

"You know perfectly. You heard my thing from beginning to end. You said it was beautiful."

She remembered as I looked at her; she showed all the things she called back. "It *was* beautiful." I went over and picked it up; I came back with it to the fire. "It was the best thing ever said about him," she went on. "It was the finest and truest."

"Well, then——!" I exclaimed.

"But what have you done to it since?"

"I haven't touched it since."

"You've put nothing else in?"

"Not a line—not a syllable. Don't you remember how you warned me against spoiling it? It's of the thing we read together, liked together, went over and over together; it's of this dear little serious thing of good sense and good faith"—and I held up my roll of proof, shaking it even as Mr Beston had shaken it—"that he expresses that opinion."

She frowned at me with an intensity that, though bringing me no pain, gave me a sense of her own. "Then that's why he has asked *me*——?"

"To do something instead. But something pure. You, he hopes, won't be indecent."

She sprang up, more mystified than enlightened; she had pieced things together, but they left the question gaping. "Is he mad? What is he talking about?"

"Oh, *I* know—now. Has he specified what he wants of you?"

She thought a moment, all before me. "Yes—to be very 'personal.'"

"Precisely. You mustn't speak of the work."

She almost glared. "Not speak of it?"

"That's indecent."

"My brother's work?"

"To speak of it."

She took this from me as she had not taken anything. "Then how can I speak of him at all?—how can I articulate? He *was* his work."

"Certainly he was. But that's not the kind of truth that will stand in Mr Beston's way. Don't you know what he means by wanting you to be personal?"

In the way she looked at me there was still for a moment a dim desire to spare him—even perhaps a little to save him. None the less, after an instant, she let herself go. "Something horrible?"

"Horrible; so long, that is, as it takes the place of something more honest and really so much more clean. He wants—what do they call the stuff?—anecdotes, glimpses, gossip, chat; a picture of his 'home life,' domestic habits, diet, dress, arrangements—all his little ways and little secrets, and even, to better it still, all your own, your relations with him, your feelings about him, his feelings about *you*: both his and yours, in short, about anything else you can think of. Don't you see what I mean?" She saw so well that, in the dismay of it, she grasped my arm an instant, half as if to steady herself, half as if to stop me. But she couldn't stop me. "He wants you just to write round and round that portrait."

She was lost in the reflections I had stirred, in apprehensions and indignations that slowly surged and spread; and for a moment she was unconscious of everything else. "What portrait?"

"Why, the beautiful one you did. The beautiful one you gave him."

"Did I give it to him? Oh, yes!" It came back to her, but this time she blushed red, and I saw what had occurred to her. It occurred, in fact, at the same instant to myself. "Ah, *par exemple*," she cried, "he shan't have it!"

I couldn't help laughing. "My dear young lady, unfortunately he *has* got it!"

"He shall send it back. He shan't use it."

"I'm afraid he *is* using it," I replied. "I'm afraid he *has* used it. They've begun to work on it."

She looked at me almost as if I were Mr Beston. "Then they must stop working on it." Something in her decision somehow thrilled me. "Mr Beston must send it straight back. Indeed I'll wire to him to bring it to-night."

"Is he coming to-night?" I ventured to inquire.

She held her head very high. "Yes, he's coming to-night. It's most happy!" she bravely added, as if to forestall any suggestion that it could be anything else.

I thought a moment; first about that, then about something that presently made me say: "Oh, well, if he brings it back——!"

She continued to look at me. "Do you mean you doubt his doing so?"

I thought again. "You'll probably have a stiff time with him."

She made, for a little, no answer to this but to sound me again with her eyes; our silence, however, was carried off by her then abruptly turning to her tea-tray and pouring me out a cup. "Will you do me a favour?" she asked as I took it.

"Any favour in life."

"Will you be present?"

"Present?"—I failed at first to imagine.

"When Mr Beston comes."

It was so much more than I had expected that I of course looked stupid in my surprise. "This evening—here?"

"This evening—here. Do you think my request very strange?"

I pulled myself together. "How can I tell when I'm so awfully in the dark?"

"In the dark——?" She smiled at me as if I were a person who carried such lights!

"About the nature, I mean, of your friendship."

"With Mr Beston?" she broke in. Then in the wonderful way that women say such things: "It has always been so pleasant."

"Do you think it will be pleasant for *me*?" I laughed.

"Our friendship? I don't care whether it is or not!"

"I mean what you'll have out with him—for of course you *will* have it out. Do you think it will be pleasant for *him*?"

"To find you here—or to see you come in? I don't feel obliged to think. This is a matter in which I now care for no one but my brother—for nothing but his honour. I stand only on that."

I can't say how high, with these words, she struck me as standing, nor how the look that she gave me with them seemed to make me spring up beside her. We were at this elevation together a moment. "I'll do anything in the world you say."

"Then please come about nine."

That struck me as so tantamount to saying "And please therefore go this minute" that I immediately turned to the door. Before I passed it, however, I gave her time to ring out clear: "I know what I'm about!" She proved it the next moment by following me into the hall with the request that I would leave her my proof. I placed it in her hands, and if she knew what she was about I wondered, outside, what *I* was.

VI

I DARE say it was the desire to make this out that, in the evening, brought me back a little before my time. Mr Beston had not arrived, and it's worth mentioning—for it was rather odd—that while we waited for him I sat with my hostess in silence. She spoke of my paper, which she had read over—but simply to tell me she had done so; and that was practically all that passed between us for a time at once so full and so quiet that it struck me neither as short nor as long. We felt, in the matter, so indivisible that we might have been united in some observance or some sanctity—to go through something decorously appointed. Without an observation we listened to the door-bell, and, still without one, a minute later, saw the person we expected stand there and show his surprise. It was at me he looked as he spoke to her.

"I'm not to see you alone?"

"Not just yet, please," Miss Delavoy answered. "Of what has suddenly come between us this gentleman is essentially a part, and I really think he'll be less present if we speak before him than if we attempt to deal with the question without him." Mr Beston was amused, but not enough amused to sit down, and we stood there while, for the third time, my proof-sheets were shaken for emphasis. "I've been reading these over," she said as she held them up.

Mr Beston, on what he had said to me of them, could only look grave; but he tried also to look pleasant, and I foresaw that, on the whole, he would really behave well. "They're remarkably clever."

"And yet you wish to publish instead of them something from so different a hand?"

He smiled now very kindly. "If you'll only let me have it! *Won't* you let me have it? I'm sure you know exactly the thing I want."

"Oh, perfectly!"

"I've tried to give her an idea of it," I threw in.

Mr Beston promptly saw his way to make this a reproach to me. "Then, after all, you had one yourself?"

"I think I couldn't have kept so clear of it if I hadn't had!" I laughed.

"I'll write you something," Miss Delavoy went on, "if you'll print this as it stands." My proof was still in her keeping.

Mr Beston raised his eyebrows. "Print two? Whatever do I want with two? What do I want with the wrong one if I can get the beautiful right?"

She met this, to my surprise, with a certain gaiety. "It's a big subject—a subject to be seen from different sides. Don't you want a full, a various treatment? Our papers will have nothing in common."

"I should hope not!" Mr Beston said good-humouredly. "You have command, dear lady, of a point of view too good to spoil. It so happens that your brother has been really less handled than anyone, so that there's a kind of obscurity about him, and in consequence a kind of curiosity, that it seems to me quite a crime not to work. There's just the perfection, don't you know? of a little sort of mystery—a tantalizing *demi-jour.*" He continued to smile at her as if he thoroughly hoped to kindle her, and it was interesting at that moment to get this vivid glimpse of his conception.

I could see it quickly enough break out in Miss Delavoy, who sounded for an instant almost assenting. "And you want the obscurity and the mystery, the tantalizing *demi-jour*, cleared up?"

"I want a little lovely, living thing! Don't be perverse," he pursued, "don't stand in your own light and in your brother's and in this young man's—in the long run, and in mine too and in every one's: just let us have him out as no one but you can bring him and as, by the most charming of chances and a particular providence, he has been kept all this time just on purpose for you to bring. Really, you know"—his vexation *would* crop up—"one could howl to see such good stuff wasted!"

"Well," our young lady returned, "that holds good of one thing as well as of another. I can never hope to describe or express my brother as these pages describe and express him; but, as I tell you, approaching him from a different direction, I promise to do my very best. Only, my condition remains."

Mr Beston transferred his eyes from her face to the little bundle in her hand, where they rested with an intensity that made me privately wonder if it represented some vain vision of a snatch defeated in advance by the stupidity of his having suffered my copy to be multiplied. "My printing that?"

"Your printing this."

Mr Beston wavered there between us: I could make out in him a vexed inability to keep us as distinct as he would have liked. But he was triumphantly light. "It's impossible. Don't be a pair of fools!"

"Very well, then," said Miss Delavoy; "please send me back my drawing."

"Oh dear, no!" Mr Beston laughed. "Your drawing we must have at any rate."

"Ah, but I forbid you to use it! This gentleman is my witness that my prohibition is absolute."

"Was it to be your witness that you sent for the gentleman? You take immense precautions!" Mr Beston exclaimed. Before she could retort, however, he came back to his strong point. "Do you coolly ask of me to sacrifice ten thousand subscribers?"

The number, I noticed, had grown since the morning, but Miss Delavoy faced it boldly. "If you do, you'll be well rid of them. They must be ignoble, your ten thousand subscribers."

He took this perfectly. "You dispose of them easily! Ignoble or not, what I have to do is to keep them and if possible add to their number; not to get rid of them."

"You'd rather get rid of my poor brother instead?"

"I don't get rid of him. I pay him a signal attention. Reducing it to the least, I publish his portrait."

"His portrait—the only one worth speaking of? Why, you turn it out with horror."

"Do you call the only one worth speaking of that misguided effort?" And, obeying a restless impulse, he appeared to reach for my tribute; not, I think, with any conscious plan, but with a vague desire in some way again to point his moral with it.

I liked immensely the motion with which, in reply to this, she put it behind her: her gesture expressed so distinctly her vision of her own lesson. From that moment, somehow, they struck me as forgetting me, and I seemed to see them as they might have been alone together; even to see a little what, for each, had held and what had divided them. I remember how, at this, I almost held my breath, effacing myself to let them go, make them show me whatever they might. "It's the only one," she insisted, "that tells, about its subject, anything that's anyone's business. If you really want John Delavoy, there he is. If you don't want him, don't insult him with an evasion and a pretence. Have at least the courage to say that you're afraid of him!"

I figured Mr Beston here as much incommoded; but all too simply, doubtless, for he clearly held on, smiling through flushed discomfort and on the whole bearing up. "Do you think I'm afraid of *you*?" He might forget me, but he would have to forget me a little more to yield completely to his visible impulse to take her hand. It was visible enough to herself to make her show that she declined to meet it, and even that his effect on her was at last distinctly exasperating. Oh, how I saw at that moment that in the really touching good faith of his personal sympathy he didn't measure his effect! If he had done so he wouldn't have tried to rush it, to carry it off with tenderness. He dropped to that now so rashly that I was in truth sorry for him. "You *could* do so gracefully, so naturally what we want. What we want, don't you see? is perfect taste. I know better than you do yourself how perfect yours would be. I always know better than people do themselves." He jested and pleaded, getting in, benightedly, deeper. Perhaps I didn't literally hear him ask in the same accents if she didn't care for him at all, but I distinctly saw him look as if he were on the point of it, and something, at any rate, in a lower tone, dropped from him that he followed up with the statement that if she did even just a little she would help him.

VII

SHE made him wait a deep minute for her answer to this, and that gave me time to read into it what he accused her of failing to do. I recollect that I was startled at their having come so far, though I was reassured, after a little, by seeing that he had come much the furthest. I had now I scarce know what amused sense of knowing our hostess so much better than he. "I think you strangely inconsequent," she said at last. "If you associate with—what you speak of—the idea of help, does it strike you as helping *me* to treat in that base fashion the memory I most honour and cherish?" As I was quite sure of what he spoke of I could measure the force of this challenge. "Have you never discovered, all this time, that my brother's work is my pride and my joy?"

"Oh, my dear thing!"—and Mr Beston broke into a cry that combined in the drollest way the attempt to lighten his guilt with the attempt to deprecate hers. He let it just flash upon us that, should he be pushed, he would show as—well, scandalised.

The tone in which Miss Delavoy again addressed him offered a reflection of this gleam. "Do you know what my brother would think of you?"

He was quite ready with his answer, and there was no moment in the whole business at which I thought so well of him. "I don't care a hang what your brother would think!"

"Then why do you wish to commemorate him?"

"How can you ask so innocent a question? It isn't for *him*."

"You mean it's for the public?"

"It's for the magazine," he said with a noble simplicity.

"The magazine *is* the public," it made me so far forget myself as to suggest.

"You've discovered it late in the day! Yes," he went on to our companion, "I don't in the least mind saying I don't care. I don't—I don't!" he repeated with a sturdiness in which I somehow recognised that he was, after all, a great editor. He looked at me a moment as if he even guessed what I saw, and, not unkindly, desired to force it home. "I don't care for anybody. It's not my business to care. That's not the way to run a magazine. Except of course as a mere man!"—and he added a smile for Miss Delavoy. He covered the whole ground again. "Your reminiscences would make a talk!"

She came back from the greatest distance she had yet reached. "My reminiscences?"

"To accompany the head." He must have been as tender as if I had been away. "Don't I see how you'd do them?"

She turned off, standing before the fire and looking into it; after which she faced him again. "If you'll publish our friend here, I'll do them."

"Why are you so awfully wound up about our friend here?"

"Read his article over—with a little intelligence—and your question will be answered."

Mr Beston glanced at me and smiled as if with a loyal warning; then, with a good conscience, he let me have it. "Oh, damn his article!"

I was struck with her replying exactly what I should have replied if I had not been so detached. "Damn it as much as you like, but publish it." Mr Beston, on this, turned to me as if to ask me if I had not heard enough to satisfy me: there was a visible offer in his face to give me more if I insisted. This amounted to an appeal to me to leave the room at least for a minute; and it was perhaps from the fear of what might pass between us that Miss Delavoy once more took him up. "If my brother's as vile as you say——!"

"Oh, I don't say *he's* vile!" he broke in.

"You only say *I* am!" I commented.

"You've entered so into him," she replied to me, "that it

comes to the same thing. And Mr Beston says further that out of this unmentionableness he wants somehow to make something—some money or some sensation."

"My dear lady," said Mr Beston, "it's a very great literary figure!"

"Precisely. You advertise yourself with it because it's a very great literary figure, and it's a very great literary figure because it wrote very great literary things that you wouldn't for the world allow to be intelligibly or critically named. So you bid for the still more striking tribute of an intimate picture—an unveiling of God knows what!—without even having the pluck or the logic to say on what ground it is that you go in for naming him at all. Do you know, dear Mr Beston," she asked, "that you make me very sick? I count on receiving the portrait," she concluded, "by to-morrow evening at latest."

I felt, before this speech was over, so sorry for her interlocutor that I was on the point of asking her if she mightn't finish him without my help. But I had lighted a flame that was to consume me too, and I was aware of the scorch of it while I watched Mr Beston plead frankly, if tacitly, that, though there was something in him not to be finished, she must yet give him a moment and let him take his time to look about him at pictures and books. He took it with more coolness than I; then he produced his answer. "You shall receive it to-morrow morning if you'll do what I asked the last time." I could see more than he how the last time had been overlaid by what had since come up; so that, as she opposed a momentary blank, I felt almost a coarseness in his recall of it with an "Oh, you know—you know!"

Yes, after a little she knew, and I need scarcely add that I did. I felt, in the oddest way, by this time, that she was conscious of my penetration and wished to make me, for the loss now so clearly beyond repair, the only compensation in her power. This compensation consisted of her showing me that she was indifferent to my having guessed the full extent of the privilege that, on the occasion to which he alluded, she had permitted Mr Beston to put before her. The balm for my wound was therefore to see what she resisted. She resisted Mr Beston in more ways than one. "And if I don't do it?" she demanded.

"I'll simply keep your picture!"

"To what purpose if you don't use it?"

"To keep it *is* to use it," Mr Beston said.

"He has only to keep it long enough," I added, and with the intention that may be imagined, "to bring you round, by the mere sense of privation, to meet him on the other ground."

Miss Delavoy took no more notice of this speech than if she had not heard it, and Mr Beston showed that he had heard it only enough to show, more markedly, that he followed her example. "I'll do anything, I'll do everything for you in life," he declared to her, "but publish such a thing as that."

She gave in all decorum to this statement the minute of concentration that belonged to it; but her analysis of the matter had for sole effect to make her at last bring out, not with harshness, but with a kind of wondering pity: "I think you're really very dreadful!"

"In what esteem then, Mr Beston," I asked, "do you hold John Delavoy's work?"

He rang out clear. "As the sort of thing that's out of our purview!" If for a second he had hesitated it was partly, I judge, with just resentment at my so directly addressing him, and partly, though he wished to show our friend that he fairly faced the question, because experience had not left him in such a case without two or three alternatives. He had already made plain indeed that he mostly preferred the simplest.

"Wonderful, wonderful purview!" I quite sincerely, or at all events very musingly, exclaimed.

"Then, if you could ever have got one of his novels——?" Miss Delavoy inquired.

He smiled at the way she put it; it made such an image of the attitude of *The Cynosure*. But he was kind and explicit. "There isn't one that wouldn't have been beyond us. We could never have run him. We could never have handled him. We could never, in fact, have touched him. We should have dropped to —oh, Lord!" He saw the ghastly figure he couldn't name— he brushed it away with a shudder.

I turned, on this, to our companion. "I wish awfully you'd do what he asks!" She stared an instant, mystified; then I quickly explained to which of his requests I referred. "I mean I wish you'd do the nice familiar chat about the sweet home-life. You might make it inimitable, and, upon my word, I'd give you for it the assistance of my general lights. The thing is —don't you see?—that it would put Mr Beston in a grand position. Your position would be grand," I hastened to add as I looked at him, "because it would be so admirably false." Then, more seriously, I felt the impulse even to warn him. "I don't think you're quite aware of what you'd make it. Are you really quite conscious?" I went on with a benevolence that struck him, I was presently to learn, as a depth of fatuity.

He was to show once more that he was a rock. "Conscious? Why should I be? Nobody's conscious."

He was splendid; yet before I could control it I had risked the challenge of a "Nobody?"

"Who's anybody? The public isn't!"

"Then why are you afraid of it?" Miss Delavoy demanded.

"Don't ask him that," I answered; "you expose yourself to his telling you that, if the public isn't anybody, that's still more the case with your brother."

Mr Beston appeared to accept as a convenience this somewhat inadequate protection; he at any rate under cover of it again addressed us lucidly. "There's only one false position— the one you seem so to wish to put me in."

I instantly met him. "That of losing——?"

"That of losing——!"

"Oh, fifty thousand—yes. And they wouldn't see anything the matter——?"

"With the position," said Mr Beston, "that you qualify, I neither know nor care why, as false." Suddenly, in a different tone, almost genially, he continued: "For what do you take them?"

For what indeed?—but it didn't signify. "It's enough that I take *you*—for one of the masters." It's literal that as he stood there in his florid beauty and complete command I felt his infinite force, and, with a gush of admiration, wondered how, for our young lady, there could be at such a moment another man. "We represent different sides," I rather lamely said. However, I picked up. "It isn't a question of where we are, but of what. You're not on a side—you *are* a side. You're the right one. What a misery," I pursued, "for us not to be 'on' you!"

His eyes showed me for a second that he yet saw how our not being on him did just have for it that it could facilitate such a speech; then they rested afresh on Miss Delavoy, and that brought him back to firm ground. "I don't think you can imagine how it will come out."

He was astride of the portrait again, and presently again she had focussed him. "If it does come out——!" she began, poor girl; but it was not to take her far.

"Well, if it does——?"

"He means what will you do then?" I observed, as she had nothing to say.

"Mr Beston will see," she at last replied with a perceptible lack of point.

He took this up in a flash. "My dear young lady, it's *you* who'll see; and when you've seen you'll forgive me. Only wait till you do!" He was already at the door, as if he quite believed in what he should gain by the gain, from this moment, of time. He stood there but an instant—he looked from one of us to the other. "It will be a ripping little thing!" he remarked; and with that he left us gaping.

VIII

THE first use I made of our rebound was to say with intensity: "What *will* you do if he does?"

"Does publish the picture?" There was an instant charm to me in the privacy of her full collapse and the sudden high tide of our common defeat. "What *can* I? It's all very well; but there's nothing to be done. I want never to see him again. There's only something," she went on, "that *you* can do."

"Prevent him?—get it back? I'll do, be sure, my utmost; but it will be difficult without a row."

"What do you mean by a row?" she asked.

"I mean it will be difficult without publicity. I don't think we want publicity."

She turned this over. "Because it will advertise him?"

"His magnificent energy. Remember what I just now told him. He's the right side."

"And we're the wrong!" she laughed. "We mustn't make that known—I see. But, all the same, save my sketch!"

I held her hands. "And if I do?"

"Ah, get it back first!" she answered, ever so gently and with a smile, but quite taking them away.

I got it back, alas! neither first nor last; though indeed at the end this was to matter, as I thought and as I found, little enough. Mr Beston rose to his full height and was not to abate an inch even on my offer of another article on a subject notoriously unobjectionable. The only portrait of John Delavoy was going, as he had said, to take, and nothing was to stand in its way. I besieged his office, I waylaid his myrmidons, I haunted his path, I poisoned, I tried to flatter myself, his life; I wrote him at any rate letters by the dozen and showed him up to his friends and his enemies. The only thing I didn't do was to urge Miss Delavoy to write to her solicitors or to the newspapers. The final result, of course, of what I did and what I didn't was to create, on the subject of the sole copy of so rare an original, a curiosity that, by the time *The Cynosure* appeared with the reproduction, made the month's sale, as I was destined to learn, take a tremendous jump. The portrait of John Delavoy, prodigiously "paragraphed" in advance and with its authorship flushing through, was accompanied by a page or two, from an anonymous hand, of the pleasantest, liveliest comment. The press was genial, the success immense, current criticism had never flowed so full, and it was universally felt that the handsome thing had been done. The process employed by Mr Beston had left, as he had promised, nothing to be desired; and the sketch itself, the next week, arrived in safety, and with only a smutch or two, by the post. I placed my article, naturally, in another magazine, but was disappointed, I confess, as to what it discoverably did in literary circles for its subject. This ache, however, was muffled. There was a worse victim than I, and there was consolation of a sort in our having out together the question of literary circles. The great orb of *The Cynosure*, wasn't that a literary circle? By the time we had fairly to face this question we had achieved the union that—at least for resistance or endurance—is supposed to be strength.

PASTE

"I'VE found a lot more things," her cousin said to her the day after the second funeral; "they're up in her room—but they're things I wish *you'd* look at."

The pair of mourners, sufficiently stricken, were in the garden of the vicarage together, before luncheon, waiting to be summoned to that meal, and Arthur Prime had still in his face the intention, she was moved to call it rather than the expression, of feeling something or other. Some such appearance was in itself of course natural within a week of his stepmother's death, within three of his father's; but what was most present to the girl, herself sensitive and shrewd, was that he seemed somehow to brood without sorrow, to suffer without what she in her own case would have called pain. He turned away from her after this last speech—it was a good deal his habit to drop an observation and leave her to pick it up without assistance. If the vicar's widow, now in her turn finally translated, had not really belonged to him it was not for want of her giving herself, so far as he ever would take her; and she had lain for three days all alone at the end of the passage, in the great cold chamber of hospitality, the dampish, greenish room where visitors slept and where several of the ladies of the parish had, without effect, offered, in pairs and successions, piously to watch with her. His personal connection with the parish was now slighter than ever, and he had really not waited for this opportunity to show the ladies what he thought of them. She felt that she herself had, during her doleful month's leave from Bleet, where she was governess, rather taken her place in the same snubbed order; but it was presently, none the less, with a better little hope of coming in for some remembrance, some relic, that she went up to look at the things he had spoken of, the identity of which, as a confused cluster of bright objects on a table in the darkened room, shimmered at her as soon as she had opened the door.

They met her eyes for the first time, but in a moment, before touching them, she knew them as things of the theatre, as very much too fine to have been, with any verisimilitude, things of the vicarage. They were too dreadfully good to be true, for her aunt had had no jewels to speak of, and these were coronets and girdles, diamonds, rubies and sapphires. Flagrant tinsel and glass, they looked strangely vulgar, but if, after the first queer shock of them, she found herself taking them up, it was for the very proof, never yet so distinct to her, of a far-off faded story. An honest widowed cleric with a small son and a large sense of Shakespeare had, on a brave latitude of habit as well as of taste—since it implied his having in very fact dropped deep into the "pit"—conceived for an obscure actress, several years older than himself, an admiration of which the prompt offer of his reverend name and hortatory hand was the sufficiently candid sign. The response had perhaps, in those dim years, in the way of eccentricity, even bettered the proposal, and Charlotte, turning the tale over, had long since drawn from it a measure of the career renounced by the undistinguished *comédienne*—doubtless also tragic, or perhaps pantomimic, at a pinch—of her late uncle's dreams. This career could not have been eminent and must much more probably have been comfortless.

"You see what it is—old stuff of the time she never liked to mention."

Our young woman gave a start; her companion had, after all, rejoined her and had apparently watched a moment her slightly scared recognition. "So I said to myself," she replied. Then, to show intelligence, yet keep clear of twaddle: "How peculiar they look!"

"They look awful," said Arthur Prime. "Cheap gilt, diamonds as big as potatoes. These are trappings of a ruder age than ours. Actors do themselves better now."

"Oh now," said Charlotte, not to be less knowing, "actresses have real diamonds."

"Some of them." Arthur spoke drily.

"I mean the bad ones—the nobodies too."

"Oh, some of the nobodies have the biggest. But mamma wasn't of that sort."

"A nobody?" Charlotte risked.

"Not a nobody to whom somebody—well, not a nobody with diamonds. It isn't all worth, this trash, five pounds."

There was something in the old gewgaws that spoke to her, and she continued to turn them over. "They're relics. I think they have their melancholy and even their dignity."

Arthur observed another pause. "Do you care for them?" he then asked. "I mean," he promptly added, "as a souvenir."

"Of you?" Charlotte threw off.

"Of me? What have I to do with it? Of your poor dead aunt who was so kind to you," he said with virtuous sternness.

"Well, I would rather have them than nothing."

"Then please take them," he returned in a tone of relief which expressed somehow more of the eager than of the gracious.

"Thank you." Charlotte lifted two or three objects up and set them down again. Though they were lighter than the materials they imitated they were so much more extravagant that they struck her in truth as rather an awkward heritage, to which she might have preferred even a matchbox or a penwiper. They were indeed shameless pinchbeck. "Had you any idea she had kept them?"

"I don't at all believe she *had* kept them or knew they were there, and I'm very sure my father didn't. They had quite equally worked off any tenderness for the connection. These odds and ends, which she thought had been given away or destroyed, had simply got thrust into a dark corner and been forgotten."

Charlotte wondered. "Where then did you find them?"

"In that old tin box"—and the young man pointed to the receptacle from which he had dislodged them and which stood on a neighbouring chair. "It's rather a good box still, but I'm afraid I can't give you *that*."

The girl gave the box no look; she continued only to look at the trinkets. "What corner had she found?"

"She hadn't 'found' it," her companion sharply insisted; "she had simply lost it. The whole thing had passed from her mind. The box was on the top shelf of the old schoolroom closet, which, until one put one's head into it from a step-ladder, looked, from below, quite cleared out. The door is narrow and the part of the closet to the left goes well into the wall. The box had stuck there for years."

Charlotte was conscious of a mind divided and a vision vaguely troubled, and once more she took up two or three of the subjects of this revelation; a big bracelet in the form of a gilt serpent with many twists and beady eyes, a brazen belt studded with emeralds and rubies, a chain, of flamboyant architecture, to which, at the Theatre Royal Little Peddlington, Hamlet's mother had probably been careful to attach the portrait of the successor to Hamlet's father. "Are you very sure they're not really worth something? Their mere weight alone——!" she vaguely observed, balancing a moment a royal diadem that might have crowned one of the creations of the famous Mrs Jarley.

But Arthur Prime, it was clear, had already thought the question over and found the answer easy. "If they had been worth anything to speak of she would long ago have sold them. My father and she had unfortunately never been in a position to keep any considerable value locked up." And while his companion took in the obvious force of this he went on with a flourish just marked enough not to escape her: "If they're worth anything at all—why, you're only the more welcome to them."

Charlotte had now in her hand a small bag of faded, figured silk—one of those antique conveniences that speak to us, in the terms of evaporated camphor and lavender, of the part they have played in some personal history; but, though she had for the first time drawn the string, she looked much more at the young man than at the questionable treasure it appeared to contain. "I shall like them. They're all I have."

"All you have——?"

"That belonged to her."

He swelled a little, then looked about him as if to appeal—as against her avidity—to the whole poor place. "Well, what else do you want?"

"Nothing. Thank you very much." With which she bent her eyes on the article wrapped, and now only exposed, in her superannuated satchel—a necklace of large pearls, such as might once have graced the neck of a provincial Ophelia and borne company to a flaxen wig. "This perhaps *is* worth something. Feel it." And she passed him the necklace, the weight of which she had gathered for a moment into her hand.

He measured it in the same way with his own, but remained quite detached. "Worth at most thirty shillings."

"Not more?"

"Surely not if it's paste?"

"But *is* it paste?"

He gave a small sniff of impatience. "Pearls nearly as big as filberts?"

"But they're heavy," Charlotte declared.

"No heavier than anything else." And he gave them back with an allowance for her simplicity. "Do you imagine for a moment they're real?"

She studied them a little, feeling them, turning them round. "Mightn't they possibly be?"

"Of that size—stuck away with that trash?"

"I admit it isn't likely," Charlotte presently said. "And pearls are so easily imitated."

"That's just what—to a person who knows—they're not. These have no lustre, no play."

"No—they *are* dull. They're opaque."

"Besides," he lucidly inquired, "how could she ever have come by them?"

"Mightn't they have been a present?"

Arthur stared at the question as if it were almost improper. "Because actresses are exposed——?" He pulled up, however, not saying to what, and before she could supply the deficiency had, with the sharp ejaculation of "No, they mightn't!" turned his back on her and walked away. His manner made her feel that she had probably been wanting in tact, and before he returned to the subject, the last thing that evening, she had satisfied herself of the ground of his resentment. They had been talking of her departure the next morning, the hour of her train and the fly that would come for her, and it was precisely these things that gave him his effective chance. "I really can't allow you to leave the house under the impression that my stepmother was at *any* time of her life the sort of person to allow herself to be approached——"

"With pearl necklaces and that sort of thing?" Arthur had made for her somehow the difficulty that she couldn't show him she understood him without seeming pert.

It at any rate only added to his own gravity. "That sort of thing, exactly."

"I didn't think when I spoke this morning—but I see what you mean."

"I mean that she was beyond reproach," said Arthur Prime.

"A hundred times yes."

"Therefore if she couldn't, out of her slender gains, ever have paid for a row of pearls——"

"She couldn't, in that atmosphere, ever properly have had one? Of course she couldn't. I've seen perfectly since our talk," Charlotte went on, "that that string of beads isn't even, as an imitation, very good. The little clasp itself doesn't seem even gold. With false pearls, I suppose," the girl mused, "it naturally wouldn't be."

"The whole thing's rotten paste," her companion returned as if to have done with it. "If it were *not*, and she had kept it all these years hidden——"

"Yes?" Charlotte sounded as he paused.

"Why, I shouldn't know what to think!"

"Oh, I see." She had met him with a certain blankness, but adequately enough, it seemed, for him to regard the subject as dismissed; and there was no reversion to it between them before, on the morrow, when she had with difficulty made a place for them in her trunk, she carried off these florid survivals.

At Bleet she found small occasion to revert to them and, in an air charged with such quite other references, even felt, after she had laid them away, much enshrouded, beneath various piles of clothing, as if they formed a collection not wholly without its note of the ridiculous. Yet she was never, for the joke, tempted to show them to her pupils, though Gwendolen and Blanche, in particular, always wanted, on her return, to know what she had brought back; so that without an accident by which the case was quite changed they might have appeared to enter on a new phase of interment. The essence of the accident was the sudden illness, at the last moment, of Lady Bobby, whose advent had been so much counted on to spice the five days' feast laid out for the coming of age of the eldest son of the house; and its equally marked effect was the despatch of a pressing message, in quite another direction, to Mrs Guy, who, could she by a miracle be secured

—she was always engaged ten parties deep—might be trusted to supply, it was believed, an element of exuberance scarcely less active. Mrs Guy was already known to several of the visitors already on the scene, but she was not yet known to our young lady, who found her, after many wires and counter-wires had at last determined the triumph of her arrival, a strange, charming little red-haired, black-dressed woman, with the face of a baby and the authority of a commodore. She took on the spot the discreet, the exceptional young governess into the confidence of her designs and, still more, of her doubts; intimating that it was a policy she almost always promptly pursued.

"To-morrow and Thursday are all right," she said frankly to Charlotte on the second day, "but I'm not half satisfied with Friday."

"What improvement then do you suggest?"

"Well, my strong point, you know, is *tableaux vivants*."

"Charming. And what is your favourite character?"

"Boss!" said Mrs Guy with decision; and it was very markedly under that ensign that she had, within a few hours, completely planned her campaign and recruited her troop. Every word she uttered was to the point, but none more so than, after a general survey of their equipment, her final inquiry of Charlotte. She had been looking about, but half appeased, at the muster of decoration and drapery. "We shall be dull. We shall want more colour. You've nothing else?"

Charlotte had a thought. "No—I've *some* things."

"Then why don't you bring them?"

The girl hesitated. "Would you come to my room?"

"No," said Mrs Guy—"bring them to-night to mine."

So Charlotte, at the evening's end, after candlesticks had flickered through brown old passages bedward, arrived at her friend's door with the burden of her aunt's relics. But she promptly expressed a fear. "Are they too garish?"

When she had poured them out on the sofa Mrs Guy was

but a minute, before the glass, in clapping on the diadem. "Awfully jolly—we can do Ivanhoe!"

"But they're only glass and tin."

"Larger than life they are, *rather*!—which is exactly what, for tableaux, is wanted. *Our* jewels, for historic scenes, don't tell—the real thing falls short. Rowena must have rubies as big as eggs. Leave them with me," Mrs Guy continued—"they'll inspire me. Good-night."

The next morning she was in fact—yet very strangely—inspired. "Yes, *I'll* do Rowena. But I don't, my dear, understand."

"Understand what?"

Mrs Guy gave a very lighted stare. "How you come to have such things."

Poor Charlotte smiled. "By inheritance."

"Family jewels?"

"They belonged to my aunt, who died some months ago. She was on the stage a few years in early life, and these are a part of her trappings."

"She left them to you?"

"No; my cousin, her stepson, who naturally has no use for them, gave them to me for remembrance of her. She was a dear kind thing, always so nice to me, and I was fond of her."

Mrs Guy had listened with visible interest. "But it's *he* who must be a dear kind thing!"

Charlotte wondered. "You think so?"

"Is *he*," her friend went on, "also 'always so nice' to you?"

The girl, at this, face to face there with the brilliant visitor in the deserted breakfast-room, took a deeper sounding. "What is it?"

"Don't you know?"

Something came over her. "The pearls——?" But the question fainted on her lips.

"Doesn't *he* know?"

Charlotte found herself flushing. "They're *not* paste?"

"Haven't you looked at them?"

She was conscious of two kinds of embarrassment. "*You* have?"

"Very carefully."

"And they're real?"

Mrs Guy became slightly mystifying and returned for all answer: "Come again, when you've done with the children, to my room."

Our young woman found she had done with the children, that morning, with a promptitude that was a new joy to them, and when she reappeared before Mrs Guy this lady had already encircled a plump white throat with the only ornament, surely, in all the late Mrs Prime's—the effaced Miss Bradshaw's—collection, in the least qualified to raise a question. If Charlotte had never yet once, before the glass, tied the string of pearls about her own neck, this was because she had been capable of no such condescension to approved "imitation"; but she had now only to look at Mrs Guy to see that, so disposed, the ambiguous objects might have passed for frank originals. "What in the world have you done to them?"

"Only handled them, understood them, admired them and put them on. That's what pearls want; they want to be worn—it wakes them up. They're alive, don't you see? How *have* these been treated? They must have been buried, ignored, despised. They were half dead. Don't you *know* about pearls?" Mrs Guy threw off as she fondly fingered the necklace.

"How *should* I? Do *you*?"

"Everything. These were simply asleep, and from the moment I really touched them—well," said their wearer lovingly, "it only took one's eye!"

"It took more than mine—though I did just wonder; and than Arthur's," Charlotte brooded. She found herself almost panting. "Then their value——?"

"Oh, their value's excellent."

The girl, for a deep moment, took another plunge into the

wonder, the beauty and mystery, of them. "Are you *sure*?"

Her companion wheeled round for impatience. "Sure? For what kind of an idiot, my dear, do you take me?"

It was beyond Charlotte Prime to say. "For the same kind as Arthur—and as myself," she could only suggest. "But my cousin didn't know. He thinks they're worthless."

"Because of the rest of the lot? Then your cousin's an ass. But what—if, as I understood you, he gave them to you—has he to do with it?"

"Why, if he gave them to me as worthless and they turn out precious——"

"You must give them back? I don't see that—if he was such a fool. He took the risk."

Charlotte fed, in fancy, on the pearls, which, decidedly, were exquisite, but which at the present moment somehow presented themselves much more as Mrs Guy's than either as Arthur's or as her own. "Yes—he did take it; even after I had distinctly hinted to him that they looked to me different from the other pieces."

"Well, then!" said Mrs Guy with something more than triumph—with a positive odd relief.

But it had the effect of making our young woman think with more intensity. "Ah, you see he thought they couldn't be different, because—so peculiarly—they shouldn't be."

"Shouldn't? I don't understand."

"Why, how would she have got them?"—so Charlotte candidly put it.

"She? Who?" There was a capacity in Mrs Guy's tone for a sinking of persons—!

"Why, the person I told you of: his stepmother, my uncle's wife—among whose poor old things, extraordinarily thrust away and out of sight, he happened to find them."

Mrs Guy came a step nearer to the effaced Miss Bradshaw. "Do you mean she may have stolen them?"

"No. But she had been an actress."

"Oh, well then," cried Mrs Guy, "wouldn't that be just how?"

"Yes, except that she wasn't at all a brilliant one, nor in receipt of large pay." The girl even threw off a nervous joke. "I'm afraid she couldn't have been our Rowena."

Mrs Guy took it up. "Was she very ugly?"

"No. She may very well, when young, have looked rather nice."

"Well, then!" was Mrs Guy's sharp comment and fresh triumph.

"You mean it was a present? That's just what he so dislikes the idea of her having received—a present from an admirer capable of going such lengths."

"Because she wouldn't have taken it for nothing? *Speriamo*—that she wasn't a brute. The 'length' her admirer went was the length of a whole row. Let us hope she was just a little kind!"

"Well," Charlotte went on, "that she was 'kind' might seem to be shown by the fact that neither her husband, nor his son, nor I, his niece, knew or dreamed of her possessing anything so precious; by her having kept the gift all the rest of her life beyond discovery—out of sight and protected from suspicion."

"As if, you mean"—Mrs Guy was quick—"she had been wedded to it and yet was ashamed of it? Fancy," she laughed while she manipulated the rare beads, "being ashamed of *these*!"

"But you see she had married a clergyman."

"Yes, she must have been 'rum.' But at any rate he had married *her*. What did he suppose?"

"Why, that she had never been of the sort by whom such offerings are encouraged."

"Ah, my dear, the sort by whom they are *not*——!" But Mrs Guy caught herself up. "And her stepson thought the same?"

"Overwhelmingly."

"Was he, then if only her stepson——"

"So fond of her as that comes to? Yes; he had never known, consciously, his real mother, and, without children of her own, she was very patient and nice with him. And *I* liked her so," the girl pursued, "that at the end of ten years, in so strange a manner, to 'give her away'——"

"Is impossible to you? Then don't!" said Mrs Guy with decision.

"Ah, but if they're real I can't keep them!" Charlotte, with her eyes on them, moaned in her impatience. "It's too difficult."

"Where's the difficulty, if he has such sentiments that he would rather sacrifice the necklace than admit it, with the presumption it carries with it, to be genuine? You've only to be silent."

"And keep it? How can *I* ever wear it?"

"You'd have to hide it, like your aunt?" Mrs Guy was amused. "You can easily sell it."

Her companion walked round her for a look at the affair from behind. The clasp was certainly, doubtless intentionally, misleading, but everything else was indeed lovely. "Well, I must think. Why didn't *she* sell them?" Charlotte broke out in her trouble.

Mrs Guy had an instant answer. "Doesn't that prove what they secretly recalled to her? You've only to be silent!" she ardently repeated.

"I must think—I must think!"

Mrs Guy stood with her hands attached but motionless. "Then you want them back?"

As if with the dread of touching them Charlotte retreated to the door. "I'll tell you to-night."

"But may I wear them?"

"Meanwhile?"

"This evening—at dinner."

It was the sharp, selfish pressure of this that really, on the spot, determined the girl; but for the moment, before closing the door on the question, she only said: "As you like!"

They were busy much of the day with preparation and rehearsal, and at dinner, that evening, the concourse of guests was such that a place among them for Miss Prime failed to find itself marked. At the time the company rose she was therefore alone in the schoolroom, where, towards eleven o'clock, she received a visit from Mrs Guy. This lady's white shoulders heaved, under the pearls, with an emotion that the very red lips which formed, as if for the full effect, the happiest opposition of colour, were not slow to translate. "My dear, you should have seen the sensation—they've had a success!"

Charlotte, dumb a moment, took it all in. "It *is* as if they knew it—they're more and more alive. But so much the worse for both of us! I can't," she brought out with an effort, "be silent."

"You mean to return them?"

"If I don't I'm a thief."

Mrs Guy gave her a long, hard look: what was decidedly not of the baby in Mrs Guy's face was a certain air of established habit in the eyes. Then, with a sharp little jerk of her head and a backward reach of her bare beautiful arms, she undid the clasp and, taking off the necklace, laid it on the table. "If you do, you're a goose."

"Well, of the two——!" said our young lady, gathering it up with a sigh. And as if to get it, for the pang it gave, out of sight as soon as possible, she shut it up, clicking the lock, in the drawer of her own little table; after which, when she turned again, her companion, without it, looked naked and plain. "But what will you say?" it then occurred to her to demand.

"Downstairs—to explain?" Mrs Guy was, after all, trying at least to keep her temper. "Oh, I'll put on something else and say that clasp is broken. And you won't of course name *me* to him," she added.

"As having undeceived me? No—I'll say that, looking at the thing more carefully, it's my own private idea."

"And does he know how little you really know?"

"As an expert—surely. And he has much, always, the conceit of his own opinion."

"Then he won't believe you—as he so hates to. He'll stick to his judgment and maintain his gift, and we shall have the darlings back!" With which reviving assurance Mrs Guy kissed for good-night.

She was not, however, to be gratified or justified by any prompt event, for, whether or no paste entered into the composition of the ornament in question, Charlotte shrank from the temerity of despatching it to town by post. Mrs Guy was thus disappointed of the hope of seeing the business settled—"by return," she had seemed to expect—before the end of the revels. The revels, moreover, rising to a frantic pitch, pressed for all her attention, and it was at last only in the general confusion of leave-taking that she made, parenthetically, a dash at her young friend.

"Come, what will you take for them?"

"The pearls? Ah, you'll have to treat with my cousin."

Mrs Guy, with quick intensity, lent herself. "Where then does he live?"

"In chambers in the Temple. You can find him."

"But what's the use, if *you* do neither one thing nor the other?"

"Oh, I *shall* do the 'other,'" Charlotte said: "I'm only waiting till I go up. You want them so awfully?" She curiously, solemnly again, sounded her.

"I'm dying for them. There's a special charm in them—I don't know what it is: they tell so their history."

"But what do you know of that?"

"Just what they themselves say. It's all *in* them—and it

comes out. They breathe a tenderness—they have the white glow of it. My dear," hissed Mrs Guy in supreme confidence and as she buttoned her glove—"they're things of love!"

"Oh!" our young woman vaguely exclaimed.

"They're things of passion!"

"Mercy!" she gasped, turning short off. But these words remained, though indeed their help was scarce needed, Charlotte being in private face to face with a new light, as she by this time felt she must call it, on the dear dead, kind, colourless lady whose career had turned so sharp a corner in the middle. The pearls had quite taken their place as a revelation. She might have received them for nothing—admit that; but she couldn't have kept them so long and so unprofitably hidden, couldn't have enjoyed them only in secret, for nothing; and she had mixed them, in her reliquary, with false things, in order to put curiosity and detection off the scent. Over this strange fact poor Charlotte interminably mused: it became more touching, more attaching for her than she could now confide to any ear. How bad, or how happy—in the sophisticated sense of Mrs Guy and the young man at the Temple—the effaced Miss Bradshaw must have been to have had to be so mute! The little governess at Bleet put on the necklace now in secret sessions; she wore it sometimes under her dress; she came to feel, verily, a haunting passion for it. Yet in her penniless state she would have parted with it for money; she gave herself also to dreams of what in this direction it would do for her. The sophistry of her so often saying to herself that Arthur had after all definitely pronounced her welcome to any gain from his gift that might accrue—this trick remained innocent, as she perfectly knew it for what it was. Then there was always the possibility of his—as she could only picture it—rising to the occasion. Mightn't he have a grand magnanimous moment?—mightn't he just say: "Oh, of course I couldn't have afforded to let you have it if I had known; but since you *have* got it, and have made out the truth by your own wit, I really can't screw myself down to the shabbiness of taking it back"?

She had, as it proved, to wait a long time—to wait till, at the end of several months, the great house of Bleet had, with due deliberation, for the season, transferred itself to town; after which, however, she fairly snatched at her first freedom to knock, dressed in her best and armed with her disclosure, at the door of her doubting kinsman. It was still with doubt and not quite with the face she had hoped that he listened to her story. He had turned pale, she thought, as she produced the necklace, and he appeared, above all, disagreeably affected. Well, perhaps there was reason, she more than ever remembered; but what on earth was one, in close touch with the fact, to do? She had laid the pearls on his table, where, without his having at first put so much as a finger to them, they met his hard, cold stare.

"I don't believe in them," he simply said at last.

"That's exactly then," she returned with some spirit, "what I wanted to hear!"

She fancied that at this his colour changed; it was indeed vivid to her afterwards—for she was to have a long recall of the scene—that she had made him quite angrily flush. "It's a beastly unpleasant imputation, you know!"—and he walked away from her as he had always walked at the vicarage.

"It's none of *my* making, I'm sure," said Charlotte Prime. "If you're afraid to believe they're real——"

"Well?"—and he turned, across the room, sharp round at her.

"Why, it's not my fault."

He said nothing more, for a moment, on this; he only came back to the table. "They're what I originally said they were. They're rotten paste."

"Then I may keep them?"

"No. I want a better opinion."

"Than your own?"

"Than *your* own." He dropped on the pearls another queer stare, then, after a moment, bringing himself to touch them, did exactly what she had herself done in the presence of Mrs Guy at Bleet—gathered them together, marched off with them to a drawer, put them in and clicked the key. "You say I'm afraid," he went on as he again met her; "but I shan't be afraid to take them to Bond Street."

"And if the people say they're real——?"

He hesitated—then had his strangest manner. "They won't say it! They shan't!"

There was something in the way he brought it out that deprived poor Charlotte, as she was perfectly aware, of any manner at all. "Oh!" she simply sounded, as she had sounded for her last word to Mrs Guy; and, within a minute, without more conversation, she had taken her departure.

A fortnight later she received a communication from him, and towards the end of the season one of the entertainments in Eaton Square was graced by the presence of Mrs Guy. Charlotte was not at dinner, but she came down afterwards, and this guest, on seeing her, abandoned a very beautiful young man on purpose to cross and speak to her. The guest had on a lovely necklace and had apparently not lost her habit of overflowing with the pride of such ornaments.

"Do you see?" She was in high joy.

They were indeed splendid pearls—so far as poor Charlotte could feel that she knew, after what had come and gone, about such mysteries. Charlotte had a sickly smile. "They're almost as fine as Arthur's."

"Almost? Where, my dear, are your eyes? They *are* 'Arthur's!'" After which, to meet the flood of crimson that accompanied her young friend's start: "I tracked them—after your folly, and, by miraculous luck, recognised them in the Bond Street window to which he had disposed of them."

"*Disposed* of them?" the girl gasped. "He wrote me that

I had insulted his mother and that the people had shown him he was right—had pronounced them utter paste."

Mrs Guy gave a stare. "Ah, I told you he wouldn't bear it! No. But I had, I assure you," she wound up, "to drive my bargain!"

Charlotte scarce heard or saw; she was full of her private wrong. "He wrote me," she panted, "that he had smashed them."

Mrs Guy could only wonder and pity. "He's really morbid!" But it was not quite clear which of the pair she pitied; though Charlotte felt really morbid too after they had separated and she found herself full of thought. She even went the length of asking herself what sort of a bargain Mrs Guy had driven and whether the marvel of the recognition in Bond Street had been a veracious account of the matter. Hadn't she perhaps in truth dealt with Arthur directly? It came back to Charlotte almost luridly that she had had his address.

THE GREAT GOOD PLACE

I

GEORGE DANE had waked up to a bright new day, the face of nature well washed by last night's downpour and shining as with high spirits, good resolutions, lively intentions—the great glare of recommencement, in short, fixed in his patch of sky. He had sat up late to finish work—arrears overwhelming; then at last had gone to bed with the pile but little reduced. He was now to return to it after the pause of the night; but he could only look at it, for the time, over the bristling hedge of letters planted by the early postman an hour before and already, on the customary table by the chimney-piece, formally rounded and squared by his systematic servant. It was something too merciless, the domestic perfection of Brown. There were newspapers on another table, ranged with the same rigour of custom, newspapers too many—what could any creature want of so much news?—and each with its hand on the neck of the other, so that the row of their bodiless heads was like a series of decapitations. Other journals, other periodicals of every sort, folded and in wrappers, made a huddled mound that had been growing for several days and of which he had been wearily, helplessly aware. There were new books, also in wrappers as well as disenveloped and dropped again—books from publishers, books from authors, books from friends, books from enemies, books from his own bookseller, who took, it sometimes struck him, inconceivable things for granted. He touched nothing, approached nothing, only turned a heavy eye over the work, as it were, of the night—the fact, in his high, wide-windowed room, where the hard light of duty could penetrate every corner, of the unashamed admonition of the day. It was the old rising tide, and it rose and rose even under a minute's watching. It had been up to his shoulders last night—it was up to his chin now.

Nothing had passed while he slept—everything had stayed; nothing, that he could yet feel, had died—many things had been born. To let them alone, these things, the new things, let them utterly alone and see if that, by chance, wouldn't somehow prove the best way to deal with them: this fancy brushed his face for a moment as a possible solution, just giving it, as many a time before, a cool wave of air. Then he knew again as well as ever that leaving was difficult, leaving impossible—that the only remedy, the true, soft, effacing sponge, would be to *be* left, to be forgotten. There was no footing on which a man who had ever liked life—liked it, at any rate, as *he* had—could now escape from it. He must reap as he had sown. It was a thing of meshes; he had simply gone to sleep under the net and had simply waked up there. The net was too fine; the cords crossed each other at spots so near together, making at each a little tight, hard knot that tired fingers, this morning, were too limp and too tender to touch. Our poor friend's touched nothing—only stole significantly into his pockets as he wandered over to the window and faintly gasped at the energy of nature. What was most overwhelming was that she herself was so ready. She had soothed him rather, the night before, in the small hours by the lamp. From behind the drawn curtain of his study the rain had been audible and in a manner merciful; washing the window in a steady flood, it had seemed the right thing, the retarding, interrupting thing, the thing that, if it would only last, might clear the ground by floating out to a boundless sea the innumerable objects among which his feet stumbled and strayed. He had positively laid down his pen as on a sense of friendly pressure from it. The kind, full swash had been on the glass when he turned out his lamp; he had left his phrase unfinished and his papers lying quite as if for the flood to bear them away on its bosom. But there still, on the table, were the bare bones of the sentence—and not all of those; the single thing borne away and that he could never recover was the missing half that might have paired with it and begotten a figure.

Yet he could at last only turn back from the window; the world was everywhere, without and within, and, with the great staring egotism of its health and strength, was not to be trusted for tact or delicacy. He faced about precisely to meet his servant and the absurd solemnity of two telegrams on a tray. Brown ought to have kicked them into the room—then he himself might have kicked them out.

"And you told me to remind you, sir——"

George Dane was at last angry. "Remind me of nothing!"

"But you insisted, sir, that I was to insist!"

He turned away in despair, speaking with a pathetic quaver at absurd variance with his words: "If you insist, Brown, I'll kill you!" He found himself anew at the window, whence, looking down from his fourth floor, he could see the vast neighbourhood, under the trumpet-blare of the sky, beginning to rush about. There was a silence, but he knew Brown had not left him—knew exactly how straight and serious and stupid and faithful he stood there. After a minute he heard him again.

"It's only because, sir, you know, sir, you can't remember——"

At this Dane did flash round; it was more than at such a moment he could bear. "Can't remember, Brown? I can't forget. That's what's the matter with me."

Brown looked at him with the advantage of eighteen years of consistency. "I'm afraid you're not well, sir."

Brown's master thought. "It's a shocking thing to say, but I wish to heaven I weren't! It would be perhaps an excuse."

Brown's blankness spread like the desert. "To put them off?"

"Ah!" The sound was a groan; the plural pronoun, *any* pronoun, so mistimed. "Who is it?"

"Those ladies you spoke of—to lunch."

"Oh!" The poor man dropped into the nearest chair and stared a while at the carpet. It was very complicated.

"How many will there be, sir?" Brown asked.

"Fifty!"

"Fifty, sir?"

Our friend, from his chair, looked vaguely about; under his hand were the telegrams, still unopened, one of which he now tore asunder. "'Do hope you sweetly won't mind, to-day, 1.30, my bringing poor dear Lady Mullet, who is so awfully bent,'" he read to his companion.

His companion weighed it. "How many does *she* make, sir?"

"Poor dear Lady Mullet? I haven't the least idea."

"Is she—a—deformed, sir?" Brown inquired, as if in this case she might make more.

His master wondered, then saw he figured some personal curvature. "No; she's only bent on coming!" Dane opened the other telegram and again read out: "'So sorry it's at eleventh hour impossible, and count on you here, as very greatest favour, at two sharp instead.'"

"How many does *that* make?" Brown imperturbably continued.

Dane crumpled up the two missives and walked with them to the waste-paper basket, into which he thoughtfully dropped them. "I can't say. You must do it all yourself. I shan't be there."

It was only on this that Brown showed an expression. "You'll go instead——"

"I'll go instead!" Dane raved.

Brown, however, had had occasion to show before that *he*

would never desert their post. "Isn't that rather sacrificing the three?" Between respect and reproach he paused.

"*Are* there three?"

"I lay for four in all."

His master had, at any rate, caught his thought. "Sacrificing the three to the one, you mean? Oh, I'm not going to *her*!"

Brown's famous "thoroughness"—his great virtue—had never been so dreadful. "Then where *are* you going?"

Dane sat down to his table and stared at his ragged phrase. "'There is a happy land—far, far away!'" He chanted it like a sick child and knew that for a minute Brown never moved. During this minute he felt between his shoulders the gimlet of criticism.

"Are you quite sure you're all right?"

"It's my certainty that overwhelms me, Brown. Look about you and judge. Could anything be more 'right,' in the view of the envious world, than everything that surrounds us here; that immense array of letters, notes, circulars; that pile of printers' proofs, magazines and books; these perpetual telegrams, these impending guests; this retarded, unfinished and interminable work? What could a man want more?"

"Do you mean there's too much, sir?"—Brown had sometimes these flashes.

"There's too much. There's too much. But *you* can't help it, Brown."

"No, sir," Brown assented. "Can't *you*?"

"I'm thinking—I must see. There are hours——!" Yes, there were hours, and this was one of them: he jerked himself up for another turn in his labyrinth, but still not touching, not even again meeting, his interlocutor's eye. If he was a genius for any one he was a genius for Brown; but it was terrible what that meant, being a genius for Brown. There had been times when he had done full justice to the way it kept him up; now, however, it was almost the worst of the avalanche.

"Don't trouble about me," he went on insincerely and looking askance through his window again at the bright and beautiful world. "Perhaps it will rain—that *may* not be over. I do love the rain," he weakly pursued. "Perhaps, better still, it will snow."

Brown now had indeed a perceptible expression, and the expression was fear. "Snow, sir—the end of May?" Without pressing this point he looked at his watch. "You'll feel better when you've had breakfast."

"I dare say," said Dane, whom breakfast struck in fact as a pleasant alternative to opening letters. "I'll come in immediately."

"But without waiting——?"

"Waiting for what?"

Brown had at last, under his apprehension, his first lapse from logic, which he betrayed by hesitating in the evident hope that his companion would, by a flash of remembrance, relieve him of an invidious duty. But the only flashes now were the good man's own. "You say you can't forget, sir; but you do forget——"

"Is it anything very horrible?" Dane broke in.

Brown hung fire. "Only the gentleman you told me you had asked——"

Dane again took him up; horrible or not, it came back—indeed its mere coming back classed it. "To breakfast to-day? It *was* to-day; I see." It came back, yes, came back; the appointment with the young man—he supposed him young—and whose letter, the letter about—what was it?—had struck him. "Yes, yes; wait, wait."

"Perhaps he'll do you good, sir," Brown suggested.

"Sure to—sure to. All right!" Whatever he might do, he would at least prevent some other doing: that was present to our friend as, on the vibration of the electric bell at the door of the flat, Brown moved away. Two things, in the short interval that followed, were present to Dane: his having utterly forgotten the connection, the whence, whither and why of his guest; and his continued disposition not to touch—no, not with the finger. Ah, if he might *never* again touch! All the unbroken seals and neglected appeals lay there while, for a pause that he couldn't measure, he stood before the chimney-piece with his hands still in his pockets. He heard a brief exchange of words in the hall, but never afterward recovered the time taken by Brown to reappear, to precede and announce another person—a person whose name, somehow, failed to reach Dane's ear. Brown went off again to serve breakfast, leaving host and guest confronted. The duration of this first stage also, later on, defied measurement; but that little mattered, for in the train of what happened came promptly the second, the third, the fourth, the rich succession of the others. Yet what happened was but that Dane took his hand from his pocket, held it straight out and felt it taken. Thus indeed, if he had wanted never again to touch, it was already done.

II

HE might have been a week in the place—the scene of his new consciousness—before he spoke at all. The occasion of it then was that one of the quiet figures he had been idly watching drew at last nearer and showed him a face that was the highest expression—to his pleased but as yet slightly confused perception—of the general charm. What *was* the general charm? He couldn't, for that matter, easily have phrased it; it was such an abyss of negatives, such an absence of everything. The oddity was that, after a minute, he was struck as by the reflection of his own very image in this first interlocutor seated with him, on the easy bench, under the high, clear portico and above the wide, far-reaching garden, where the things that most showed in the greenness were the surface of still water and the white note of old statues. The absence of everything was, in the aspect of the Brother who had thus informally joined him—a man of his own age, tired, distinguished, modest, kind—really, as he could soon see, but the absence of what he didn't want. He didn't want, for the time, anything but just to *be* there, to stay in the bath. He was in the bath yet, the broad, deep bath of stillness. They sat in it together now, with the water up to their chins. He had not had to talk, he had not had to think, he had scarce even had to feel. He had been sunk that way before, sunk—when and where?—in another flood; only a flood of rushing waters, in which bumping and gasping were all. This was a current so slow and so tepid that one floated practically without motion and without chill. The break of silence was not immediate, though Dane seemed indeed to feel it begin before a sound passed. It could pass quite sufficiently without words that he and his mate were Brothers, and what that meant.

Dane wondered, but with no want of ease—for want of ease was impossible—if his friend found in *him* the same likeness, the proof of peace, the gage of what the place could do. The long afternoon crept to its end; the shadows fell further and the sky glowed deeper; but nothing changed—nothing *could* change—in the element itself. It was a conscious security. It was wonderful! Dane had lived into it, but he was still immensely aware. He would have been sorry to lose that, for just this fact, as yet, the blessed fact of consciousness, seemed the greatest thing of all. Its only fault was that, being in itself such an occupation, so fine an unrest in the heart of gratitude, the life of the day all went to it. But what even then was the harm? He had come only to come, to take what he found. This was the part where the great cloister, inclosed externally on three sides and probably the largest, lightest, fairest effect, to his charmed sense, that human hands could ever have expressed in dimensions of length and breadth, opened to the south its splendid fourth quarter, turned to the great view an outer gallery that combined with the rest of the portico to form a high, dry loggia, such as he a little pretended to himself he had, in Italy, in old days, seen in old cities, old convents, old villas. This recall of the disposition of some great abode of an Order, some mild Monte Cassino, some Grande Chartreuse more accessible, was his main term of comparison; but he knew he had really never anywhere beheld anything at once so calculated and so generous.

Three impressions in particular had been with him all the week, and he could only recognise in silence their happy effect on his nerves. How it was all managed he couldn't have told —he had been content moreover till now with his ignorance of cause and pretext; but whenever he chose to listen with a certain intentness he made out, as from a distance, the sound of slow, sweet bells. How could they be so far and yet so audible? How could they be so near and yet so faint? How, above all, could they, in such an arrest of life, be, to *time* things, so frequent? The very essence of the bliss of Dane's whole change had been precisely that there was nothing now to time. It was the same with the slow footsteps that always, within earshot, to the vague attention, marked the space and the leisure, seemed, in long, cool arcades, lightly to fall and perpetually to recede. This was the second impression, and it melted into the third, as, for that matter, every form of softness, in the great good place, was but a further turn, without jerk or gap, of the endless roll of serenity. The quiet footsteps were quiet figures; the quiet figures that, to the eye, kept the picture human and brought its perfection within reach. This perfection, he felt on the bench by his friend, was now more in reach that ever. His friend at last turned to him a look different from the looks of friends in London clubs.

"The thing was to find it out!"

It was extraordinary how this remark fitted into his thought. "Ah, wasn't it? And when I think," said Dane, "of all the people who haven't and who never will!" He sighed over these unfortunates with a tenderness that, in its degree, was practically new to him, feeling, too, how well his companion would know the people he meant. He only meant some, but they were all who would want it; though of these, no doubt—well, for reasons, for things that, in the world, he had observed—there would never be too many. Not all perhaps who wanted would really find; but none at least would find who didn't really want. And then what the need would have to have been first! What it at first had to be for himself! He felt afresh, in the light of his companion's face, what it might still be even when deeply satisfied, as well as what communication was established by the mere mutual knowledge of it.

"Every man must arrive by himself and on his own feet—isn't that so? We're brothers here for the time, as in a great monastery, and we immediately think of each other and recognise each other as such; but we must have first got here as we can, and we meet after long journeys by complicated ways. Moreover we meet—don't we?—with closed eyes."

"Ah, don't speak as if we were dead!" Dane laughed.

"I shan't mind death if it's like this," his friend replied.

It was too obvious, as Dane gazed before him, that one wouldn't; but after a moment he asked, with the first articulation, as yet, of his most elementary wonder: "Where is it?"

"I shouldn't be surprised if it were much nearer than one ever suspected."

"Nearer town, do you mean?"

"Nearer everything—nearer every one."

George Dane thought. "Somewhere, for instance, down in Surrey?"

His Brother met him on this with a shade of reluctance. "Why should we call it names? It must have a climate, you see."

"Yes," Dane happily mused; "without that——!" All it so securely did have overwhelmed him again, and he couldn't help breaking out: "*What* is it?"

"Oh, it's positively a part of our ease and our rest and our change, I think, that we don't at all know and that we may really call it, for that matter, anything in the world we like—the thing, for instance, we love it most for being."

"I know what *I* call it," said Dane after a moment. Then as his friend listened with interest: "Just simply 'The Great Good Place.'"

"I see—what can you say more? I've put it to myself perhaps a little differently." They sat there as innocently as small boys confiding to each other the names of toy animals. "The Great Want Met."

"Ah, yes, that's it!"

"Isn't it enough for us that it's a place carried on, for our benefit, so admirably that we strain our ears in vain for a creak of the machinery? Isn't it enough for us that it's simply a thorough hit?"

"Ah, a hit!" Dane benignantly murmured.

"It does for us what it pretends to do," his companion went on; "the mystery isn't deeper than that. The thing is probably simple enough in fact, and on a thoroughly practical basis; only it has had its origin in a splendid thought, in a real stroke of genius."

"Yes," Dane exclaimed, "in a sense—on somebody or other's part—so exquisitely personal!"

"Precisely—it rests, like all good things, on experience. The 'great want' comes home—that's the great thing it does! On the day it came home to the right mind this dear place was constituted. It always, moreover, in the long run, *has* been met—it always must be. How can it not require to be, more and more, as pressure of every sort grows?"

Dane, with his hands folded in his lap, took in these words of wisdom. "Pressure of every sort *is* growing!" he placidly observed.

"I see well enough what that fact has done to *you*," his Brother returned.

Dane smiled. "I couldn't have borne it longer. I don't know what would have become of me."

"I know what would have become of *me*."

"Well, it's the same thing."

"Yes," said Dane's companion, "it's doubtless the same thing." On which they sat in silence a little, seeming pleasantly to follow, in the view of the green garden, the vague movements of the monster—madness, surrender, collapse—they had escaped. Their bench was like a box at the opera. "And I may perfectly, you know," the Brother pursued, "have seen you before. I may even have known you well. We don't know."

They looked at each other again serenely enough, and at last Dane said: "No, we don't know."

"That's what I meant by our coming with our eyes closed. Yes—there's something out. There's a gap—a link missing, the great hiatus!" the Brother laughed. "It's as simple a story as the old, old rupture—the break that lucky Catholics have always been able to make, that they are still, with their innumerable religious houses, able to make, by going into 'retreat.' I don't speak of the pious exercises; I speak only of the material simplification. I don't speak of the putting off of one's self; I speak only—if one has a self worth sixpence—of the getting it back. The place, the time, the way were, for those of the old persuasion, always there—are indeed practically there for them as much as ever. They can always get off—the blessed houses receive. So it was high time that we—we of the great Protestant peoples, still more, if possible, in the sensitive individual case, overscored and overwhelmed, still more congested with mere quantity and prostituted, through our 'enterprise,' to mere profanity—should learn how to get off, should find somewhere *our* retreat and remedy. There was such a huge chance for it!"

Dane laid his hand on his companion's arm. "It's charming, how, when we speak for ourselves, we speak for each other. That was exactly what I said!" He had fallen to recalling from over the gulf the last occasion.

The Brother, as if it would do them both good, only desired to draw him out. "What you said——?"

"To *him*—that morning." Dane caught a far bell again and heard a slow footstep. A quiet figure passed somewhere—neither of them turned to look. What was, little by little, more present to him was the perfect taste. It was supreme—it was everywhere. "I just dropped my burden—and he received it."

"And was it very great?"

"Oh, such a load!" Dane laughed.

"Trouble, sorrow, doubt?"

"Oh, no; worse than that!"

"Worse?"

"'Success'—the vulgarest kind!" And Dane laughed again.

"Ah, I know that, too! No one in future, as things are going, will be able to face success."

"Without something of this sort—never. The better it is the worse—the greater the deadlier. But my one pain here," Dane continued, "is in thinking of my poor friend."

"The person to whom you've already alluded?"

"My substitute in the world. Such an unutterable benefactor. He turned up that morning when everything had somehow got on my nerves, when the whole great globe indeed, nerves, or no nerves, seemed to have squeezed itself into my study. It wasn't a question of nerves, it was a mere question of the displacement of everything—of submersion by our eternal too much. I didn't know *où donner de la tête*—I couldn't have gone a step further."

The intelligence with which the Brother listened kept them as children feeding from the same bowl. "And then you got the tip?"

"I got the tip!" Dane happily sighed.

"Well, we all get it. But I dare say differently."

"Then how did *you*——?"

The Brother hesitated, smiling. "You tell me first."

III

"WELL," said George Dane, "it was a young man I had never seen—a man, at any rate, much younger than myself—who had written to me and sent me some article, some book. I read the stuff, was much struck with it, told him so and thanked him—on which, of course, I heard from him again. He asked me things—his questions were interesting; but to save time and writing I said to him: 'Come to see me—we can talk a little; but all I can give you is half an hour at breakfast.' He turned up at the hour on a day when, more than ever in my life before, I seemed, as it happened, in the endless press and stress, to have lost possession of my soul and to be surrounded only with the affairs of other people and the irrelevant, destructive, brutalising sides of life. It made me literally ill—made me feel as I had never felt that if I should once really, for an hour, lose hold of the thing itself, the thing I was trying for, I should never recover it again. The wild waters would close over me, and I should drop straight to the bottom where the vanquished dead lie."

"I follow you every step of your way," said the friendly Brother. "The wild waters, you mean, of our horrible time."

"Of our horrible time—precisely. Not, of course—as we sometimes dream—of any other."

"Yes, any other is only a dream. We really know none but our own."

"No, thank God—that's enough," Dane said. "Well, my young man turned up, and I hadn't been a minute in his presence before making out that practically it would be in him somehow or other to help me. He came to me with envy, envy extravagant—really passionate. I was, heaven save us, the great 'success' for him; he himself was broken and beaten. How can I say what passed between us?—it was so strange, so swift, so much a matter, from one to the other, of instant perception and agreement. He was so clever and haggard and hungry!"

"Hungry?" the Brother asked.

"I don't mean for bread, though he had none too much, I think, even of that. I mean for—well, what *I* had and what I was a monument of to him as I stood there up to my neck in preposterous evidence. He, poor chap, had been for ten years serenading closed windows and had never yet caused a shutter to show that it stirred. My dim blind was the first to be raised an inch; my reading of his book, my impression of it, my note and my invitation, formed literally the only response ever dropped into his dark street. He saw in my littered room, my shattered day, my bored face and spoiled temper—it's embarrassing, but I must tell you—the very blaze of my glory. And he saw in the blaze of my glory—deluded innocent!—what he had yearned for in vain."

"What he had yearned for was to *be* you," said the Brother. Then he added: "I see where you're coming out."

"At my saying to him by the end of five minutes: 'My dear fellow, I wish you'd just try it—wish you'd, for a while, just *be* me!' You go straight to the mark, and that was exactly what occurred—extraordinary though it was that we should both have understood. I saw what he could give, and he did too. He saw moreover what I could take; in fact what he saw was wonderful."

"He must be very remarkable!" the Brother laughed.

"There's no doubt of it whatever—far more remarkable than I. That's just the reason why what I put to him in joke —with a fantastic, desperate irony—became, on his hands, with his vision of his chance, the blessed guarantee of my sitting on this spot in your company. 'Oh, if I could just shift it all—make it straight over for an hour to other shoulders! If there only *were* a pair!'—that's the way I put it to him. And then at something in his face, 'Would *you*, by a miracle, undertake it?' I asked. I let him know all it meant—how it meant that he should at that very moment step in. It meant that he should finish my work and open my letters and keep my engagements and be subject, for better or worse, to my contacts and complications. It meant that he should live with my life, and think with my brain, and write with my hand, and speak with my voice. It meant, above all, that I should get off. He accepted with magnificence—rose to it like a hero. Only he said: 'What will become of *you*?' "

"There was the hitch!" the Brother admitted.

"Ah, but only for a minute. He came to my help again," Dane pursued, "when he saw I couldn't quite meet that, could at least only say that I wanted to think, wanted to cease, wanted to do the thing itself—the thing I was trying for, miserable me, and that thing only—and therefore wanted first of all really to *see* it again, planted out, crowded out, frozen out as it now so long had been. 'I know what you want,' he after a moment quietly remarked to me. 'Ah, what I want doesn't exist!' 'I know what you want,' he repeated. At that I began to believe him."

"Had you any idea yourself?" the Brother asked.

"Oh, yes," said Dane, "and it was just my idea that made me despair. There it was as sharp as possible in my imagination and my longing—there it was so utterly *not* in fact. We were sitting together on my sofa as we waited for breakfast. He presently laid his hand on my knee—showed me a face that the sudden great light in it had made, for me, indescribably beautiful. 'It exists—it exists,' he at last said. And so, I remember, we sat a while and looked at each other, with the final effect of my finding that I absolutely believed him. I remember we weren't at all solemn—we smiled with the joy of discoverers. He was as glad as I—he was tremendously glad. That came out in the whole manner of his reply to the appeal that broke from me: 'Where is it, then, in God's name? Tell me without delay where it is!' "

The Brother had attended with a sympathy! "He gave you the address?"

"He was thinking it out—feeling for it, catching it. He has a wonderful head of his own and must be making of the whole thing, while we sit here gossiping, something much better than ever *I* did. The mere sight of his face, the sense of his hand on my knee, made me, after a little, feel that he not only knew what I wanted, but was getting nearer to it than I could have got in ten years. He suddenly sprang up and went over to my study-table—sat straight down there as if to write me my passport. Then it was—at the mere sight of his back, which was turned to me—that I felt the spell work. I simply sat and watched him with the queerest, deepest, sweetest sense in the world—the sense of an ache that had stopped. All life was lifted; I myself at least was somehow off the ground. He was already where I had been."

"And where were you?" the Brother amusedly inquired.

"Just on the sofa always, leaning back on the cushion and feeling a delicious ease. He was already me."

"And who were you?" the Brother continued.

"Nobody. That was the fun."

"That *is* the fun," said the Brother, with a sigh like soft music.

Dane echoed the sigh, and, as nobody talking with nobody, they sat there together still and watched the sweet wide picture darken into tepid night.

IV

AT the end of three weeks—so far as time was distinct—Dane began to feel there was something he had recovered. It was the thing they never named—partly for want of the need and partly for lack of the word; for what indeed was the description that would cover it all? The only real need was to know it, to see it, in silence. Dane had a private, practical sign for it, which, however, he had appropriated by theft—"the vision and the faculty divine." That, doubtless, was a flattering phrase for his idea of his genius; the genius, at all events, was what he had been in danger of losing and had at last held by a thread that might at any moment have broken. The change was that, little by little, his hold had grown firmer, so that he drew in the line—more and more each day—with a pull that he was delighted to find it would bear. The mere dream-sweetness of the place was superseded; it was more and more a world of reason and order, of sensible, visible arrangement. It ceased to be strange—it was high, triumphant clearness. He cultivated, however, but vaguely, the question of where he was, finding it near enough the mark to be almost sure that if he was not in Kent he was probably in Hampshire. He paid for everything but that—that wasn't one of the items. Payment, he had soon learned, was definite; it consisted of sovereigns and shillings—just like those of the world he had left, only parted with more ecstatically—that he put, in his room, in a designated place and that were taken away in his absence by one of the unobtrusive, effaced agents—shadows projected on the hours like the noiseless march of the sundial—that were always at work. The institution had sides that had their recalls, and a pleased, resigned perception of these things was at once the effect and the cause of its grace.

Dane picked out of his dim past a dozen halting similes. The sacred, silent convent was one; another was the bright country-house. He did the place no outrage to liken it to an hotel; he permitted himself on occasion to trace its resemblance to a club. Such images, however, but flickered and went out—they lasted only long enough to light up the difference. An hotel without noise, a club without newspapers—when he turned his face to what it was "without" the view opened wide. The only approach to a real analogy was in himself and his companions. They were brothers, guests, members; they were even, if one liked—and they didn't in the least mind what they were called—"regular boarders." It was not they who made the conditions, it was the conditions that made them. These conditions found themselves accepted, clearly, with an appreciation, with a rapture, it was rather to be called, that had to do—as the very air that pervaded them and the force that sustained—with their quiet and noble assurance. They combined to form the large, simple idea of a general refuge—an image of embracing arms, of liberal accommodation. What was the effect, really, but the poetisation by perfect taste of a type common enough? There was no daily miracle; the perfect taste, with the aid of space, did the trick. What underlay and overhung it all, better yet, Dane mused, was some original inspiration, but confirmed, unquenched, some happy thought of an individual breast. It had been born somehow and somewhere—it had had to insist on being—the blessed conception. The author might remain in the obscure, for that was part of the perfection: personal service so hushed and regulated that you scarce caught it in the act and only knew it by its results. Yet the wise mind was everywhere—the whole thing, infallibly, centred, at the core, in a consciousness. And what a consciousness it had been, Dane thought, a consciousness how like his own! The wise mind had felt, the wise mind had suffered; then, for all the worried company of minds, the wise mind had seen a chance. Of the creation thus arrived at you could none the less never have said if it were the last echo of the old or the sharpest note of the modern.

Dane again and again, among the far bells and the soft footfalls, in cool cloister and warm garden, found himself wanting not to know more and yet liking not to know less. It was part of the general beauty that there was no personal publicity, much less any personal success. Those things were in the world—in what he had left; there was no vulgarity here of credit or claim or fame. The real exquisite was to be without the complication of an identity, and the greatest boon of all, doubtless, the solid security, the clear confidence one could feel in the keeping of the contract. That was what had been most in the wise mind—the importance of the absolute sense, on the part of its beneficiaries, that what was offered was guaranteed. They had no concern but to pay—the wise mind knew what they paid for. It was present to Dane each hour that he could never be overcharged. Oh, the deep, deep bath, the soft, cool plash in the stillness!—this, time after time, as if under regular treatment, a sublimated German "cure," was the vivid name for his luxury. The inner life woke up again, and it was the inner life, for people of his generation, victims of the modern madness, mere maniacal extension and motion, that was returning health. He had talked of independence and written of it, but what a cold, flat word it had been! This was the wordless fact itself—the uncontested possession of the long, sweet, stupid day. The fragrance of flowers just wandered through the void, and the quiet recurrence of delicate, plain fare in a high, clean refectory where the soundless, simple service was the triumph of art. That, as he analysed, remained the constant explanation: all the sweetness and serenity were created, calculated things. He analysed, however, but in a desultory way and with a positive delight in the residuum of mystery that made for the great artist in the background the innermost shrine of the idol of a temple; there were odd moments for it, mild meditations when, in the broad cloister of peace or some garden-nook where the air was light, a special glimpse of beauty or reminder of felicity seemed, in passing, to hover and linger. In the mere ecstasy of change that had at first possessed him he had not discriminated—had only let himself sink, as I have mentioned, down to hushed depths. Then had come the slow, soft stages of intelligence and notation, more marked and more fruitful perhaps after that long talk with his mild mate in the twilight, and seeming to wind up the process by putting the key into his hand. This key, pure gold, was simply the cancelled list. Slowly and blissfully he read into the general wealth of his comfort all the particular absences of which it was composed. One by one he touched, as it were, all the things it was such rapture to be without.

It was the paradise of his own room that was most indebted to them—a great square, fair chamber, all beautified with omissions, from which, high up, he looked over a long valley to a far horizon, and in which he was vaguely and pleasantly reminded of some old Italian picture, some Carpaccio or some early Tuscan, the representation of a world without newspapers and letters, without telegrams and photographs, without the dreadful, fatal too much. There, for a blessing, he *could* read and write; there, above all, he could do nothing—he could live. And there were all sorts of freedoms—always, for the occasion, the particular right one. He could bring a book from the library—he could bring two, he could bring three. An effect produced by the charming place was that, for some reason, he never wanted to bring more. The library was a benediction—high and clear and plain, like everything else, but with something, in all its arched amplitude, unconfused and brave and gay. He should never forget, he knew, the throb of immediate perception with which he first stood there, a single glance round sufficing so to show him that it would give him what for years he had desired. He had not had detachment, but there was detachment here—the sense of a great silver bowl from which he could ladle up the melted hours. He strolled about from wall to wall, too pleasantly in tune on that occasion to sit down punctually or to choose; only recognising from shelf to shelf every dear old book that he had had to put off or never returned to; every deep, distinct voice of another time that, in the hubbub of the world, he had had to take for lost and unheard. He came back, of course, soon, came back every day; enjoyed there, of all the rare, strange moments, those that were at once most quickened and most caught—moments in which every apprehension counted double and every act of the mind was a lover's embrace. It was the quarter he perhaps, as the days went on, liked best; though indeed it only shared with the rest of the place, with every aspect to which his face happened to be turned, the power to remind him of the masterly general control.

There were times when he looked up from his book to lose himself in the mere tone of the picture that never failed at any moment or at any angle. The picture was always there, yet was made up of things common enough. It was in the way an open window in a broad recess let in the pleasant morning; in the way the dry air pricked into faint freshness the gilt of old bindings; in the way an empty chair beside a table unlittered showed a volume just laid down; in the way a happy Brother—as detached as oneself and with his innocent back presented—lingered before a shelf with the slow sound of turned pages. It was a part of the whole impression that, by some extraordinary law, one's vision seemed less from the facts than the facts from one's vision; that the elements were determined at the moment by the moment's need or the moment's sympathy. What most prompted this reflection was the degree in which, after a while, Dane had a consciousness of company. After that talk with the good Brother on the bench there were other good Brothers in other places—always in cloister or garden some figure that stopped if he himself stopped and with which a greeting became, in the easiest way in the world, a sign of the diffused amenity. Always, always, however, in all contacts, was the balm of a happy ignorance. What he had felt the first time recurred: the friend was always new and yet at the same time—it was amusing, not disturbing—suggested the possibility that he might be but an old one altered. That was only delightful—as positively delightful in the particular, the actual conditions as it might have been the reverse in the conditions abolished. These others, the abolished, came back to Dane at last so easily that he could exactly measure each difference, but with what he had finally been hustled on to hate in them robbed of its terror in consequence of something that had happened. What had happened was that in tranquil walks and talks the deep spell had worked and he had got his soul again. He had drawn in by this time, with his lightened hand, the whole of the long line, and that fact just dangled at the end. He could put his other hand on it, he could unhook it, he was once more in possession. This, as it befell, was exactly what he supposed he must have said to a comrade beside whom, one afternoon in the cloister, he found himself measuring steps.

"Oh, it comes—comes of itself, doesn't it, thank goodness?—just by the simple fact of finding room and time!"

The comrade was possibly a novice or in a different stage from his own; there was at any rate a vague envy in the recognition that shone out of the fatigued, yet freshened face. "It has come to *you* then?—you've got what you wanted?" That was the gossip and interchange that could pass to and fro. Dane, years before, had gone in for three months of hydropathy, and there was a droll echo, in this scene, of the old questions of the water-cure, the questions asked in the periodical pursuit of the "reaction"—the ailment, the progress of each, the action of the skin and the state of the appetite. Such memories worked in now—all familiar reference, all easy play of mind; and among them our friends, round and round, fraternised ever so softly, until, suddenly stopping short, Dane, with a hand on his companion's arm, broke into the happiest laugh he had yet sounded.

V

"WHY, it's raining!" And he stood and looked at the splash of the shower and the shine of the wet leaves. It was one of the summer sprinkles that bring out sweet smells.

"Yes—but why not?" his mate demanded.

"Well—because it's so charming. It's so exactly right."

"But everything *is*. Isn't that just why we're here?"

"Just exactly," Dane said; "only I've been living in the beguiled supposition that we've somehow or other a climate."

"So have I; so, I dare say, has every one. Isn't that the blessed moral?—that we live in beguiled suppositions. They come so easily here, and nothing contradicts them." The good Brother looked placidly forth—Dane could identify his phase. "A climate doesn't consist in its never raining, does it?"

"No, I dare say not. But somehow the good I've got has been half the great, easy absence of all that friction of which the question of weather mostly forms a part—has been indeed largely the great, easy, perpetual air-bath."

"Ah, yes—that's not a delusion; but perhaps the sense comes a little from our breathing an emptier medium. There are fewer things *in* it! Leave people alone, at all events, and the air is what they take to. Into the closed and the stuffy they have to be driven. I've had, too—I think we must all have—a fond sense of the south."

"But imagine it," said Dane, laughing, "in the beloved British islands and so near as we are to Bradford!"

His friend was ready enough to imagine. "To Bradford?" he asked, quite unperturbed. "How near?"

Dane's gaiety grew. "Oh, it doesn't matter!"

His friend, quite unmystified, accepted it. "There are things to puzzle out—otherwise it would be dull. It seems to me one can puzzle them."

"It's because we're so well disposed," Dane said.

"Precisely—we find good in everything."

"In everything," Dane went on. "The conditions settle that—they determine us."

They resumed their stroll, which evidently represented on the good Brother's part infinite agreement. "Aren't they probably in fact very simple?" he presently inquired. "Isn't simplification the secret?"

"Yes, but applied with a tact!"

"There it is. The thing's so perfect that it's open to as many interpretations as any other great work—a poem of Goethe, a dialogue of Plato, a symphony of Beethoven."

"It simply stands quiet, you mean," said Dane, "and lets us call it names?"

"Yes, but all such loving ones. We're 'staying' with some one—some delicious host or hostess who never shows."

"It's liberty-hall—absolutely," Dane assented.

"Yes—or a convalescent home."

To this, however, Dane demurred. "Ah, that, it seems to me, scarcely puts it. You weren't *ill*—were you? I'm very sure *I* really wasn't. I was only, as the world goes, too 'beastly well'!"

The good Brother wondered. "But if we couldn't keep it up——?"

"We couldn't keep it *down*—that was all the matter!"

"I see—I see." The good Brother sighed contentedly; after which he brought out again with kindly humour: "It's a sort of kindergarten!"

"The next thing you'll be saying that we're babes at the breast!"

"Of some great mild, invisible mother who stretches away into space and whose lap is the whole valley——?"

"And her bosom"—Dane completed the figure—"the noble eminence of our hill? That will do; anything will do that covers the essential fact."

"And what do you call the essential fact?"

"Why, that—as in old days on Swiss lake-sides—we're *en pension*."

The good Brother took this gently up. "I remember—I remember: seven francs a day without wine! But, alas, it's more than seven francs here."

"Yes, it's considerably more," Dane had to confess. "Perhaps it isn't particularly cheap."

"Yet should you call it particularly dear?" his friend after a moment inquired.

George Dane had to think. "How do I know, after all? What practice has one ever had in estimating the inestimable? Particular cheapness certainly isn't the note that we feel struck all round; but don't we fall naturally into the view that there *must* be a price to anything so awfully sane?"

The good Brother in his turn reflected. "We fall into the view that it must pay—that it does pay."

"Oh, yes; it does pay!" Dane eagerly echoed. "If it didn't it wouldn't last. It has *got* to last, of course!" he declared.

"So that we can come back?"

"Yes—think of knowing that we shall be able to!"

They pulled up again at this and, facing each other, thought of it, or at any rate pretended to; for what was really in their eyes was the dread of a loss of the clue. "Oh, when we want it again we shall find it," said the good Brother. "If the place really pays, it will keep on."

"Yes, that's the beauty; that it isn't, thank heaven, carried on only for love."

"No doubt, no doubt; and yet, thank heaven, there's love in it too." They had lingered as if, in the mild, moist air, they were charmed with the patter of the rain and the way the garden drank it. After a little, however, it did look rather as if they were trying to talk each other out of a faint, small fear. They saw the increasing rage of life and the recurrent need, and they wondered proportionately whether to return to the front when their hour should sharply strike would be the end of the dream. Was this a threshold perhaps, after all, that could only be crossed one way? They must return to the front sooner or later—that was certain: for each his hour would strike. The flower would have been gathered and the trick played—the sands, in short, would have run.

There, in its place, *was* life—with all its rage; the vague unrest of the need for action knew it again, the stir of the faculty that had been refreshed and reconsecrated. They seemed each, thus confronted, to close their eyes a moment for dizziness; then they were again at peace, and the Brother's confidence rang out. "Oh, we shall meet!"

"Here, do you mean?"

"Yes—and I dare say in the world too."

"But we shan't recognise or know," said Dane.

"In the world, do you mean?"

"Neither in the world nor here."

"Not a bit—not the least little bit, you think?"

Dane turned it over. "Well, so it is that it seems to me all best to hang together. But we shall see."

His friend happily concurred. "We shall see." And at this, for farewell, the Brother held out his hand.

"You're going?" Dane asked.

"No, but I thought *you* were."

It was odd, but at this Dane's hour seemed to strike—his consciousness to crystallise. "Well, I am. I've got it. You stay?" he went on.

"A little longer."

Dane hesitated. "You haven't yet got it?"

"Not altogether—but I think it's coming."

"Good!" Dane kept his hand, giving it a final shake, and at that moment the sun glimmered again through the shower, but with the rain still falling on the hither side of it and seeming to patter even more in the brightness. "Hallo—how charming!"

The Brother looked a moment from under the high arch—then again turned his face to our friend. He gave this time his longest, happiest sigh. "Oh, it's all right!"

But why was it, Dane after a moment found himself wondering, that in the act of separation his own hand was so long retained? Why but through a queer phenomenon of change, on the spot, in his companion's face—change that gave it another, but an increasing and above all a much more familiar identity, an identity not beautiful, but more and more distinct, an identity with that of his servant, with the most conspicuous, the physiognomic seat of the public propriety of Brown? To this anomaly his eyes slowly opened; it was not his good Brother, it was verily Brown who possessed his hand. If his eyes had to open, it was because they had been closed and because Brown appeared to think he had better wake up. So much as this Dane took in, but the effect of his taking it was a relapse into darkness, a recontraction of the lids just prolonged enough to give Brown time, on a second thought, to withdraw his touch and move softly away. Dane's next consciousness was that of the desire to make sure he *was* away, and this desire had somehow the result of dissipating the obscurity. The obscurity was completely gone by the time he had made out that the back of a person writing at his study-table was presented to him. He recognised a portion of a figure that he had somewhere described to somebody—the intent shoulders of the unsuccessful young man who had come that bad morning to breakfast. It was strange, he at last reflected, but the young man was still there. How long had he stayed—days, weeks, months? He was exactly in the position in which Dane had last seen him. Everything—stranger still

—was exactly in that position; everything, at least, but the light of the window, which came in from another quarter and showed a different hour. It wasn't after breakfast now; it was after—well, what? He suppressed a gasp—it was after everything. And yet—quite literally—there were but two other differences. One of these was that if he was still on the sofa he was now lying down; the other was the patter on the glass that showed him how the rain—the great rain of the night—had come back. It was the rain of the night, yet when had he last heard it? But two minutes before? Then how many were there before the young man at the table, who seemed intensely occupied, found a moment to look round at him and, on meeting his open eyes, get up and draw near?

"You've slept all day," said the young man.

"All day?"

The young man looked at his watch. "From ten to six. You were extraordinarily tired. I just, after a bit, let you alone, and you were soon off." Yes, that was it; he had been "off"—off, off, off. He began to fit it together; while he had been off the young man had been on. But there were still some few confusions; Dane lay looking up. "Everything's done," the young man continued.

"Everything?"

"Everything."

Dane tried to take it all in, but was embarrassed and could only say weakly and quite apart from the matter: "I've been so happy!"

"So have I," said the young man. He positively looked so; seeing which George Dane wondered afresh, and then, in his wonder, read it indeed quite as another face, quite, in a puzzling way, as another person's. Every one was a little some one else. While he asked himself who else then the young man was, this benefactor, struck by his appealing stare, broke again into perfect cheer. "It's all right!" That answered Dane's question; the face was the face turned to him by the good Brother there in the portico while they listened together to the rustle of the shower. It was all queer, but all pleasant and all distinct, so distinct that the last words in his ear—the same from both quarters—appeared the effect of a single voice. Dane rose and looked about his room, which seemed disencumbered, different, twice as large. It *was* all right.

A GUIDE TO FURTHER READING

(i) Bibliographies

A Bibliography of Henry James, The Soho Bibliographies, edited by Leon Edel and Dan H. Laurence and revised with the assistance of James Rambeau (New York, 1957; third edition, Clarendon Press, Oxford and New York, 1982).

Henry James, 1917-1959: A Reference Guide, A Reference Publication in Literature (Hall, Boston, Mass., 1979), compiled by Kristian P. McColgan.

Henry James, 1960-1974: A Reference Guide, A Reference Publication in Literature (Hall, Boston, Mass., 1979), compiled by Dorothy M. Scura.

(ii) Letters

The Letters of Henry James, 2 vols., edited by Percy Lubbock (Macmillan, London and New York, 1920).

Henry James Letters, vol. I-, edited by Leon Edel (Belknap Press, Cambridge Mass., and Macmillan, London, 1974-).

(iii) Autobiography and Biography

Henry James: Autobiography, edited with an introduction by Frederick W. Dupee (W.H. Allen, London, 1956); this comprises Henry James, *A Small Boy and Others* (1913), *Notes of a Son and a Brother* (1914), and *The Middle Years* (1917).

F.O. Matthiessen, *The James Family* (Alfred A. Knopf, New York, 1947; reprinted, Random House, New York, 1980).

Leon Edel, *The Life of Henry James*, 2 vols. (Peregrine Books, London, 1977). This is a revised and condensed version of his five-volume biography.

(iv) Tales

The Complete Tales of Henry James, edited with an introduction by Leon Edel, 12 vols. (Rupert Hart-Davis, London, and J.B. Lippincott, Philadelphia and New York, 1962-4).

The Tales of Henry James, edited with an introduction by Maqbool Aziz, vol.I- (Clarendon Press, Oxford, 1973-).

(v) Other Writings

The Complete Plays of Henry James, edited with an introduction and notes by Leon Edel (Rupert Hart-Davis, London, and J.B. Lippincott, Philadelphia and New York, 1949).

The Notebooks of Henry James, edited with an introduction and notes by F.O. Matthiessen and Kenneth B. Murdock (Oxford University Press, New York, 1947; reprinted, the University of Chicago Press, Chicago and London, 1981).

The Art of the Novel: Critical Prefaces by Henry James, with an introduction by Richard P. Blackmur (Scribner's, New York, 1934, and London, 1935).

Henry James Selected Literary Criticism, edited by Morris Shapira (Heinemann Educational, London, 1963; reprinted, Cambridge University Press, Cambridge, 1981).

(vi) Background

Ian Fletcher (ed.), *Decadence and the 1890s*, Stratford-Upon-Avon Studies 17 (Edward Arnold, London, 1979).

Wendell V. Harris, *British Short Fiction in the Nineteenth Century: A Literary and Bibliographical Guide* (Wayne State University Press, Detroit, 1979).

Holbrook Jackson, *The Eighteen Nineties* (Grant Richards, London, 1913; reprinted, Harvester Press, Brighton, 1976).

Valerie Shaw, *The Short Story: A Critical Introduction* (Longman, London and New York, 1983).

Eric Warner and Graham Hough (eds.), *Strangeness and Beauty: An Anthology of Aesthetic Criticism, 1840-1910*, 2 vols. (Cambridge University Press, Cambridge, 1983).

(vii) Criticism

Wayne C. Booth, *The Rhetoric of Fiction* (University of Chicago Press, Chicago and London, 1961; second edition, 1983).

F.W. Dupee, *Henry James*, The American Men of Letters Series (Methuen, London and New York, 1951).

Laurence Bedwell Holland, *The Expense of Vision: Essays on the Craft of Henry James* (Princeton University Press, Princeton, 1964; reprinted John Hopkins University Press, Baltimore and London, 1982).

F.O. Matthiessen, *Henry James: The Major Phase* (London and New York, 1944). This concentrates on the later novels and tales; still the best book on James.

Tzvetan Todorov, 'The Structural Analysis of Literature: the Tales of Henry James', in *Structuralism: an Introduction*, edited by David Robey (Oxford, 1973), pp.73-103.

T.M. Segnitz, 'The Actual Genesis of Henry James's "Paste"' *American Literature* (May, 1964), pp.216-19.

NOTE ON THE TEXTS

The complicated publishing history of Henry James' tales indicates the extent of the opportunity he took to be, like Dencombe in 'The Middle Years', 'a passionate corrector, a fingerer of style'. The introduction to volume I of Maqbool Aziz's *The Tales of Henry James*, (Clarendon Press, Oxford, 1973) together with his '"Four Meetings": A Caveat for James Critics' in *Essays in Criticism*, XVIII (July, 1968), pp. 258-74 are useful initiations into this contentious area of textual criticism. All but nine of the 112 tales originally appeared in periodicals and eighty-seven of these, mostly revised, were published in various collections in book form. The most considerable revisions were made for the twenty-four volumes of *The Novels and Tales of Henry James*, New York Edition (New York, 1907-9; London, 1908-9) and in which James included only fifty-five of his tales. The degree and nature of the revisions at each stage shift enormously and, following the usual editorial practice, the text of James' work most widely available is often that, if included in that edition, of his revision for the New York Edition. One of the problems with this policy is that it is difficult to develop a sense of James' changing style over the six decades of his writing career. And the perspective on his work inevitably becomes that of the late period, particularly from the vantage point of 1907-9, with its characteristically more involuted mode. For these reasons the text here is that of the first authorised book edition, often corrected at this stage instead of radically revised, and not that of its periodical publication nor, where available, New York Edition.

All the tales in this volume were originally reprinted by James in two volumes: *Embarrassments* (1896) and *The Soft Side* (1900). 'The Next Time' and 'The Figure in the Carpet' were revised for volume XV of the New York Edition. The original appearance of 'The Next Time' was in the *Yellow Book*, VI (July, 1895), pp.11-59 and 'The Figure in the Carpet' was first published in *Cosmopolis*, I (January-February, 1896), pp.41-59, 373-92. 'The Way it Came' was revised under the title of 'The Friends of the Friends' for volume XVII of the New York Edition; its initial appearance was in the *Chap Book*, IV (1 May 1896), pp.562-93 and simultaneously in *Chapman's Magazine of Fiction*, IV (May 1896), pp.95-120. 'John Delavoy' was not included in the New York Edition but 'Paste' and 'The Great Good Place' formed part of volume XVI. 'John Delavoy' had its first appearance in *Cosmopolis*, IX (January-February, 1898), pp.1-21, 317-32. 'Paste' was first published in *Frank Leslie's Popular Monthly*, XLIX (December, 1899), pp.175-89 and 'The Great Good Place' in *Scribner's Magazine*, XXVII (January, 1900), pp.99-112.